U B I K

NOVELS BY PHILIP K. DICK

PHILIP K. DICK

UBIK

VINTAGE BOOKS

A Division of Random House, Inc.

New York

FOR TONY BOUCHER

First Vintage Books Edition, December 1991

Copyright © 1969 by Philip K. Dick

All rights reserved under International and Pan-American Copyright
Conventions. Published in the United States by Vintage Books, a
division of Random House, Inc., New York, and distributed in
Canada by Random House of Canada Limited, Toronto.
Originally published by Doubleday & Company, Inc.,
New York, in 1969.

Library of Congress Cataloging-in-Publication Data
Dick, Philip K.
Ubik / Philip K. Dick.—1st Vintage Books ed.
p. cm.
ISBN 0-679-73664-6
I. Title.
PS3554.I3U24   1991
813′.54—dc20   91-50097
CIP

Book design by Debbie Glasserman

For information about the Philip K. Dick Society, write to:
PKDS, Box 611, Glen Ellen, CA 95442.

Manufactured in the United States of America
B9

U B I K

1

Friends, this is clean-up time and we're discounting all our silent, electric Ubiks by this much money. Yes, we're throwing away the bluebook. And remember: every Ubik on our lot has been used only as directed.

At three-thirty A.M. on the night of June 5, 1992, the top telepath in the Sol System fell off the map in the offices of Runciter Associates in New York City. That started vidphones ringing. The Runciter organization had lost track of too many of Hollis' psis during the last two months; this added disappearance wouldn't do.

"Mr. Runciter? Sorry to bother you." The technician in charge of the night shift at the map room coughed nervously as the massive, sloppy head of Glen Runciter swam up to fill the vidscreen. "We got this news from one of our inertials. Let me look." He fiddled with a disarranged stack of tapes from the recorder which monitored incoming messages. "Our Miss Dorn reported it; as you may recall she had followed him to Green River, Utah, where—"

Sleepily, Runciter grated, "Who? I can't keep in mind at all times which inertials are following what teep or precog." With his hand he smoothed down his ruffled gray mass of wirelike hair. "Skip the rest and tell me which of Hollis' people is missing now."

"S. Dole Melipone," the technician said.

"What? Melipone's gone? You kid me."

"I not kid you," the technician assured him. "Edie Dorn and two other inertials followed him to a motel named the Bonds of Erotic Polymorphic Experience, a sixty-unit sub-surface structure catering to businessmen and their hookers who don't want to be entertained. Edie and her colleagues didn't think he was active, but just to be on the safe side we had one of our own telepaths, Mr. G. G. Ashwood, go in and read him. Ashwood found a scramble pattern surrounding Melipone's mind, so he couldn't do anything; he therefore went back to Topeka, Kansas, where he's currently scouting a new possibility."

Runciter, more awake now, had lit a cigarette; chin in hand, he sat propped up somberly, smoke drifting across the scanner of his end of the bichannel circuit. "You're sure the teep was Melipone? Nobody seems to know what he looks like; he must use a different physiognomic template every month. What about his field?"

"We asked Joe Chip to go in there and run tests on the magnitude and minitude of the field being generated there at the Bonds of Erotic Polymorphic Experience Motel. Chip says it registered, at its height, 68.2 blr units of telepathic aura, which only Melipone, among all the known telepaths, can produce." The technician finished, "So that's where we stuck Melipone's identflag on the map. And now he—it—is gone."

"Did you look on the floor? Behind the map?"

"It's gone electronically. The man it represents is no longer on Earth or, as far as we can make out, on a colony world either."

Runciter said, "I'll consult my dead wife."

"It's the middle of the night. The moratoriums are closed now."

"Not in Switzerland," Runciter said, with a grimacing smile, as if some repellent midnight fluid had crept up into his aged throat. "Goodeve." Runciter hung up.

As owner of the Beloved Brethren Moratorium, Herbert Schoenheit von Vogelsang, of course, perpetually came to work before his employees. At this moment, with the chilly, echoing building just beginning to stir, a worried-looking clerical individual with nearly opaque glasses and wearing a tabby-fur blazer and pointed yellow shoes waited at the reception counter, a claim-check stub in his hand. Obviously, he had shown up to holiday-greet a relative. Resurrection Day—the holiday on which the half-lifers were publicly honored—lay just around the corner; the rush would soon be beginning.

"Yes, sir," Herbert said to him with an affable smile. "I'll take your stub personally."

"It's an elderly lady," the customer said. "About eighty, very small and wizened. My grandmother."

"Twill only be a moment." Herbert made his way back to the cold-pac bins to search out number 3054039-B.

When he located the correct party he scrutinized the lading report attached. It gave only fifteen days of half-life remaining. Not very much, he reflected; automatically he pressed a portable protophason amplifier into the transparent plastic hull of the casket, tuned it, listened at the proper frequency for indication of cephalic activity.

Faintly from the speaker a voice said, ". . . and then Tillie sprained her ankle and we never thought it'd heal; she was so foolish about it, wanting to start walking immediately . . ."

Satisfied, he unplugged the amplifier and located a union man to perform the actual task of carting 3054039-B to the consultation lounge, where the customer would be put in touch with the old lady.

"You checked her out, did you?" the customer asked as he paid the poscreds due.

"Personally," Herbert answered. "Functioning perfectly." He kicked a series of switches, then stepped back. "Happy Resurrection Day, sir."

"Thank you." The customer seated himself facing the casket, which steamed in its envelope of cold-pac; he pressed an earphone against the side of his head and spoke firmly into the microphone. "Flora, dear, can you hear me? I think I can hear you already. Flora?"

When I pass, Herbert Schoenheit von Vogelsang said to himself, I think I'll will my heirs to revive me one day a century. That way I can observe the fate of all mankind. But that meant a rather high maintenance cost to the heirs—and he knew what that meant. Sooner or later they would rebel, have his body taken out of cold-pac and—god forbid—buried.

"Burial is barbaric," Herbert muttered aloud. "Remnant of the primitive origins of our culture."

"Yes, sir," his secretary agreed, at her typewriter.

In the consultation lounge several customers now communed with their half-lifer relations, in rapt quiet, distributed at intervals each with his separate casket. It was a tranquil sight, these faithfuls, coming as they did so regularly to pay homage. They brought messages, news of what took place in the outside world; they cheered the gloomy half-lifers in these intervals of cerebral activity. And—they paid Herbert Schoenheit von Vogelsang. It was a profitable business, operating a moratorium.

"My dad seems a little frail," a young man said, catching Herbert's attention. "I wonder if you could take a moment of your time to check him over. I'd really appreciate it."

"Certainly," Herbert said, accompanying the customer across the lounge to his deceased relative. The lading for this one showed only a few days remaining; that explained the vitiated quality of cerebration. But still . . . he turned up the gain of the protophason amplifier, and the voice from the half-lifer became a trifle stronger in the earphone. He's almost at an end, Herbert thought. It seemed obvious to him that the son did not want to see the lading, did not actually care to know that contact with his dad was diminishing, finally. So Herbert said nothing; he merely walked off, leaving the son to commune. Why tell him that this was probably the last time he would come here? He would find out soon enough in any case.

A truck had now appeared at the loading platform at the rear of the moratorium; two men hopped down from it, wearing familiar pale-blue uniforms. Atlas Interplan Van and Storage, Herbert perceived. Delivering another half-lifer who had just now passed, or here to pick up one which had expired. Leisurely, he started in that direction, to supervise; at that moment, however, his secretary called to him. "Herr Schoenheit von Vogelsang; sorry to break into your meditation, but a customer wishes you to assist in revving up his relative." Her voice took on special coloration as she said, "The customer is Mr. Glen Runciter, all the way here from the North American Confederation."

A tall, elderly man, with large hands and a quick, sprightly stride, came toward him. He wore a varicolored Dacron wash-and-wear suit, knit cummerbund and dip-dyed cheese-cloth cravat. His head, massive like a tomcat's, thrust forward as he peered through slightly protruding, round and warm and highly alert eyes. Runciter kept, on his face, a professional expression of greeting, a fast attentiveness which fixed on Herbert, then almost at once strayed past him, as if Runciter had already fastened onto future matters. "How is Ella?" Runciter boomed, sounding as if he possessed a voice electronically augmented. "Ready to be cranked up for a talk? She's only twenty; she ought to be in better shape than you or me." He chuckled, but it had an abstract quality; he always smiled and he always chuckled, his voice always boomed, but inside he did not notice anyone, did not care; it was his body which smiled, nodded and shook hands. Nothing touched his mind, which remained remote; aloof, but amiable, he propelled Herbert along with him, sweeping his way in great strides back into the chilled bins where the half-lifers, including his wife, lay.

"You have not been here for some time, Mr. Runciter," Herbert pointed out; he could not recall the data on Mrs. Runciter's lading sheet, how much half-life she retained.

Runciter, his wide, flat hand pressing against Herbert's back to urge him along, said, "This is a moment of importance, von Vogelsang. We, my associates and myself, are in a line of business that surpasses all rational understanding. I'm not at liberty to make disclosures at this time, but we consider matters at present to be ominous but not however hopeless. Despair is not indicated—not by any means. Where's Ella?" He halted, glanced rapidly about.

"I'll bring her from the bin to the consultation lounge for you," Herbert said; customers should not be here in the bins. "Do you have your numbered claim-check, Mr. Runciter?"

"God, no," Runciter said. "I lost it months ago. But you know who my wife is; you can find her. Ella Runciter, about twenty. Brown hair and eyes." He looked around him impatiently. "Where did you put the lounge? It used to be located where I could find it."

"Show Mr. Runciter to the consultation lounge," Herbert said to one of his employees, who had come meandering by, curious to see what the world-renowned owner of an anti-psi organization looked like.

Peering into the lounge, Runciter said with aversion, "It's full. I can't talk to Ella in there." He strode after Herbert, who had made for the moratorium's files. "Mr. von Vogelsang," he said, overtaking him and once more dropping his big paw onto the man's shoulder; Herbert felt the weight of the hand, its persuading vigor. "Isn't there a more private sanctum sanctorum for confidential communications? What I have to discuss with Ella my wife is not a matter which we at Runciter Associates are ready at this time to reveal to the world."

Caught up in the urgency of Runciter's voice and presence, Herbert found himself readily mumbling, "I can make Mrs. Runciter available to you in one of our offices, sir." He wondered what had happened, what pressure had forced Runciter out of his bailiwick to make this belated pilgrimage to the Beloved Brethren Moratorium to crank up—as Runciter crudely phrased it—his half-lifer wife. A business crisis of some sort, he theorized. Ads over TV and in the homeopapes by the various anti-psi prudence establishments had shrilly squawked their harangues of late. Defend your privacy, the ads yammered on the hour, from all media. Is a stranger tuning in on you? Are you *really* alone? That for the telepaths. . . and then the queasy worry about precogs. Are your actions being predicted by someone you never met? Someone you would not want to meet or invite into your home? Terminate anxiety; contacting your nearest prudence organization will first tell you if in fact you are the victim of unauthorized intrusions, and then, on your instructions, nullify these intrusions—at moderate cost to you.

"Prudence organizations." He liked the term; it had dignity and it was accurate. He knew this from personal experience; two years ago a telepath had infiltrated his moratorium staff, for reasons which he had never discovered. To monitor confidences between half-lifers and their visitors, probably; perhaps those of one specific half-lifer—anyhow, a scout from one of the anti-psi organizations had picked up the telepathic field, and he had been notified. Upon his signing of a work contract an anti-telepath had been dispatched, had installed himself on the moratorium premises. The telepath had not been located but it had been nullified, exactly as the TV ads promised. And so, eventually, the defeated telepath had gone away. The moratorium was now psi-free, and, to be sure it stayed so, the anti-psi prudence organization surveyed his establishment routinely once a month.

"Thanks very much, Mr. Vogelsang," Runciter said, following Herbert through an outer office in which clerks worked to an empty inner room that smelled of drab and unnecessary micro-documents.

Of course, Herbert thought musingly to himself, I took their word for it that a telepath got in here; they showed me a graph they had obtained, citing it as proof. Maybe they faked it, made up the graph in their own labs. And I took their word for it that the telepath left; he came, he left— and I paid two thousand poscreds. Could the prudence organizations be, in fact, rackets? Claiming a need for their services when sometimes no need actually exists?

Pondering this he set off in the direction of the files once more. This time Runciter did not follow him; instead, he thrashed about noisily, making his big frame comfortable in terms of a meager chair. Runciter sighed, and it seemed to Herbert, suddenly, that the massively built old man was tired, despite his customary show of energy.

I guess when you get up into that bracket, Herbert decided, you have to act in a certain way; you have to appear more than a human with merely ordinary failings. Probably Runciter's body contained a dozen artiforgs, artificial organs grafted into place in his physiological apparatus as the genuine, original ones, failed. Medical science, he conjectured, supplies the material groundwork, and out of the authority of his mind Runciter supplies the remainder. I wonder how old he is, he wondered. Impossible any more to tell by looks, especially after ninety.

"Miss Beason," he instructed his secretary, "have Mrs. Ella Runciter located and bring me the ident number. She's to be taken to office 2-A." He seated himself across from her, busied himself with a pinch or two of Fribourg & Treyer *Princes* snuff as Miss Beason began the relatively simple job of tracking down Glen Runciter's wife.

2

The best way to ask for beer is to sing out Ubik. Made from select hops, choice water, slow-aged for perfect flavor, Ubik is the nation's number-one choice in beer. Made only in Cleveland.

Upright in her transparent casket, encased in an effluvium of icy mist, Ella Runciter lay with her eyes shut, her hands lifted permanently toward her impassive face. It had been three years since he had seen Ella, and of course she had not changed. She never would, now, at least not in the outward physical way. But with each resuscitation into active half-life, into a return of cerebral activity, however short, Ella died somewhat. The remaining time left to her pulse-phased out and ebbed.

Knowledge of this underwrote his failure to rev her up more often. He rationalized this way: that it doomed her, that to activate her constituted a sin against her. As to her own stated wishes, before her death and in early half-life encounters—this had become handily nebulous in his mind. Anyway, he would know better, being four times as old as she. What had she wished? To continue to function with him as co-owner of Runciter Associates; something vague on that order. Well, he had granted this wish. Now, for example. And six or seven times in the past. He did consult her at each crisis of the organization. He was doing so at this moment.

Damn this earphone arrangement, he grumbled as he fitted the plastic disc against the side of his head. And this microphone; all impediments to *natural* communication. He felt impatient and uncomfortable as he shifted about on the inadequate chair which Vogelsang or whatever his name was had provided him; he watched her rev back into sentience and wished she would hurry. And then in panic he thought, Maybe she isn't going to make it; maybe she's worn out and they didn't tell me. Or they don't know. Maybe, he thought, I ought to get that Vogelsang creature in here to explain. Maybe something terrible is wrong.

Ella, pretty and light-skinned; her eyes, in the days when they had been open, had been bright and luminous blue. That would not again occur; he could talk to her and hear her answer; he could communicate with her . . . but he would never again see her with eyes opened; nor would her mouth move. She would not smile at his arrival. When he departed she would not cry. Is this worth it? he asked himself. Is this better than the old way, the direct road from full-life to the grave? I still do have her with me, in a sense, he decided. The alternative is nothing.

In the earphone words, slow and uncertain, formed: circular thoughts of no importance, fragments of the mysterious dream which she now dwelt in. How did it feel, he wondered, to be in half-life? He could never fathom it from what Ella had told him; the basis of it, the experience of it, couldn't really be transmitted. Gravity, she had told him, once; it begins not to affect you and you float, more and more. When half-life is over, she had said, I think you float out of the System, out into the stars. But she did not know either; she only wondered and conjectured. She did not, however, seem afraid. Or unhappy. He felt glad of that.

"Hi, Ella," he said clumsily into the microphone.

"Oh," her answer came, in his ear; she seemed startled. And yet of course her face remained stable. Nothing showed; he looked away. "Hello, Glen," she said, with a sort of childish wonder, surprised, taken aback, to find him here. "What—" She hesitated. "How much time has passed?"

"Couple years," he said.

"Tell me what's going on."

"Aw, christ," he said, "everything's going to pieces, the whole organization. That's why I'm here; you wanted to be brought into major policy-planning decisions, and god knows we need that now, a new policy, or anyhow a revamping of our scout structure."

"I was dreaming," Ella said. "I saw a smoky red light, a horrible light. And yet I kept moving toward it. I couldn't stop."

"Yeah," Runciter said, nodding. "The *Bardo Thödol,* the *Tibetan Book of the Dead,* tells about that. You remember reading that; the doctors made you read it when you were " He hesitated. "Dying," he said then.

"The smoky red light is bad, isn't it?" Ella said.

"Yeah, you want to avoid it." He cleared his throat. "Listen, Ella, we've got problems. You feel up to hearing about it? I mean, I don't want to overtax you or anything; just say if you're too tired or if there's something else you want to hear about or discuss."

"It's so weird. I think I've been dreaming all this time, since you last talked to me. Is it really two years? Do you know, Glen, what I think? I think that other people who are around me—we seem to be progressively growing together. A lot of my dreams aren't about me at all. Sometimes I'm a man and sometimes a little boy; sometimes I'm an old fat woman with varicose veins . . . and I'm in places I've never seen, doing things that make no sense."

"Well, like they say, you're heading for a new womb to be born out of. And that smoky red light—that's a bad womb; you don't want to go that way. That's a humiliating, low sort of womb. You're probably anticipating your next life, or whatever it is." He felt foolish, talking like this; normally he had no theological convictions. But the half-life experience was real and it had made theologians out of all of them. "Hey," he said, changing the subject. "Let me tell you what's happened, what made me come here and bother you. S. Dole Melipone has dropped out of sight."

A moment of silence, and then Ella laughed. "Who or what is an S. Dole Melipone? There can't be any such thing." The laugh, the unique and familiar warmth of it, made his spine tremble; he remembered that about her, even after so many years. He had not heard Ella's laugh in over a decade.

"Maybe you've forgotten," he said.

Ella said, "I haven't forgotten; I wouldn't forget an S. Dole Melipone. Is it like a hobbit?"

"It's Raymond Hollis' top telepath. We've had at least one inertial sticking close to him ever since G. G. Ashwood first scouted him, a year and a half ago. We *never* lose Melipone; we can't afford to. Melipone can when necessary generate twice the psi field of any other Hollis employee. And Melipone is only one of a whole string of Hollis people who've disappeared—anyhow, disappeared as far as we're concerned. As far as all prudence organizations in the Society can make out. So I thought, Hell, I'll go ask Ella what's up and what we should do. Like you specified in your will—remember?"

"I remember." But she sounded remote. "Step up your ads on TV. Warn people. Tell them . . ." Her voice trailed off into silence then.

"This bores you," Runciter said gloomily.

"No. I—" She hesitated and he felt her once more drift away. "Are they all telepaths?" she asked after an interval.

"Telepaths and precogs mostly. They're nowhere on Earth; I know that. We've got a dozen inactive inertials with nothing to do because the Psis they've been nullifying aren't around, and what worries me even more, a lot more, is that requests for anti-psis have dropped—which you would expect, given the fact that so many Psis are missing. But I know they're on one single project; I mean, I believe. Anyhow, I'm sure of it; somebody's hired the bunch of them, but only

Hollis knows who it is or where it is. Or what it's all about."
He lapsed into brooding silence then. How would Ella be
able to help him figure it out? he asked himself. Stuck here
in this casket, frozen out of the world—she knew only what
he told her. Yet, he had always relied on her sagacity, that
particular female form of it, a wisdom not based on knowledge or experience but on something innate. He had not,
during the period she had lived, been able to fathom it; he
certainly could not do so now that she lay in chilled immo-
bility. Other women he had known since her death—there
had been several—had a little of it, trace amounts perhaps.
Intimations of a greater potentiality which, in them, never
emerged as it had in Ella.

"Tell me," Ella said, "what this Melipone person is like."

"A screwball."

"Working for money? Or out of conviction? I always feel
wary about that, when they have that psi mystique, that sense
of purpose and cosmic identity. Like that awful Sarapis had;
remember him?"

"Sarapis isn't around any more. Hollis allegedly bumped
him off because he connived to set up his own outfit in com-
petition with Hollis. One of his precogs tipped Hollis off."
He added, "Melipone is much tougher on us than Sarapis
was. When he's hot it takes three inertials to balance his
field, and there's no profit in that; we collect—or *did* collect—the same fee we get with one inertial. Because the
Society has a rate schedule now which we're bound by." He
liked the Society less each year; it had become a chronic
obsession with him, its uselessness, its cost. Its vainglory.
"As near as we can tell, Melipone is a money-Psi. Does that
make you feel better? Is that less bad?" He waited, but heard
no response from her. "Ella," he said. Silence. Nervously
he said, "Hey, hello there, Ella; can you hear me? Is something wrong?" Oh, god, he thought. She's gone.

A pause, and then thoughts materialized in his right ear.
"My name is Jory." Not Ella's thoughts; a different *élan*,
more vital and yet clumsier. Without her deft subtlety.

"Get off the line," Runciter said in panic. "I was talking to my wife Ella; where'd you come from?"

"I am Jory," the thoughts came, "and no one talks to me. I'd like to visit with you awhile, mister, if that's okay with you. What's your name?"

Stammering, Runciter said, "I want my wife, Mrs. Ella Runciter; I paid to talk to her, and that's who I want to talk to, not you."

"I know Mrs. Runciter," the thoughts clanged in his ear, much stronger now. "She talks to me, but it isn't the same as somebody like you talking to me, somebody in the world. Mrs. Runciter is here where we are; it doesn't count because she doesn't know any more than we do. What year is it, mister? Did they send that big ship to proxima? I'm very interested in that; maybe you can tell me. And if you want, I can tell Mrs. Runciter later on. Okay?"

Runciter popped the plug from his ear, hurriedly set down the earphone and the rest of the gadgetry; he left the stale, dust-saturated office and roamed about among the chilling caskets, row after row, all of them neatly arranged by number. Moratorium employees swam up before him and then vanished as he churned on, searching for the owner.

"Is something the matter, Mr. Runciter?" the von Vogelsang person said, observing him as he floundered about. "Can I assist you?"

"I've got some *thing* coming in over the wire," Runciter panted, halting. "Instead of Ella. Damn you guys and your shoddy business practices; this shouldn't happen, and what does it mean?" He followed after the moratorium owner, who had already started in the direction of office 2-A. "If I ran my business this way—"

"Did the individual identify himself?"

"Yeah, he called himself Jory."

Frowning with obvious worry, von Vogelsang said, "That would be Jory Miller. I believe he's located next to your wife. In the bin."

"But I can see it's Ella!"

"After prolonged proximity," von Vogelsang explained, "there is occasionally a mutual osmosis, a suffusion between the mentalities of half-lifers. Jory Miller's cephalic activity is particularly good; your wife's is not. That makes for an unfortunately one-way passage of protophasons."

"Can you correct it?" Runciter asked hoarsely; he found himself still spent, still panting and shaking. "Get that thing out of my wife's mind and get her back—that's your job!"

Von Vogelsang said, in a stilted voice, "If this condition persists your money will be returned to you."

"Who cares about the money? Snirt the money." They had reached office 2-A now; Runciter unsteadily reseated himself, his heart laboring so that he could hardly speak. "If you don't get this Jory person off the line," he half gasped, half snarled, "I'll sue you; I'll close down this place!"

Facing the casket, von Vogelsang pressed the audio outlet into his ear and spoke briskly into the microphone. "Phase out, Jory; that's a good boy." Glancing at Runciter he said, "Jory passed at fifteen; that's why he has so much vitality. Actually, this has happened before; Jory has shown up several times where he shouldn't be." Once more into the microphone he said, "This is very unfair of you, Jory; Mr. Runciter has come a long way to talk to his wife. Don't dim her signal, Jory; that's not nice." A pause as he listened to the earphone. "I know her signal is weak." Again he listened, solemn and froglike, then removed the earphone and rose to his feet.

"What'd he say?" Runciter demanded. "Will he get out of there and let me talk to Ella?"

Von Vogelsang said, "There's nothing Jory can do. Think of two AM radio transmitters, one close by but limited to only five-hundred watts of operating power. Then another, far off, but on the same or nearly the same frequency, and utilizing five-thousand watts. When night comes—"

"And night," Runciter said, *"has* come." At least for Ella. And maybe himself as well, if Hollis' missing teeps, parakineticists, precogs, resurrectors and animators couldn't be found. He had not only lost Ella; he had also lost her advice, Jory having supplanted her before she could give it.

"When we return her to the bin," von Vogelsang was blabbing, "we won't install her near Jory again. In fact, if you're agreeable as to paying the somewhat larger monthly fee, we can place her in a high-grade isolated chamber with walls coated and reinforced with Teflon-26 so as to inhibit hetero-psychic infusion—from Jory or anybody else."

"Isn't it too late?" Runciter said, surfacing momentarily from the depression into which this happening had dropped him.

"She may return. Once Jory phases out. Plus anyone else who may have gotten into her because of her weakened state. She's accessible to almost anyone." Von Vogelsang chewed his lip, palpably pondering. "She may not like being isolated, Mr. Runciter. We keep the containers—the caskets, as they're called by the lay public—close together for a reason. Wandering through one another's mind gives those in half-life the only—"

"Put her in solitary right now," Runciter broke in. "Better she be isolated than not exist at all."

"She exists," von Vogelsang corrected. "She merely can't contact you. There's a difference."

Runciter said, "A metaphysical difference which means nothing to me."

"I will put her in isolation," von Vogelsang said, "but I think you're right; it's too late. Jory has permeated her permanently, to some extent at least. I'm sorry."

Runciter said harshly, "So am I."

3

*Instant Ubik has all the fresh flavor
of just-brewed drip coffee. Your
husband will say, Christ, Sally, I
used to think your coffee was only
so-so. But now, wow! Safe when
taken as directed.*

Still in gay pinstripe clown-style pajamas, Joe Chip hazily
seated himself at his kitchen table, lit a cigarette and, after
inserting a dime, twiddled the dial of his recently rented 'pape
machine. Having a hangover, he dialed off *interplan news,*
hovered momentarily at *domestic news* and then selected
gossip.

"Yes sir," the 'pape machine said heartily. "Gossip. Guess
what Stanton Mick, the reclusive, interplanetarily known
speculator and financier, is up to at this very moment." Its
works whizzed and a scroll of printed matter crept from its
slot; the ejected roll, a document in four colors, niftily incised
with bold type, rolled across the surface of the neo-teakwood
table and bounced to the floor. His head aching, Chip re-
trieved it, spread it out flat before him.

MICK HITS WORLD BANK FOR TWO TRIL
(AP) London. What could Stanton Mick, the reclusive, interplanetarily known speculator and financier be up to? the
business community asked itself as rumor leaked out of White-
hall that the dashing but peculiar industrial magnate, who
once offered to build free of charge a fleet by which Israel
could colonize and make fertile otherwise desert areas of

Mars, had asked for and may possibly receive a staggering and unprecedented loan of

"This isn't gossip," Joe Chip said to the 'pape machine. "This is speculation about fiscal transactions. Today I want to read about which TV star is sleeping with whose drug-addicted wife." He had as usual not slept well, at least in terms of REM—rapid eye movement—sleep. And he had resisted taking a soporific because, very unfortunately, his week's supply of stimulants, provided him by the autonomic pharmacy of his conapt building, had run out—due, admittedly, to his own oral greed, but nonetheless gone. By law he could not approach the pharmacy for more until next Tuesday. Two days away, two *long* days.

The 'pape machine said, "Set the dial for *low gossip*."

He did so and a second scroll, excreted by the 'pape machine without delay, emerged; he zommed in on an excellent caricature drawing of Lola Herzburg-Wright, licked his lips with satisfaction at the naughty exposure of her entire right ear, then feasted on the text.

Accosted by a cutpurse in a fancy N.Y. after-hours mowl the other night, LOLA HERZBURG-WRIGHT bounced a swift right jab off the chops of the do-badder which sent him reeling onto the table where KING EGON GROAT OF SWEDEN and an unidentified miss with astonishingly large

The ring-construct of his conapt door jangled; startled, Joe Chip glanced up, found his cigarette attempting to burn the formica surface of his neo-teakwood table, coped with that, then shuffled blearily to the speaktube mounted handily by the release bolt of the door. "Who is it?" he grumbled; checking with his wrist watch, he saw that eight o'clock had not arrived. Probably the rent robot, he decided. Or a creditor. He did not trigger off the release bolt of the door.

An enthusiastic male voice from the door's speaker exclaimed, "I know it's early, Joe, but I just hit town. G. G. Ashwood here; I've got a firm prospect that I snared in

Topeka—I read this one as magnificent and I want your confirmation before I lay the pitch in Runciter's lap. Anyhow, he's in Switzerland."

Chip said, "I don't have my test equipment in the apt."

"I'll shoot over to the shop and pick it up for you."

"It's not at the shop." Reluctantly, he admitted, "It's in my car. I didn't get around to unloading it last night." In actuality, he had been too pizzled on papapot to get the trunk of his hovercar open. "Can't it wait until after nine?" he asked irritably. G. G. Ashwood's unstable manic energy annoyed him even at noon . . . this, at seven-forty, struck him as downright impossible: worse even than a creditor.

"Chip, dearie, this is a sweet number, a walking symposium of miracles that'll curl the needles of your gauges and, in addition, give new life to the firm, which it badly needs. And furthermore—"

"It's an anti what?" Joe Chip asked. "Telepath?"

"I'll lay it on you right out in front," G. G. Ashwood declared. "I don't know. Listen, Chip." Ashwood lowered his voice. "This is confidential, this particular one. I can't stand down here at the gate gum-flapping away out loud; somebody might overhear. In fact I'm already picking up the thoughts of some gloonk in a ground-level apt; he—"

"Okay," Joe Chip said, resigned. Once started, G. G. Ashwood's relentless monologs couldn't be aborted anyhow. He might as well listen to it. "Give me five minutes to get dressed and find out if I've got any coffee left in the apt anywhere." He had a quasi memory of shopping last night at the conapt's supermarket, in particular a memory of tearing out a green ration stamp, which could mean either coffee or tea or cigarettes or fancy imported snuff.

"You'll like her," G. G. Ashwood stated energetically. "Although, as often happens, she's the daughter of a—"

"Her?" In alarm Joe Chip said, "My apt's unfit to be seen; I'm behind in my payments to the building clean-up robots— they haven't been inside here in two weeks."

"I'll ask her if she cares."

"Don't ask her. *I* care. I'll test her out down at the shop, on Runciter's time."

"I read her mind and she doesn't care."

"How old is she?" Maybe, he thought, she's only a child. Quite a few new and potential inertials were children, having developed their ability in order to protect themselves against their psionic parents.

"How old are you, dear?" G. G. Ashwood asked faintly, turning his head away to speak to the person with him. "Nineteen," he reported to Joe Chip.

Well, that shot that. But now he had become curious. G. G. Ashwood's razzle-dazzle wound-up tightness usually manifested itself in conjunction with attractive women; maybe this girl fell into that category. "Give me fifteen minutes," he told G.G. If he worked fast, and skulked about in a clean-up campaign, and if he missed both coffee and breakfast, he could probably effect a tidy apt by then. At least it seemed worth trying.

He rang off, then searched in the cupboards of the kitchen for a broom (manual or self-powered) or vacuum cleaner (helium battery or wall socket). Neither could be found. Evidently he had never been issued any sort of cleaning equipment by the building's supply agency. Hell of a time, he thought, to find that out. And he had lived here four years.

Picking up the vidphone, he dialed 214, the extension for the maintenance circuit of the building. "Listen," he said, when the homeostatic entity answered. "I'm now in a position to divert some of my funds in the direction of settling my bill vis-à-vis your clean-up robots. I'd like them up here right now to go over my apt. I'll pay the full and entire bill when they're finished."

"Sir, you'll pay your full and entire bill before they start."

By now he had his billfold in hand; from it he dumped his supply of Magic Credit Keys—most of which, by now, had been voided. Probably in perpetuity, his relationship with money and the payment of pressing debts being such as it was. "I'll charge my overdue bill against my Triangular Magic Key," he informed his nebulous antagonist. "That will transfer the obligation out of your jurisdiction; on your books it'll show as total restitution."

"Plus fines, plus penalties."

"I'll charge those against my Heart-Shaped—"

"Mr. Chip, the Ferris & Brockman Retail Credit Auditing and Analysis Agency has published a special flier on you. Our recept-slot received it yesterday and it remains fresh in our minds. Since July you've dropped from a triple G status creditwise to quadruple G. Our department—in fact this entire conapt building—is now programed against an extension of services and/or credit to such pathetic anomalies as yourself, sir. Regarding you, everything must hereafter be handled on a basic-cash subfloor. In fact, you'll probably be on a basic-cash subfloor for the rest of your life. In fact—"

He hung up. And abandoned the hope of enticing and/or threatening the clean-up robots into entering his muddled apt. Instead, he padded into the bedroom to dress; he could do that without assistance.

After he had dressed—in a sporty maroon wrapper, twinkle-toes turned-up shoes and a felt cap with a tassel—he poked about hopefully in the kitchen for some manifestation of coffee. None. He then focused on the living room and found, by the door leading to the bathroom, last night's greatcape, every spotty blue yard of it, and a plastic bag which contained a half-pound can of authentic Kenya coffee, a great treat and one which only while pizzled would he have risen to. Especially in view of his current abominable financial situation.

Back in the kitchen he fished in his various pockets for a dime, and, with it, started up the coffeepot. Sniffing the—to him—very unusual smell, he again consulted his watch, saw that fifteen minutes had passed; he therefore vigorously strode to the apt door, turned the knob and pulled on the release bolt.

The door refused to open. It said, "Five cents, please."

He searched his pockets. No more coins; nothing. "I'll pay you tomorrow," he told the door. Again he tried the knob. Again it remained locked tight. "What I pay you," he informed it, "is in the nature of a gratuity; I don't *have* to pay you."

"I think otherwise," the door said. "Look in the purchase contract you signed when you bought this conapt."

In his desk drawer he found the contract; since signing it he had found it necessary to refer to the document many times. Sure enough; payment to his door for opening and shutting constituted a mandatory fee. Not a tip.

"You discover I'm right," the door said. It sounded smug.

From the drawer beside the sink Joe Chip got a stainless steel knife; with it he began systematically to unscrew the bolt assembly of his apt's money-gulping door.

"I'll sue you," the door said as the first screw fell out.

Joe Chip said, "I've never been sued by a door. But I guess I can live through it."

A knock sounded on the door. "Hey, Joe, baby, it's me, G. G. Ashwood. And I've got her right here with me. Open up."

"Put a nickel in the slot for me," Joe said. "The mechanism seems to be jammed on my side."

A coin rattled down into the works of the door; it swung open and there stood G. G. Ashwood with a brilliant look on his face. It pulsed with sly intensity, an erratic, gleaming triumph as he propelled the girl forward and into the apt.

She stood for a moment staring at Joe, obviously no more than seventeen, slim and copper-skinned, with large dark eyes. My god, he thought, she's beautiful. She wore an ersatz canvas workshirt and jeans, heavy boots caked with what appeared to be authentic mud. Her tangle of shiny hair was tied back and knotted with a red bandanna. Her rolled-up sleeves showed tanned, competent arms. At her imitation leather belt she carried a knife, a field-telephone unit and an emergency pack of rations and water. On her bare, dark forearm he made out a tattoo. CAVEAT EMPTOR, it read. He wondered what that meant.

"This is Pat," G. G. Ashwood said, his arm, with ostentatious familiarity, around the girl's waist. "Never mind her last name." Square and puffy, like an overweight brick, wearing his usual mohair poncho, apricot-colored felt hat, argyle ski socks and carpet slippers, he advanced toward Joe Chip, self-satisfaction smirking from every molecule in his body: He had found something of value here, and he meant to make the most of it. "Pat, this is the company's highly skilled, first-line electrical type tester."

Coolly, the girl said to Joe Chip, "Is it you that's electrical? Or your tests?"

"We trade off," Joe said. He felt, from all around him, the miasma of his uncleaned-up apt; it radiated the specter of debris and clutter, and he knew that Pat had already noticed. "Sit down," he said awkwardly. "Have a cup of actual coffee."

"Such luxury," Pat said, seating herself at the kitchen table; reflexively she gathered the week's heap of 'papes into a neater pile. "How can you afford real coffee, Mr. Chip?"

G. G. Ashwood said, "Joe gets paid a hell of a lot. The firm couldn't operate without him." Reaching out he took a cigarette from the package lying on the table.

"Put it back," Joe Chip said. "I'm almost out and I used up my last green ration stamp on the coffee."

"I paid for the door," G.G. pointed out. He offered the pack to the girl. "Joe puts on an act; pay no attention. Like look how he keeps his place. Shows he's creative; all geniuses live like this. Where's your test equipment, Joe? We're wasting time."

To the girl, Joe said, "You're dressed oddly."

"I maintain the subsurface vidphone lines at the Topeka Kibbutz," Pat said. "Only women can hold jobs involving manual labor at that particular kibbutz. That's why I applied there, instead of the Wichita Falls Kibbutz." Her black eyes blazed pridefully.

Joe said, "That inscription on your arm, that tattoo; is that Hebrew?"

"Latin." Her eyes veiled her amusement. "I've never seen an apt so cluttered with rubbish. Don't you have a mistress?"

"These electrical-expert types have no time for tarradiddle," G. G. Ashwood said irritably. "Listen, Chip, this girl's parents work for Ray Hollis. If they knew she was here they'd give her a frontal lobotomy."

To the girl, Joe Chip said, "They don't know you have a counter talent?"

"No." She shook her head. "I didn't really understand it either until your scout sat down with me in the kibbutz cafeteria and told me. Maybe it's true." She shrugged. "Maybe not. He said you could show me objective proof of it, with your testing battery."

"How would you feel," he asked her, "if the tests show that you have it?"

Reflecting, Pat said, "It seems so—negative. I don't do anything; I don't move objects or turn stones into bread or give birth without impregnation or reverse the illness process in sick people. Or read minds. Or look into the future—not even common talents like that. I just negate somebody else's ability. It seems—" She gestured. "Stultifying."

"As a survival factor for the human race," Joe said, "it's as useful as the psi talents. Especially for us Norms. The anti-psi factor is a natural restoration of ecological balance. One insect learns to fly, so another learns to build a web to trap him. Is that the same as no flight? Clams developed hard shells to protect them; therefore, birds learn to fly the clam up high in the air and drop him on a rock. In a sense, you're a life form preying on the Psis, and the Psis are life forms that prey on the Norms. That makes you a friend of the Norm class. Balance, the full circle, predator and prey. It appears to be an eternal system; and, frankly, I can't see how it could be improved."

"I might be considered a traitor," Pat said.

"Does it bother you?"

"It bothers me that people will feel hostile toward me. But I guess you can't live very long without arousing hostility; you can't please everybody, because people want different things. Please one and you displease another."

Joe said, "What is your anti-talent?"

"It's hard to explain."

"Like I say," G. G. Ashwood said, "it's unique; I've never heard of it before."

"Which psi talent does it counteract?" Joe asked the girl.

"Precog," Pat said. "I guess." She indicated G. G. Ashwood, whose smirk of enthusiasm had not dimmed. "Your scout Mr. Ashwood explained it to me. I knew I did something funny; I've always had these strange periods in my life, starting in my sixth year. I never told my parents, because I sensed that it would displease them."

"Are they precogs?" Joe asked.

"Yes.

"You're right. It would have displeased them. But if you used it around them—even once—they would have known. Didn't they suspect? Didn't you interfere with their ability?"

Pat said, "I—" She gestured. "I think I did interfere but they didn't know it." Her face showed bewilderment.

"Let me explain," Joe said, "how the anti-precog generally functions. Functions, in fact, in every case we know of. The precog sees a variety of futures, laid out side by side like cells in a beehive. For him one has greater luminosity, and this he picks. Once he has picked it the anti-precog can do nothing; the anti-precog has to be present when the precog is in the process of deciding, not after. The anti-precog makes all futures seem equally real to the precog; he aborts his talent to choose at all. A precog is instantly aware when an anti-precog is nearby because his entire relation to the future is altered. In the case of telepaths a similar impairment—"

"She goes back in time," G. G. Ashwood said.

Joe stared at him.

"Back in time," G.G. repeated, savoring this; his eyes shot shafts of significance to every part of Joe Chip's kitchen. "The precog affected by her still sees one predominant future; like you said, the one luminous possibility. And he chooses it, and he's right. But why is it right? Why is it luminous? Because this girl—" He shrugged in her direction. "Pat controls the future; that one luminous possibility is luminous because she's gone into the past and changed it. By changing it she changes the present, which includes the precog; he's affected without knowing it and his talent seems to work, whereas it really doesn't. So that's one advantage of her anti-talent over other anti-precog talents. The other— and greater—is that she can cancel out the precog's decision *after he's made it*. She can enter the situation later on, and this problem has always hung us up, as you know; if we didn't get in there from the start we couldn't do anything. In a way, we never could truly abort the precog ability as we've done with the others; right? Hasn't that been a weak link in our services?" He eyed Joe Chip expectantly.

"Interesting," Joe said presently.

"Hell—'interesting'?" G. G. Ashwood thrashed about indignantly. "This is the greatest anti-talent to emerge thus far!"

In a low voice Pat said, "I don't go back in time." She raised her eyes, confronted Joe Chip half apologetically, half belligerently. "I do something, but Mr. Ashwood has built it up all out of proportion to reality."

"I can read your mind," G.G. said to her, looking a little nettled. "I know you can change the past; you've done it."

Pat said, "I can change the past but I don't *go* into the past; I don't time-travel, as you want your tester to think."

"How do you change the past?" Joe asked her.

"I think about it. One specific aspect of it, such as one incident, or something somebody said. Or a little thing that

happened that I wish hadn't happened. The first time I did
this, as a child—"

"When she was six years old," G.G. broke in, "living in
Detroit, with her parents of course, she broke a ceramic
antique statue that her father treasured."

"Didn't your father foresee it?" Joe asked her. "With his
precog ability?"

"He foresaw it," Pat answered, "and he punished me the
week before I broke the statue. But he said it was inevitable;
you know the precog talent: They can foresee but they can't
change anything. Then after the statue did break—after I
broke it, I should say—I brooded about it, and I thought
about that week before it broke when I didn't get any dessert
at dinner and had to go to bed at five P.M. I thought Christ—
or whatever a kid says—isn't there some way these unfortunate events can be averted? My father's precog ability
didn't seem very spectacular to me, since he couldn't alter
events; I still feel that way, a sort of contempt. I spent a
month trying to will the damn statue back into one piece; in
my mind I kept going back to before it broke, imagining what
it had looked like . . . which was awful. And then one morning when I got up—I even dreamed about it at night—there
it stood. As it used to be." Tensely, she leaned toward Joe
Chip; she spoke in a sharp, determined voice. "But neither
of my parents noticed anything. It seemed perfectly normal
to them that the statue was in one piece; they thought it had
always been in one piece. I was the only one who remembered." She smiled, leaned back, took another of his cigarettes from the pack and lit up.

"I'll go get my test equipment from the car," Joe said,
starting toward the door.

"Five cents, please," the door said as he seized its knob.

"Pay the door," Joe said to G. G. Ashwood.

When he had lugged his armload of testing apparatus from
the car to his apt he told the firm's scout to hit the road.

"What?" G.G. said, astounded. "But I found her; the bounty is mine. I spent almost ten days tracing the field to her; I—"

Joe said to him, "I can't test her with your field present, as you well know. Talent and anti-talent fields deform each other; if they didn't we wouldn't be in this line of business." He held out his hand as G.G. got grumpily to his feet. "And leave me a couple of nickels. So she and I can get out of here."

"I have change," Pat murmured. "In my purse."

"You can measure the force she creates," G.G. said, "by the loss within my field. I've seen you do it that way a hundred times."

Joe said, briefly, "This is different."

"I don't have any more nickels," G.G. said. "I can't get out."

Glancing at Joe, then at G.G., Pat said, "Have one of mine." She tossed G.G. a coin, which he caught, an expression of bewilderment on his face. The bewilderment then, by degrees, changed to aggrieved sullenness.

"You sure shot me down," he said as he deposited the nickel in the door's slot. "Both of you," he muttered as the door closed after him. "I discovered her. This is really a cutthroat business, when—" His voice faded out as the door clamped shut. There was, then, silence.

Presently Pat said, "When his enthusiasm goes, there isn't much left of him."

"He's okay," Joe said; he felt a usual feeling: guilt. But not very much. "Anyhow he did his part. Now—"

"Now it's your turn," Pat said. "So to speak. May I take off my boots?"

"Sure," he said. He began to set up his test equipment, checking the drums, the power supply; he started trial motions of each needle, releasing specific surges and recording their effect.

"A shower?" she asked as she set her boots neatly out of the way.

"A quarter," he murmured. "It costs a quarter." He glanced up at her and saw that she had begun unbuttoning her blouse. "I don't have a quarter," he said.

"At the kibbutz," Pat said, "everything is free."

"Free!" He stared at her. "That's not economically feasible. How can it operate on that basis? For more than a month?"

She continued unperturbedly unbuttoning her blouse. "Our salaries are paid in and we're credited with having done our job. The aggregate of our earnings underwrites the kibbutz as a whole. Actually, the Topeka Kibbutz has shown a profit for several years; we, as a group, are putting in more than we're taking out." Having unbuttoned her blouse, she laid it over the back of her chair. Under the blue, coarse blouse she wore nothing, and he perceived her breasts. hard and high, held well by the accurate muscles of her shoulders.

"Are you sure you want to do that?" he said. "Take off your clothes, I mean?"

Pat said, "You don't remember."

"Remember what?"

"My not taking off my clothes. In another present. You didn't like that very well, so I eradicated that; hence this." She stood up lithely.

"What did I do," he asked cautiously, "when you didn't take off your clothes? Refuse to test you?"

"You mumbled something about Mr. Ashwood having overrated my anti-talent."

Joe said, "I don't work that way; I don't do that."

"Here." Bending, her breasts wagging forward, she rummaged in the pocket of her blouse, brought forth a folded sheet of paper which she handed him. "From the previous present, the one I abolished."

He read it, read his one-line evaluation at the end. "Antipsi field generated—inadequate. Below standard throughout. No value against precog ratings now in existence." And then the codemark which he employed, a circle with a stroke dividing it. *Do not hire,* the symbol meant. And only he and

Glen Runciter knew that. Not even their scouts knew the meaning of the symbol, so Ashwood could not have told her. Silently he returned the paper to her; she refolded it and returned it to her blouse pocket.

"Do you need to test me?" she asked. "After seeing that?"

"I have a regular procedure," Joe said. "Six indices which—"

Pat said, "You're a little, debt-stricken, ineffective bureaucrat who can't even scrape together enough coins to pay his door to let him out of his apt." Her tone, neutral but devastating, rebounded in his ears; he felt himself stiffen, wince and violently flush.

"This is a bad spot right now," he said. "I'll be back on my feet financially any day now. I can get a loan. From the firm, if necessary." He rose unsteadily, got two cups and two saucers, poured coffee from the coffeepot. "Sugar?" he said. "Cream?"

"Cream," Pat said, still standing barefoot, without her blouse.

He fumbled for the doorhandle of the refrigerator, to get out a carton of milk.

"Ten cents, please," the refrigerator said. "Five cents for opening my door; five cents for the cream."

"It isn't cream," he said. "It's plain milk." He continued to pluck—futilely—at the refrigerator door. "Just this one time," he said to it. "I swear to god I'll pay you back. Tonight."

"Here," Pat said; she slid a dime across the table toward him. "She should have money," she said as she watched him put the dime in the slot of the refrigerator. "Your mistress. You really have failed, haven't you? I knew it when Mr. Ashwood—"

"It isn't," he grated, "always like this."

"Do you want me to bail you out of your problems, Mr. Chip?" Hands in the pockets of her jeans, she regarded him expressionlessly, no emotion clouding her face. Only alertness. "You know I can. Sit down and write out your evaluation report on me. Forget the tests. My talent is unique anyway; you can't measure the field I produce—it's in the past and you're testing me in the present, which simply takes place as an automatic consequence. Do you agree?"

He said, "Let me see that evaluation sheet you have in your blouse. I want to look at it one more time. Before I decide."

From her blouse she once more brought forth the folded-up yellow sheet of paper; she calmly passed it across the table to him and he reread it. My writing, he said to himself; yes, it's true. He returned it to her and, from the collection of testing items, took a fresh, clean sheet of the same familiar yellow paper.

On it he wrote her name, then spurious, extraordinarily high test results, and then at last his conclusions. His new conclusions. "Has unbelievable power. Anti-psi field unique in scope. Can probably negate any assembly of precogs imaginable." After that he scratched a symbol: this time two crosses, both underlined. Pat, standing behind him, watched him write; he felt her breath on his neck.

"What do the two underlined crosses mean?" she asked.

" 'Hire her,' " Joe said. " 'At whatever cost required.' "

"Thank you." She dug into her purse, brought out a handful of poscred bills, selected one and presented it to him. A big one. "This will help you with expenses. I couldn't give it to you earlier, before you made your official evaluation of me. You would have canceled very nearly everything and you would have gone to your grave thinking I had bribed you. Ultimately you would have even decided that I had no counter-talent." She then unzipped her jeans and resumed her quick, furtive undressing.

Joe Chip examined what he had written, not watching her. The underlined crosses did not symbolize what he had told her. They meant: Watch this person. She is a hazard to the firm. She is dangerous.

He signed the test paper, folded it and passed it to her. She at once put it away in her purse.

"When can I move my things in here?" she asked as she padded toward the bathroom. "I consider it mine as of now, since I've already paid you what must be virtually the entire month's rent."

"Anytime," he said.

The bathroom said, "Fifty cents, please. Before turning on the water."

Pat padded back into the kitchen to reach into her purse.

4

*Wild new Ubik salad dressing, not
Italian, not French, but an entirely
new and different taste treat that's
waking up the world. Wake up to
Ubik and be wild! Safe when taken
as directed.*

Back in New York once more, his trip to the Beloved Brethren Moratorium completed, Glen Runciter landed via a silent and impressive all-electric hired limousine on the roof of the central installation of Runciter Associates. A descent chute dropped him speedily to his fifth-floor office. Presently—at nine-thirty A.M. local time—he sat in the massive, old-fashioned, authentic walnut-and-leather swivel chair, behind his desk, talking on the vidphone to his public-relations department.

"Tamish, I just now got back from Zürich. I conferred with Ella there." Runciter glared at his secretary, who had cautiously entered his personal oversized office, shutting the door behind her. "What do you want, Mrs. Frick?" he asked her.

Withered, timorous Mrs. Frick, her face dabbed with spots of artificial color to compensate for her general ancient grayness, made a gesture of disavowal; she had no choice but to bother him.

"Okay, Mrs. Frick," he said patiently. "What is it?"

"A new client, Mr. Runciter. I think you should see her." She both advanced toward him and retreated, a difficult maneuver which Mrs. Frick alone could carry off. It had taken her ten decades of practice.

"As soon as I'm off the phone," Runciter told her. Into the phone he said, "How often do our ads run on prime-time TV planetwide? Still once every third hour?"

"Not quite that, Mr. Runciter. Over the course of a full day, prudence ads appear on an average of once every third hour per UHF channel, but the cost of prime time—"

"I want them to appear every hour," Runciter said. "Ella thinks that would be better." On the trip back to the Western Hemisphere he had decided which of their ads he liked the most. "You know that recent Supreme Court ruling where a husband can legally murder his wife if he can prove she wouldn't under any circumstances give him a divorce?"

"Yes, the so-called—"

"I don't care what it's called; what matters is that we have a TV ad made up on that already. How does that ad go? I've been trying to remember it."

Tamish said, "There's this man, an ex-husband, being tried. First comes a shot of the jury, then the judge, then a pan-up on the prosecuting attorney, cross-examining the ex-husband. He says, 'It would seem, sir, that your wife—' "

"That's right," Runciter said with satisfaction; he had, originally, helped write the ad. It was, in his opinion, another manifestation of the marvelous multifacetedness of his mind.

"Is it not the assumption, however," Tamish said, "that the missing Psis are at work, as a group, for one of the larger investment houses? Seeing as how this is probably so, perhaps we should stress one of our business-establishment commercials. Do you perhaps recall this one, Mr. Runciter? It shows a husband home from his job at the end of the day; he still has on his electric-yellow cummerbund, petal skirt, knee-hugging hose and military-style visored cap. He seats himself wearily on the living-room couch, starts to take off one of his gauntlets, then hunches over, frowns and says, 'Gosh, Jill, I wish I knew what's been wrong with me lately. Sometimes, with greater frequency almost every day, the least little remark at the office makes me think that, well, somebody's reading my mind!' Then she says, 'If you're worried about that, why don't we contact our nearest prudence organization? They'll lease us an inertial at prices easy on our budget, and then you'll feel like your old self again!' Then this great smile appears on his face and he says, 'Why, this nagging feeling is already—' "

Again appearing in the doorway to Runciter's office, Mrs. Frick said, "Please, Mr. Runciter." Her glasses quivered.

He nodded. "I'll talk to you later, Tamish. Anyhow, get hold of the networks and start our material on the hour basis as I outlined." He rang off, then regarded Mrs. Frick silently. "I went all the way to Switzerland," he said presently, "and had Ella roused, to get that information, that advice."

"Mr. Runciter is free, Miss Wirt." His secretary tottered to one side, and a plump woman rolled into the office. Her head, like a basketball, bobbled up and down; her great round body propelled itself toward a chair, and there, at once, she seated herself, narrow legs dangling. She wore an unfashionable spider-silk coat, looking like some amiable bug wound up in a cocoon not spun by itself; she looked encased. However, she smiled. She seemed fully at ease. In her late forties, Runciter decided. Past any period in which she might have had a good figure.

"Ah, Miss Wirt," he said. "I can't give you too much time; maybe you should get to the point. What's the problem?"

In a mellow, merry, incongruous voice Miss Wirt said, "We're having a little trouble with telepaths. We think so but we're not sure. We maintain a telepath of our own—one we know about and who's supposed to circulate among our employees. If he comes across any Psis, telepaths or precogs, any kind, he's supposed to report to—" She eyed Runciter brightly. "To my principal. Late last week he made such a report. We have an evaluation, done by a private firm, on the capacities of the various prudence agencies. Yours is rated foremost."

"I know that," Runciter said; he had seen the evaluation,

as a matter of fact. As yet, however, it had brought him little if any greater business. But now this. "How many telepaths," he said, "did your man pick up? More than one?"

"Two at least."

"Possibly more?"

"Possibly." Miss Wirt nodded.

"Here is how we operate," Runciter said. "First we measure the psi field objectively, so we can tell what we're dealing with. That generally takes from one week to ten days, depending on—"

Miss Wirt interrupted, "My employer wants you to move in your inertials right away, without the time-consuming and expensive formality of making tests."

"We wouldn't know how many inertials to bring in. Or what kind. Or where to station them. Defusing a psi operation has to be done on a systematic basis; we can't wave a magic wand or spray toxic fumes into corners. We have to balance Hollis' people individual by individual, an anti-talent for every talent. If Hollis has gotten into your operation he's done it the same way: Psi by Psi. One gets into the personnel department, hires another; that person sets up a department or takes charge of a department and requisitions a couple more . . . sometimes it takes them months. We can't undo in twenty-four hours what they've constructed over a long period of time. Big-time Psi activity is like a mosaic; they can't afford to be impatient, and neither can we."

"My employer," Miss Wirt said cheerfully, "is impatient."

"I'll talk to him." Runciter reached for the vidphone. "Who is he and what's his number?"

"You'll deal through me."

"Maybe I won't deal at all. Why won't you tell me who you represent?" He pressed a covert button mounted under the rim of his desk; it would bring his resident telepath, Nina Freede, into the next office, where she could monitor Miss Wirt's thought processes. I can't work with these people, he said to himself, if I don't know who they are. For all I know, Ray Hollis is trying to hire me.

"You're hidebound," Miss Wirt said. "All we're asking for is speed. And we're only asking for that because we have to have it. I call tell you this much: Our operation which they've infested isn't on Earth. From the standpoint of potential yield, as well as from an investment standpoint, it's our primary project. My principal has put all his negotiable assets into it. Nobody is supposed to know about it. The greatest shock to us, in finding telepaths on the site—"

"Excuse me," Runciter said; he rose, walked to the office door. "I'll find out how many people we have about the place who're available for use in this connection." Shutting his office door behind him, he looked into each of the adjoining offices until he spied Nina Freede; she sat alone in a minor sideroom, smoking a cigarette and concentrating. "Find out who she represents," he said to her. "And then find out how high they'll go." We've got thirty-eight idle inertials, he reflected. Maybe we can dump all of them or most of them into this. I may finally have found where Hollis' smart-assed talents have sneaked off to. The whole goddam bunch of them.

He returned to his own office, reseated himself behind his desk.

"If telepaths have gotten into your operation," he said to Miss Wirt, his hands folded before him, "then you have to face up to and accept the realization that the operation per se is no longer secret. Independent of any specific technical info they've picked up. So why not tell me what the project is?"

Hesitating, Miss Wirt said, "I don't know what the project is."

"Or where it is?"

"No." She shook her head.

Runciter said, "Do you know who your employer is?"

"I work for a subsidiary firm which he financially controls; I know who my immediate employer is—that's a Mr. Shepard Howard—but I've never been told whom Mr. Howard represents."

"If we supply you with the inertials you need, will we know where they are being sent?"

"Probably not."

"Suppose we never get them back?"

"Why wouldn't you get them back? After they've decontaminated our operation."

"Hollis' men," Runciter said, "have been known to kill inertials sent out to negate them. It's my responsibility to see that my people are protected; I can't do that if I don't know where they are."

The concealed microspeaker in his left ear buzzed and he heard the faint, measured voice of Nina Freede, audible to him alone. "Miss Wirt represents Stanton Mick. She is his confidential assistant. There is no one named Shepard Howard. The project under discussion exists primarily on Luna; it has to do with Techprise, Mick's research facilities, the controlling stock of which Miss Wirt keeps in her name. She does not know any technical details; no scientific evaluations or memos or progress reports are ever made available to her by Mr. Mick, and she resents this enormously. From Mick's staff, however, she has picked up a general idea of the nature of the project. Assuming that her secondhand knowledge is accurate, the Lunar project involves a radical, new, low-cost interstellar drive system, approaching the velocity of light, which could be leased to every moderately affluent political or ethnological group. Mick's idea seems to be that the drive system will make colonization feasible on a mass basic understructure. And hence no longer a monopoly of specific governments."

Nina Freede clicked off, and Runciter leaned back in his leather and walnut swivel chair to ponder.

"What are you thinking?" Miss Wirt asked brightly.

"I'm wondering," Runciter said, "if you can afford our services. Since I have no test data to go on, I can only estimate how many inertials you'll need . . . but it may run as high as forty." He said this knowing that Stanton Mick could afford—or could figure out how to get someone else to underwrite—an unlimited number of inertials.

" 'Forty,' " Miss Wirt echoed. "Hmm. That is quite a few."

"The more we make use of, the sooner we can get the job done. Since you're in a hurry, we'll move them all in at one time. If you are authorized to sign a work contract in the name of your employer"—he pointed a steady, unyielding finger at her; she did not blink—"and you can come up with a retainer now, we could probably accomplish this within seventy-two hours." He eyed her then, waiting.

The microspeaker in his ear rasped, "As owner of Techprise she is fully bonded. She can legally obligate her firm up to and including its total worth. Right now she is calculating how much this would be, if converted on today's market." A pause. "Several billion poscreds, she has decided. But she doesn't want to do this; she doesn't like the idea of committing herself to both a contract and retainer. She would prefer to have Mick's attorneys do that, even if it means several days' delay."

But they're in a hurry, Runciter reflected. Or so they say.

The microspeaker said, "She has an intuition that you know—or have guessed—whom she represents. And she's afraid you'll up your fee accordingly. Mick knows his reputation. He considers himself the world's greatest mark. So he negotiates in this manner: through someone or some firm as a front. On the other hand, they want as many inertials as they can get. And they're resigned to that being enormously expensive."

"Forty inertials," Runciter said idly; he scratched with his pen at a small sheet of blank paper, on his desk for just such purposes. "Let's see. Six times fifty times three. Times forty."

Miss Wirt, still smiling her glazed, happy smile, waited with visible tension.

"I wonder," he murmured, "who paid Hollis to put his employees in the middle of your project."

"That doesn't really matter, does it?" Miss Wirt said. "What matters is that they're there."

Runciter said, "Sometimes one never finds out. But as you say—it's the same as when ants find their way into your kitchen. You don't ask why they're there; you just begin the job of getting them back out." He had arrived at a cost figure.

It was enormous.

"I'll—have to think it over," Miss Wirt said; she raised her eyes from the shocking sight of his estimate and half rose to her feet. "Is there somewhere, an office, where I can be alone? And possibly phone Mr. Howard?"

Runciter, also rising, said, "It's rare for any prudence organization to have that many inertials available at one time. If you wait, the situation will change. So if you want them you'd better act."

"And you think it would really take *that* many inertials?"

Taking Miss Wirt by the arm, he led her from his office and down the hall. To the firm's map room. "This shows," he told her, "the location of our inertials plus the inertials of other prudence organizations. In addition to that it shows—or tries to show—the location of all of Hollis' Psis." He systematically counted the psi ident-flags which, one by one, had been removed from the map; he wound up holding the final one: that of S. Dole Melipone. "I know now where they are," he said to Miss Wirt, who had lost her mechanical smile as she comprehended the significance of the unpositioned ident-flags. Taking hold of her damp hand, he deposited Melipone's flag among her damp fingers and closed them around it. "You can stay here and meditate," he said. "There's a vidphone over there—" He pointed. "No one will bother you. I'll be in my office." He left the map room, thinking, I really don't know that this is where they are, all those missing Psis. But it's possible. And—Stanton Mick had waived the routine procedure of making an objective test.

Therefore, if he wound up hiring inertials which he did not need it would be his own fault.

Legalistically speaking, Runciter Associates was required to notify the Society that some of the missing Psis—if not all—had been found. But he had five days in which to file the notification . . . and he decided to wait until the last day. This kind of business opportunity, he reflected, happens once in a lifetime.

"Mrs. Frick," he said, entering her outer office. "Type up a work contract specifying forty—" He broke off.

Across the room sat two persons. The man, Joe Chip, looked haggard and hungover and more than usually glum . . . looked, in fact, about as always, the glumness excepted. But beside him lounged a long-legged girl with brilliant, tumbling black hair and eyes; her intense, distilled beauty illuminated that part of the room, igniting it with heavy, sullen fire. It was, he thought, as if the girl resisted being attractive, disliked the smoothness of her skin and the sensual, swollen, dark quality of her lips.

She looks, he thought, as if she just now got out of bed. Still disordered. Resentful of the day—in fact, of every day.

Walking over to the two of them, Runciter said, "I gather G.G. is back from Topeka."

"This is Pat," Joe Chip said. "No last name." He indicated Runciter, then sighed. He had a peculiar defeated quality hanging over him, and yet, underneath, he did not seem to have given up. A vague and ragged hint of vitality lurked behind the resignation; it seemed to Runciter that Joe most nearly could be accused of feigning spiritual downfall . . . the real article, however, was not there.

"Anti what?" Runciter asked the girl, who still sat sprawling in her chair, legs extended.

The girl murmured, "Anti-ketogenesis."

"What's that mean?"

"The prevention of ketosis," the girl said remotely. "As by the administration of glucose."

To Joe, Runciter said, "Explain."

"Give Mr. Runciter your test sheet," Joe said to the girl.

Sitting up, the girl reached for her purse, rummaged, then produced one of Joe's wrinkled yellow score sheets, which she unfolded, glanced at and passed to Runciter.

"Amazing score," Runciter said. "Is she really this good?" he asked Joe. And then he saw the two underlined crosses, the graphic symbol of indictment—of, in fact, treachery.

"She's the best so far," Joe said.

"Come into my office," Runciter said to the girl; he led the way, and, behind them, the two of them followed.

Fat Miss Wirt, all at once, breathless, her eyes rolling, appeared. "I phoned Mr. Howard," she informed Runciter. "He has now given me my instructions." She thereupon perceived Joe Chip and the girl named Pat; for an instant she hesitated, then plunged on, "Mr. Howard would like the formal arrangements made right away. So may we go ahead now? I've already acquainted you with the urgency, the time factor." She smiled her glassy, determined smile. "Do you two mind waiting?" she asked them. "My business with Mr. Runciter is of a priority nature."

Glancing at her, Pat laughed, a low, throaty laugh of contempt.

"You'll have to wait, Miss Wirt," Runciter said. He felt afraid; he looked at Pat, then at Joe, and his fear quickened. "Sit down, Miss Wirt," he said to her, and indicated one of the outer-office chairs.

Miss Wirt said, "I can tell you exactly, Mr. Runciter, how many inertials we intend to take. Mr. Howard feels he can make an adequate determination of our needs, of our problem."

"How many?" Runciter asked.

"Eleven," Miss Wirt said.

"We'll sign the contract in a little while," Runciter said. "As soon as I'm free." With his big, wide hand he guided Joe and the girl into his inner office; he shut the door behind them and seated himself. "They'll never make it," he said to Joe. "With eleven. Or fifteen. Or twenty. Especially not with S. Dole Melipone involved on the other side." He felt tired as well as afraid. "This is, as I assumed, the potential trainee that G.G. scouted in Topeka? And you believe we should hire her? Both you and G.G. agree? Then we'll hire her, naturally." Maybe I'll turn her over to Mick, he said to himself. Make her one of the eleven. "Nobody has managed to tell me yet," he said, "which of the psi talents she counters."

"Mrs. Frick says you flew to Zürich," Joe said. "What did Ella suggest?"

"More ads," Runciter said. "On TV. Every hour." Into his intercom he said, "Mrs. Frick, draw up an agreement of employment between ourselves and a Jane Doe; specify the starting salary that we and the union agreed on last December; specify—"

"What is the starting salary?" the girl Pat asked, her voice suffused with sardonic suspicion of a cheap, childish sort.

Runciter eyed her. "I don't even know what you can do."

"It's precog, Glen," Joe Chip grated. "But in a different way." He did not elaborate; he seemed to have run down, like an old-time battery-powered watch.

"Is she ready to go to work?" Runciter asked Joe. "Or is this one we have to train and work with and wait for? We've got almost forty idle inertials and we're hiring another; forty less, I suppose, eleven. Thirty idle employees, all drawing full scale while they sit around with their thumbs in their noses. I don't know, Joe; I really don't. Maybe we ought to fire our scouts. Anyway, I think I've found the rest of Hollis' Psis. I'll tell you about it later." Into his intercom he said, "Specify that we can discharge this Jane Doe without notice, without severance pay or compensation of any kind; nor is she eligible, for the first ninety days, for pension, health or sick-pay benefits." To Pat he said, "Starting salary, in all cases, begins at four hundred 'creds per month, figuring on twenty hours a week. And you'll have to join a union. The Mine, Mill and Smelter-workers Union; they're the one that signed up all the prudence-organization employees three years ago. I have no control over that."

"I get more," Pat said, "maintaining vidphone relays at the Topeka Kibbutz. Your scout Mr. Ashwood said—"

"Our scouts lie," Runciter said. "And, in addition, we're not legally bound by anything they say. No prudence organization is." The office door opened and Mrs. Frick crept unsteadily in with the typed-out agreement. "Thank you, Mrs. Frick," Runciter said, accepting the papers. "I have a twenty-year-old wife in cold-pac," he said to Joe and Pat. "A beautiful woman who when she talks to me gets pushed out of the way by some weird kid named Jory, and then I'm talking to him, not her. Ella frozen in half-life and dimming out—and that battered crone for my secretary that I have to look at all day long." He gazed at the girl Pat, with her black, strong hair and her sensual mouth; in him he felt unhappy cravings arise, cloudy and pointless wants that led nowhere, that returned to him empty, as in the completion of a geometrically perfect circle.

"I'll sign," Pat said, and reached for the desk pen.

5

*Can't make the frug contest,
Helen; stomach's upset. I'll fix you
Ubik! Ubik drops you back in the
thick of things fast. Taken as directed, Ubik speeds relief to head
and stomach. Remember: Ubik is
only seconds away. Avoid prolonged use.*

During the long days of forced, unnatural idleness, the anti-
telepath Tippy Jackson slept regularly until noon. An elec-
trode planted within her brain perpetually stimulated
EREM—*extremely* rapid eye movement—sleep, so while
tucked within the percale sheets of her bed she had plenty
to do.

At this particular moment her artificially induced dream
state centered around a mythical Hollis functionary endowed
with enormous psionic powers. Every other inertial in the
Sol System had either given up or been melted down into
lard. By process of elimination, the task of nullifying the field
generated by this supernatural entity had devolved to her.

"I can't be myself while you're around," her nebulous
opponent informed her. On his face a feral, hateful expression formed, giving him the appearance of a psychotic squirrel.

In her dream Tippy answered, "Perhaps your definition of
your self-system lacks authentic boundaries. You've erected
a precarious structure of personality on unconscious factors
over which you have no control. That's why you feel threat-
ened by me."

"Aren't you an employee of a prudence organization?" the Hollis telepath demanded, looking nervously about.

"If you're the stupendous talent you claim to be," Tippy said, "you can tell that by reading my mind."

"I can't read anybody's mind," the telepath said. "My talent is gone. I'll let you talk to my brother Bill. Here, Bill; talk to this lady. Do you like this lady?"

Bill, looking more or less like his brother the telepath, said, "I like her fine because I'm a precog and she doesn't postscript me." He shuffled his feet and grinned, revealing great, pale teeth, as blunt as shovels. " 'I, that am curtailed of this fair proportion, cheated of feature by dissembling nature—' " He paused, wrinkling his forehead. "How does it go, Matt?" he asked his brother.

" '—deformed, unfinished, sent before my time into this breathing world, scarce half made up,' " Matt the squirrel-like telepath said, scratching meditatively at his pelt.

"Oh, yeah." Bill the precog nodded. "I remember. 'And that so lamely and unfashionable that dogs bark at me as I halt by them.' From *Richard the Third,*" he explained to Tippy. Both brothers grinned. Even their incisors were blunt. As if they lived on a diet of uncooked seeds.

Tippy said, "What does that mean?"

"It means," both Matt and Bill said in unison, "that we're going to get you."

The vidphone rang, waking Tippy up.

Stumbling groggily to it, confounded by floating colored bubbles, blinking, she lifted the receiver and said, "Hello." God, it's late, she thought, seeing the clock. I'm turning into a vegetable. Glen Runciter's face emerged on the screen. "Hello, Mr. Runciter," she said, standing out of sight of the phone's scanner. "Has a job turned up for me?"

"Ah, Mrs. Jackson," Runciter said, "I'm glad I caught you. A group is forming under Joe Chip's and my direction; eleven in all, a major work assignment for those we choose. We've been examining everyone's history. Joe thinks yours looks good, and I tend to agree. How long will it take you to get down here?" His tone seemed adequately optimistic, but on the little screen his face looked hard-pressed and careworn.

Tippy said, "For this one will I be living—"

"Yes, you'll have to pack." Chidingly he said, "We're supposed to be packed and ready to go at all times; that's a rule I don't ever want broken, especially in a case like this where there's a time factor."

"I *am* packed. I'll be at the New York office in fifteen minutes. All I have to do is leave a note for my husband, who's at work."

"Well, okay," Runciter said, looking preoccupied; he was probably already reading the next name on his list. "Goodbye, Mrs. Jackson." He rang off.

That was a strange dream, she thought as she hastily unbuttoned her pajamas and hurried back into the bedroom for her clothes. What did Bill and Matt say that poetry was from? *Richard the Third,* she remembered, seeing in her mind once more their flat, big teeth, their unformed, knoblike, identical heads with tufts of reddish hair growing from them like patches of weeds. I don't think I've ever read *Richard the Third,* she realized. Or, if I did, it must have been years ago, when I was a child.

How can you dream lines of poetry you don't know? she asked herself. Maybe an actual nondream telepath was getting at me while I slept. Or a telepath and a precog working together, the way I saw them in my dream. It might be a good idea to ask our research department whether Hollis does, by any remote chance, employ a brother team named Matt and Bill.

Puzzled and uneasy, she began as quickly as possible to dress.

Lighting a green all-Havana Cuesta-Rey palma-supreme, Glen Runciter leaned back in his noble chair, pressed a button of his intercom and said, "Make out a bounty check,

Mrs. Frick. Payable to G. G. Ashwood, for one-hundred poscreds."

"Yes, Mr. Runciter."

He watched G. G. Ashwood, who paced with manic restlessness about the big office with its genuine hardwood floor against which G.G.'s feet clacked irritatingly. "Joe Chip can't seem to tell me what she does," Runciter said.

"Joe Chip is a grunk," G.G. said.

"How come she, this Pat, can travel back into time, and no one else can? I'll bet this talent isn't new; you scouts probably just missed noticing it up until now. Anyhow, it's not logical for a prudence organization to hire her; it's a talent, not an anti-talent. We deal in—"

"As I explained, and as Joe indicated on the test report, it aborts the precogs out of business."

"But that's only a side-effect." Runciter pondered moodily. "Joe thinks she's dangerous. I don't know why."

"Did you ask him why?"

Runciter said, "He mumbled, the way he always does. Joe never has reasons, just hunches. On the other hand, he wants to include her in the Mick operation." He shuffled through, rooted among and rearranged the personnel-department documents before him on his desk. "Ask Joe to come in here so we can see if we've got our group of eleven set up." He examined his watch. "They should be arriving about now. I'm going to tell Joe to his face that he's crazy to include this Pat Conley girl if she's so dangerous. Wouldn't you say, G.G.?"

G. G. Ashwood said, "He's got a thing going with her."

"What sort of thing?"

"A sexual understanding."

"Joe has no sexual understanding. Nina Freede read his mind the other day and he's too poor even to—" He broke off, because the office door had opened; Mrs. Frick teetered her way in carrying G.G.'s bounty check for him to sign. "I know why he wants her along on the Mick operation," Runciter said as he scratched his signature on the check. "So he can keep an eye on her. He's going too; he's going to measure the psi field despite what the client stipulated. We have to know what we're up against. Thank you, Mrs. Frick." He waved her away and held the check out to G. G. Ashwood. "Suppose we don't measure the psi field and it turns out to be too intense for our inertials. Who gets blamed?"

"We do," G.G. said.

"I told them eleven wasn't enough. We're supplying our best; we're doing the best we can. After all, getting Stanton Mick's patronage is a matter of great importance to us. Amazing, that someone as wealthy and powerful as Mick could be so short-sighted, so goddam miserly. Mrs. Frick, is Joe out there? Joe Chip?"

Mrs. Frick said, "Mr. Chip is in the outer office with a number of other people."

"How many other people, Mrs. Frick? Ten or eleven?"

"I'd say about that many, Mr. Runciter. Give or take one or two."

To G. G. Ashwood, Runciter said, "That's the group. I want to see them, all of them, together. Before they leave for Luna." To Mrs. Frick he said, "Send them in." He puffed vigorously on his green-wrapped cigar.

She gyrated out.

"We know," Runciter said to G.G., "that as individuals they perform well. It's all down here on paper." He rattled the documents on his desk. "But how about together? How great a polyencephalic counter-field will they generate together? Ask yourself that, G.G. That is the question to ask."

"I guess time will tell," G. G. Ashwood said.

"I've been in this business a long time," Runciter said. From the outer office people began to file in. "This is my contribution to contemporary civilization."

"That puts it well," G.G. said. "You're a policeman guarding human privacy."

"You know what Ray Hollis says about us?" Runciter said. "He says we're trying to turn the clock back." He eyed the individuals who had begun to fill up his office; they gathered near one another, none of them speaking. They waited for him. What an ill-assorted bunch, he thought pessimistically. A young stringbean of a girl with glasses and straight lemon-yellow hair, wearing a cowboy hat, black lace mantilla and Bermuda shorts; that would be Edie Dorn. A good-looking, older, dark woman with tricky, deranged eyes who wore a silk sari and nylon obi and bobby socks; Francy something, a part-time schizophrenic who imagined that sentient beings from Betelgeuse occasionally landed on the roof of her conapt building. A woolly-haired adolescent boy wrapped in a superior and cynical cloud of pride, this one, in a floral mumu and Spandex bloomers, Runciter had never encountered before. And so it went: five females and—he counted—five males. Someone was missing.

Ahead of Joe Chip the smoldering, brooding girl, Patricia Conley, entered. That made the eleventh; the group had all appeared.

"You made good time, Mrs. Jackson," he said to the mannish, thirtyish, sand-colored lady wearing ersatz vicuna trousers and a gray sweatshirt on which had been printed a now faded full-face portrait of Bertrand Lord Russell. "You had less time than anybody else, inasmuch as I notified you last."

Tippy Jackson smiled a bloodless, sand-colored smile.

"Some of you I know," Runciter said, rising from his chair and indicating with his hands that they should find chairs and make themselves comfortable, smoking if necessary. "You, Miss Dorn; Mr. Chip and I chose you first because of your topnotch activity vis-à-vis S. Dole Melipone, whom you eventually lost through no fault of your own."

"Thank you, Mr. Runciter," Edie Dorn said in a wispy, shy trickle of a voice; she blushed and stared wide-eyed at the far wall. "It's good to be a part of this new undertaking," she added with undernourished conviction.

"Which one of you is Al Hammond?" Runciter asked, consulting his documents.

An excessively tall, stoop-shouldered Negro with a gentle expression on his elongated face made a motion to indicate himself.

"I've never met you before," Runciter said, reading the material from Al Hammond's file. "You rate highest among our anti-precogs. I should, of course, have gotten around to meeting you. How many of the rest of you are anti-precog?" Three additional hands appeared. "The four of you," Runciter said, "will undoubtedly get a great bloop out of meeting and working with G. G. Ashwood's most recent discovery, who aborts precogs on a new basis. Perhaps Miss Conley herself will describe it to us." He nodded toward Pat—

And found himself standing before a shop window on Fifth Avenue, a rare-coin shop; he was studying an uncirculated U.S. gold dollar and wondering if he could afford to add it to his collection.

What collection? he asked himself, startled. I don't collect coins. What am I doing here? And how long have I been wandering around window-shopping when I ought to be in my office supervising—he could not remember what he generally supervised; a business of some kind, dealing in people with abilities, special talents. He shut his eyes, trying to focus his mind. No, I had to give that up, he realized. Because of a coronary last year, I had to retire. But I was just there, he remembered. Only a few seconds ago. In my office. Talking to a group of people about a new project. He shut his eyes. It's gone, he thought dazedly. Everything I built up.

When he opened his eyes he found himself back in his office; he faced G. G. Ashwood, Joe Chip and a dark, intensely attractive girl whose name he did not recall. Other than that his office was empty, which for reasons he did not understand struck him as strange.

"Mr. Runciter," Joe Chip said, "I'd like you to meet Patricia Conley."

The girl said, "How nice to be introduced to you at last, Mr. Runciter." She laughed and her eyes flashed exultantly. Runciter did not know why.

Joe Chip realized, *She's been doing something.* "Pat," he said aloud, "I can't put my finger on it but things are different." He gazed wonderingly around the office; it appeared as it had always: too loud a carpet, too many unrelated art objects, on the walls original pictures of no artistic merit whatever. Glen Runciter had not changed; shaggy and gray, his face wrinkled broodingly, he returned Joe's stare—he too seemed perplexed. Over by the window G. G. Ashwood, wearing his customary natty birch-bark pantaloons, hemp-rope belt, peekaboo see-through top and train-engineer's tall hat, shrugged indifferently. He, obviously, saw nothing wrong.

"Nothing is different," Pat said.

"*Everything* is different," Joe said to her. "You must have gone back into time and put us on a different track; I can't prove it and I can't specify the nature of the changes—"

"No domestic quarreling on my time," Runciter said frowningly.

Joe, taken aback, said, " 'Domestic quarreling'?" He saw, then, on Pat's finger the ring: wrought-silver and jade; he remembered helping her pick it out. Two days, he thought, before we got married. That was over a year ago, despite how bad off I was financially. That, of course, is changed now; Pat, with her salary and her money-minding propensity, fixed that. For all time.

"Anyhow, to continue," Runciter said. "We must each of us ask ourselves why Stanton Mick took his business to a prudence organization other than ours. Logically, we should have gotten the contract; we're the finest in the business and we're located in New York, where Mick generally prefers to deal. Do you have any theory, Mrs. Chip?" He looked hopefully in Pat's direction.

Pat said, "Do you really want to know, Mr. Runciter?"

"Yes." He nodded vigorously. "I'd very much like to know."

"*I* did it," Pat said.

"How?"

"With my talent."

Runciter said, "What talent? You don't have a talent; you're Joe Chip's wife."

At the window G. G. Ashwood said, "You came in here to meet Joe and me for lunch."

"She has a talent," Joe said. He tried to remember, but already it had become foggy; the memory dimmed even as he tried to resurrect it. A different time track, he thought. The past. Other than that, he could not make it out; there the memory ended. My wife, he thought, is unique; she can do something no one else on Earth can do. In that case, why isn't she working for Runciter Associates? *Something is wrong.*

"Have you measured it?" Runciter asked him. "I mean, that's your job. You sound as if you have; you sound sure of yourself."

"I'm not sure of myself," Joe said. But I am sure about my wife, he said to himself. "I'll get my test gear," he said. "And we'll see what sort of a field she creates."

"Oh, come on, Joe," Runciter said angrily. "If your wife has a talent or an anti-talent you would have measured it at least a year ago; you wouldn't be discovering it now." He pressed a button on his desk intercom. "Personnel? Do we have a file on Mrs. Chip? Patricia Chip?"

After a pause the intercom said, "No file on Mrs. Chip. Under her maiden name, perhaps?"

"Conley," Joe said. "Patricia Conley."

Again a pause. "On a Miss Patricia Conley we have two items: an initial scout report by Mr. Ashwood, and then test findings by Mr. Chip." From the slot of the intercom repros of the two documents slowly dribbled forth and dropped to the surface of the desk.

Examining Joe Chip's findings, Runciter said, scowling, "Joe, you better look at this; come here." He jabbed a finger at the page, and Joe, coming over beside him, saw the twin underlined crosses; he and Runciter glanced at each other, then at Pat.

"I know what it reads," Pat said levelly. " 'Unbelievable power. Anti-psi field unique in scope.' " She concentrated, trying visibly to remember the exact wording. " 'Can probably—' "

"We did get the Mick contract," Runciter said to Joe Chip. "I had a group of eleven inertials in here and then I suggested to her—"

Joe said, "That she show the group what she could do. So she did. She did exactly that. And my evaluation was right." With his fingertip he traced the symbols of danger at the bottom of the sheet. "My own wife," he said.

"I'm not your wife," Pat said. "I changed that, too. Do you want it back the way it was? With no changes, not even in details? That won't show your inertials much. On the other hand, they're unaware anyhow . . . unless some of them have retained a vestigial memory as Joe has. By now, though, it should have phased out."

Runciter said bitingly, "I'd like the Mick contract back; that much, at least."

"When I scout them," G. G. Ashwood said, "I scout them." He had become gray.

"Yes, you really bring in the talent," Runciter said.

The intercom buzzed and the quaking, elderly voice of Mrs. Frick rasped, "A group of our inertials are waiting to see you, Mr. Runciter; they say you sent for them in connection with a new joint work project. Are you free to see them?"

"Send them in," Runciter said.

Pat said, "I'll keep this ring." She displayed the silver and jade wedding ring which, in another time track, she and Joe had picked out; this much of the alternate world she had elected to retain. He wondered what—if any—legal basis she had kept in addition. None, he hoped; wisely, however, he said nothing. Better not even to ask.

The office door opened and, in pairs, the inertials entered; they stood uncertainly for a moment and then began seating themselves facing Runciter's desk. Runciter eyed them, then pawed among the rat's nest of documents on his desk; obviously, he was trying to determine whether Pat had changed in any way the composition of the group.

"Edie Dorn," Runciter said. "Yes, you're here." He

glanced at her, then at the man beside her. "Hammond. Okay, Hammond. Tippy Jackson." He peered inquiringly.

"I made it as quick as I could," Mrs. Jackson said. "You didn't give me much time, Mr. Runciter."

"Jon Ild," Runciter said.

The adolescent boy with the tousled, woolly hair grunted in response. His arrogance, Joe noted, seemed to have receded; the boy now seemed introverted and even a little shaken. It would be interesting, Joe thought, to find out what he remembers—what all of them, individually and collectively, remember.

"Francesca Spanish," Runciter said.

The luminous, gypsy-like dark woman, radiating a peculiar jangled tautness, spoke up. "During the last few minutes, Mr. Runciter, while we waited in your outer office, mysterious voices appeared to me and told me things."

"You're Francesca Spanish?" Runciter asked her, patiently; he looked more than usually tired.

"I am; I have always been; I will always be." Miss Spanish's voice rang with conviction. "May I tell you what the voices revealed to me?"

"Possibly later," Runciter said, passing on to the next personnel document.

"It must be said," Miss Spanish declared vibrantly.

"All right," Runciter said. "We'll take a break for a couple of minutes." He opened a drawer of his desk, got out one of his amphetamine tablets, took it without water. "Let's hear what the voices revealed to you, Miss Spanish." He glanced toward Joe, shrugging.

"Someone," Miss Spanish said, "just now moved us, all of us, into another world. We inhabited it, lived in it, as citizens of it, and then a vast, all-encompassing spiritual agency restored us to this, our rightful universe."

"That would be Pat," Joe Chip said. "Pat Conley. Who just joined the firm today."

"Tito Apostos," Runciter said. "You're here?" He craned his neck, peering about the room at the seated people.

A bald-headed man, wagging a goatish beard, pointed to himself. He wore old-fashioned, hip-hugging gold lamé trousers, yet somehow created a stylish effect. Perhaps the egg-sized buttons of his kelp-green mitty blouse helped; in any case he exuded a grand dignity, a loftiness surpassing the average. Joe felt impressed.

"Don Denny," Runciter said.

"Right here, sir," a confident baritone like that of a Siamese cat declared; it arose from within a slender, earnest-looking individual who sat bolt-upright in his chair, his hands on his knees. He wore a polyester dirndl, his long hair in a snood, cowboy chaps with simulated silver stars. And sandals.

"You're an anti-animator," Runciter said, reading the appropriate sheet. "The only one we use." To Joe he said, "I wonder if we'll need him; maybe we should substitute another anti-telepath—the more of those the better."

Joe said, "We have to cover everything. Since we don't know what we're getting into."

"I guess so." Runciter nodded. "Okay, Sammy Mundo."

A weak-nosed young man, dressed in a maxiskirt, with an undersized, melon-like head, stuck his hand up in a spasmodic, wobbling, ticlike gesture; as if, Joe thought, the anemic body had done it by itself. He knew this particular person. Mundo looked years younger than his chronological age; both mental and physical growth processes had ceased for him long ago. Technically, Mundo had the intelligence of a raccoon; he could walk, eat, bathe himself, even—after a fashion—talk. His anti-telepathic ability, however, was considerable. Once, alone, he had blanked out S. Dole Melipone; the firm's house magazine had rambled on about it for months afterward.

"Oh, yes," Runciter said. "Now we come to Wendy Wright."

As always, when the opportunity arose, Joe took a long, astute look at the girl whom, if he could have managed it, he would have had as his mistress, or, even better, his wife. It did not seem possible that Wendy Wright had been born out of blood and internal organs like other people. In proximity to her he felt himself to be a squat, oily, sweating, uneducated nurt whose stomach rattled and whose breath wheezed. Near her he became aware of the physical mechanisms which kept him alive; within him machinery, pipes and valves and gas-compressors and fan belts had to chug away at a losing task, a labor ultimately doomed. Seeing her face, he discovered that his own consisted of a garish mask; noticing her body made him feel like a low-class windup toy. All her colors possessed a subtle quality, indirectly lit. Her eyes, those green and tumbled stones, looked impassively at everything; he had never seen fear in them, or aversion, or contempt. What she saw she accepted. Generally she seemed calm. But more than that she struck him as being durable, untroubled and cool, not subject to wear, or to fatigue, or to physical illness and decline. Probably she was twenty-five or -six, but he could not imagine her looking younger, and certainly she would never look older. She had too much control over herself and outside reality for that.

"I'm here," Wendy said, with soft tranquility.

Runciter nodded. "Okay; that leaves Fred Zafsky." He fixed his gaze on a flabby, big-footed, middle-aged, unnatural-looking individual with pasted-down hair, muddy skin plus a peculiar protruding Adam's apple—clad, for this occasion, in a shift dress the color of a baboon's ass. "That must be you."

"Right you are," Zafsky agreed, and sniggered. "How about that?"

"Christ," Runciter said, shaking his head. "Well, we have to include one anti-parakineticist, to be safe. And you're it." He tossed down his documents and looked about for his green cigar. To Joe he said, "That's the group, plus you and me. Any last-minute changes you want to make?"

"I'm satisfied," Joe said.

"You suppose this bunch of inertials is the best combination we can come up with?" Runciter eyed him intently.

"Yes," Joe said.

"And it's good enough to take on Hollis' Psis?"

"Yes," Joe said.

But he knew otherwise.

It was not something he could put his finger on. It certainly was not rational. Potentially, the counter-field capacity of the eleven inertials had to be considered enormous. And yet—

"Mr. Chip, can I have a second of your time?" Mr. Apostos, bald-headed and bearded, his gold lamé trousers glittering, plucked at Joe Chip's arm. "Could I discuss an experience I had late last night? In a hypnagogic state I seem to have contacted one, or possibly two, of Mr. Hollis' people—a telepath evidently operating in conjunction with one of their precogs. Do you think I should tell Mr. Runciter? Is it important?"

Hesitating, Joe Chip looked toward Runciter. Seated in his worthy, beloved chair, trying to relight his all-Havana cigar, Runciter appeared terribly tired; the wattles of his face sagged. "No," Joe said. "Let it go."

"Ladies and gentlemen," Runciter said, raising his voice above the general noise. "We're leaving now for Luna, you eleven inertials, Joe Chip and myself and our client's rep, Zoe Wirt; fourteen of us in all. We'll use our own ship." He got out his round, gold, anachronistic pocket watch and studied it. "Three-thirty. *Pratfall II* will take off from the main roof-field at four." He snapped his watch shut and returned it to the pocket of his silk sash. "Well, Joe," he said, "we're in this for better or worse. I wish we had a resident precog who could take a look ahead for us." Both his face and the tone of his voice drooped with worry and the cares, the irreversible burden, of responsibility and age.

6

We wanted to give you a shave like no other you ever had. We said, It's about time a man's face got a little loving. We said, With Ubik's self-winding Swiss chromium never-ending blade, the days of scrape-scrape are over. So try Ubik. And be loved. Warning: use only as directed. And with caution.

"Welcome to Luna," Zoe Wirt said cheerfully, her jolly eyes enlarged by her red-framed, triangular glasses. "Via myself, Mr. Howard says hello to each and every one of you, and most especially to Mr. Glen Runciter for making his organization—and you people, in particular—available to us. This subsurface hotel suite, decorated by Mr. Howard's artistically talented sister Lada, lies just three-hundred linear yards from the industrial and research facilities which Mr. Howard believes to have been infiltrated. Your joint presence in this room, therefore, should already be inhibiting the psionic capabilities of Hollis' agents, a thought pleasing to all of us." She paused, looked over them all. "Are there any questions?"

Tinkering with his test gear, Joe Chip ignored her; despite their client's stipulation, he intended to measure the surrounding psionic field. During the hour-long trip from Earth he and Glen Runciter had decided on this.

"I have a question," Fred Zafsky said, raising his hand. He giggled. "Where is the bathroom?"

"You will each be given a miniature map," Zoe Wirt said, "on which this is indicated." She nodded to a drab female assistant, who began passing out brightly colored, glossy paper maps. "This suite," she continued, "is complete with a kitchen all the appliances of which are free, rather than coin-operated. Obviously, outright blatant expense has been incurred in the constructing of this living unit, which is ample enough for twenty persons, possessing, as it does, its own self-regulating air, heat, water, and unusually varied food supply, plus closed-circuit TV and high-fidelity polyphonic phonograph sound-system—the two latter facilities, however, unlike the kitchen, being coin-operated. To aid you in utilizing these recreation facilities, a change-making machine has been placed in the game room."

"My map," Al Hammond said, "shows only nine bedrooms."

"Each bedroom," Miss Wirt said, "contains two bunk-type beds; hence eighteen accommodations in all. In addition, five of the beds are double, assisting those of you who wish to sleep with each other during your stay here."

"I have a rule," Runciter said irritably, "about my employees sleeping with one another."

"For or against?" Zoe Wirt inquired.

"Against." Runciter crumpled up his map and dropped it to the metal, heated floor. "I'm not accustomed to being told—"

"But you will not be staying here, Mr. Runciter," Miss Wirt pointed out. "Aren't you returning to Earth as soon as your employees begin to function?" She smiled her professional smile at him.

Runciter said to Joe Chip, "You getting any readings as to the psi field?"

"First," Joe said, "I have to obtain a reading on the counter-field our inertials are generating."

"You should have done that on the trip," Runciter said.

"Are you attempting to take measurements?" Miss Wirt inquired alertly. "Mr. Howard expressly contraindicated that, as I explained."

"We're taking a reading anyway," Runciter said.

"Mr. Howard—"

"This isn't Stanton Mick's business," Runciter told her.

To her drab assistant, Miss Wirt said, "Would you ask Mr. Mick to come down here, please?" The assistant scooted off in the direction of the syndrome of elevators. "Mr. Mick will tell you himself," Miss Wirt said to Runciter. "Meanwhile, please do nothing; I ask you kindly to wait until he arrives."

"I have a reading now," Joe said to Runciter. "On our own field. It's very high." Probably because of Pat, he decided. "Much higher than I would have expected," he said. Why are they so anxious for us not to take readings? he wondered. It's not a time factor now; our inertials are here and operating.

"Are there closets," Tippy Jackson asked, "where we can put away our clothes? I'd like to unpack."

"Each bedroom," Miss Wirt said, "has a large closet, coin-operated. And to start you all off—" She produced a large plastic bag. "Here is a complimentary supply of coins." She handed the rolls of dimes, nickels and quarters to Jon Ild. "Would you distribute these equally? A gesture of goodwill by Mr. Mick."

Edie Dorn asked, "Is there a nurse or doctor in this settlement? Sometimes I develop psychosomatic skin rashes when I'm hard at work; a cortisone-base ointment usually helps me, but in the hurry I forgot to bring some along."

"The industrial, research installations adjoining these living quarters," Miss Wirt said, "keep several doctors on standby, and in addition there is a small medical ward with beds for the ill."

"Coin-operated?" Sammy Mundo inquired.

"All our medical care," Miss Wirt said, "is free. But the burden of proof that he is genuinely ill rests on the shoulders of the alleged patient." She added, "All medication-dispensing machines, however, are coin-operated. I might say, in regard to this, that you will find in the game room of this suite a tranquilizer-dispensing machine. And, if you wish, we can probably have one of the stimulant-dispensing machines moved in from the adjoining installations."

"What about hallucinogens?" Francesca Spanish inquired. "When I'm at work I function better if I can get an ergot-base psychedelic drug; it causes me to actually see who I'm up against, and I find that helps."

Miss Wirt said, "Our Mr. Mick disapproves of all the ergot-base hallucinogenic agents; he feels they're liver-toxic. If you have brought any with you, you're free to use them. But we will not dispense any, although I understand we have them."

"Since when," Don Denny said to Francesca Spanish, "did you begin to need psychedelic drugs in order to hallucinate? Your whole life's a waking hallucination."

Unfazed, Francesca said, "Two nights ago I received a particularly impressive visitation."

"I'm not surprised," Don Denny said.

"A throng of precogs and telepaths descended from a ladder spun of finest natural hemp to the balcony outside my window. They dissolved a passageway through the wall and manifested themselves around my bed, waking me up with their chatter. They quoted poetry and languid prose from oldtime books, which delighted me; they seemed so—" She groped for the word. "Sparkling. One of them, who called himself Bill—"

"Wait a minute," Tito Apostos said. "I had a dream like that, too." He turned to Joe. "Remember, I told you just before we left Earth?" His hands convulsed excitedly. "Didn't I?"

"I dreamed that too," Tippy Jackson said. "Bill and Matt. They said they were going to get me."

His face twisting with abrupt darkness, Runciter said to Joe, "You should have told *me.*"

"At the time," Joe said, "you—" He gave up. "You looked tired. You had other things on your mind."

Francesca said sharply, "It wasn't a dream; it was an authentic visitation. I can distinguish the difference."

"Sure you can, Francy," Don Denny said. He winked at Joe.

"I had a dream," Jon Ild said. "But it was about hovercars. I was memorizing their license-plate numbers. I memorized sixty-five, and I still remember them. Want to hear them?"

"I'm sorry, Glen," Joe Chip said to Runciter. "I thought only Apostos experienced it; I didn't know about the others. I—" The sound of elevator doors sliding aside made him pause; he and the others turned to look.

Potbellied, squat and thick-legged, Stanton Mick perambulated toward them. He wore fuchsia pedal-pushers, pink yakfur slippers, a snakeskin sleeveless blouse, and a ribbon in his waist-length dyed white hair. His nose, Joe thought; it looks like the rubber bulb of a New Delhi taxi horn, soft and squeezable. And loud. The loudest noise, he thought, that I have ever seen.

"Hello, all you top anti-psis," Stanton Mick said, extending his arms in fulsome greeting. "The exterminators are here—by that, I mean yourselves." His voice had a squeaky, penetrating castrato quality to it, an unpleasant noise that one might expect to hear, Joe Chip thought, from a hive of metal bees. "The plague, in the form of various psionic riffraff, descended upon the harmless, friendly, peaceful world of Stanton Mick. What a day that was for us in Mickville— as we call our attractive and appetizing Lunar settlement here. You have, of course, already started work, as I knew you would. That's because you're tops in your field, as everyone realizes when Runciter Associates is mentioned. I'm already delighted at your activity, with one small exception that I perceive your tester there dingling with his equipment. Tester, would you look my way while I'm speaking to you?"

Joe shut off his polygraphs and gauges, killed the power supply.

"Do I have your attention now?" Stanton Mick asked him.

"Yes," Joe said.

"Leave your equipment on," Runciter ordered him.

"You're not an employee of Mr. Mick; you're my employee."

"It doesn't matter," Joe said to him. "I've already gotten a reading on the psi field being generated in this vicinity." He had done his job. Stanton Mick had been too slow in arriving.

"How great is their field?" Runciter asked him.

Joe said, *"There is no field."*

"Our inertials are nullifying it? Our counter-field is greater?"

"No," Joe said. "As I said: There is no psi field of any sort within range of my equipment. I pick up our own field, so as far as I can determine my instruments are functioning; I consider that an accurate feedback. We're producing 2000 blr units, fluctuating upward to 2100 every few minutes. Probably it will gradually increase; by the time our inertials have been functioning together, say, twelve hours, it may reach as high as—"

"I don't understand," Runciter said. All the inertials now were gathering around Joe Chip; Don Denny picked up one of the tapes which had been excreted by the polygraph, examined the unwavering line, then handed the tape to Tippy Jackson. One by one the other inertials examined it silently, then looked toward Runciter. To Stanton Mick, Runciter said, "Where did you get the idea that Psis had infiltrated your operations here on Luna? And why didn't you want us to run our normal tests? Did you know we would get this result?"

"Obviously, he knew," Joe Chip said. He felt sure of it.

Rapid, agitated activity crossed Runciter's face; he started to speak to Stanton Mick, then changed his mind and said to Joe in a low voice, "Let's get back to Earth; let's get our inertials right out of here now."

Aloud, to the others, he said, "Collect your possessions; we're flying back to New York. I want all of you in the ship within the next fifteen minutes; any of you who aren't in will be left behind. Joe, get all that junk of yours together in one heap; I'll help you lug it to the ship, if I have to—anyhow, I want it out of here and you with it." He turned in Mick's direction once again, his face puffy with anger; he started to speak—

Squeaking in his metal-insect voice, Stanton Mick floated to the ceiling of the room, his arms protruding distendedly and rigidly. "Mr. Runciter, don't let your thalamus override your cerebral cortex. This matter calls for discretion, not haste; calm your people down and let's huddle together in an effort to mutually understand." His rotund, colorful body bobbed about, twisting in a slow, transversal rotation so that now his feet, rather than his head, extended in Runciter's direction.

"I've heard of this," Runciter said to Joe. "It's a self-destruct humanoid bomb. Help me get everybody out of here. They just now put it on auto; that's why it floated upward."

The bomb exploded.

Smoke, billowing in ill-smelling masses which clung to the ruptured walls and floor, sank and obscured the prone, twitching figure at Joe Chip's feet.

In Joe's ear Don Denny was yelling, "They killed Runciter, Mr. Chip. That's Mr. Runciter." In his excitement he stammered.

"Who else?" Joe said thickly, trying to breathe; the acrid smoke constricted his chest. His head rang from the concussion of the bomb, and, feeling an oozing warmth on his neck, he found that a flying shard had lacerated him.

Wendy Wright, indistinct although close by, said, "I think everyone else is hurt but alive."

Bending down beside Runciter, Edie Dorn said, "Could we get an animator from Ray Hollis?" Her face looked crushed in and pale.

"No," Joe said; he, too, bent down. "You're wrong," he said to Don Denny. "He's not dead."

But on the twisted floor Runciter lay dying. In two minutes, three minutes, Don Denny would be correct.

"Listen, everybody," Joe said aloud. "Since Mr. Runciter is injured, I'm now in charge—temporarily, anyhow, until we can get back to Terra."

"Assuming," Al Hammond said, "we get back at all." With a folded handkerchief he patted a deep cut over his right eye.

"How many of you have hand weapons?" Joe asked. The inertials continued to mill without answering. "I know it's against Society rules," Joe said. "But I know some of you carry them. Forget the illegality; forget everything you've ever learned pertaining to inertials on the job carrying guns."

After a pause Tippy Jackson said, "Mine is with my things. In the other room."

"Mine is here with me," Tito Apostos said; he already held, in his right hand, an old-fashioned lead-slug pistol.

"If you have guns," Joe said, "and they're in the other room where you left your things, go get them."

Six inertials started toward the door.

To Al Hammond and Wendy Wright, who remained, Joe said, "We've got to get Runciter into cold-pac."

"There're cold-pac facilities on the ship," Al Hammond said.

"Then we'll lug him there," Joe said. "Hammond, take one end and I'll lift up the other. Apostos, you go ahead of us and shoot any of Hollis' employees who try to stop us."

Jon Ild, returning from the next room with a laser tube, said, "You think Hollis is in here with Mr. Mick?"

"With him," Joe said, "or by himself. We may never have been dealing with Mick; it may have been Hollis from the start." Amazing, he thought, that the explosion of the humanoid bomb didn't kill the rest of us. He wondered about Zoe Wirt. Evidently, she had gotten out before the blast; he saw no sign of her. I wonder what her reaction was, he thought, when she found out she wasn't working for Stanton Mick, that her employer—her real employer—had hired us, brought us here, to assassinate us. They'll probably have to kill her too. Just to be on the safe side. She certainly won't be of any more use; in fact, she'll be a witness to what happened.

Now armed, the other inertials returned; they waited for Joe to tell them what to do. Considering their situation, the eleven inertials seemed reasonably self-possessed.

"If we can get Runciter into cold-pac soon enough," Joe explained, as he and Al Hammond carried their apparently dying employer toward the elevators, "he can still run the firm. The way his wife does." He stabbed the elevator button with his elbow. "There's really very little chance," he said, "that the elevator will come. They probably cut off all power at the same moment as the blast."

The elevator, however, did appear. With haste he and Al Hammond carried Runciter aboard it.

"Three of you who have guns," Joe said, "come along with us. The rest of you—"

"The hell with that," Sammy Mundo said. "We don't want to be stuck down here waiting for the elevator to come back. It may never come back." He started forward, his face constricted with panic.

Joe said harshly, "Runciter goes first." He touched a button and the doors shut, enclosing him, Al Hammond, Tito Apostos, Wendy Wright, Don Denny—and Glen Runciter. "It has to be done this way," he said to them as the elevator ascended. "And anyhow, if Hollis' people are waiting they'll get us first. Except that they probably don't expect us to be armed."

"There is that law," Don Denny put in.

"See if he's dead yet," Joe said to Tito Apostos.

Bending, Apostos examined the inert body. "Still some shallow respiration," he said presently. "So we still have a chance."

"Yes, a chance," Joe said. He remained numb, as he had been both physically and psychologically since the blast; he felt cold and torpid and his eardrums appeared to be damaged. Once we're back in our own ship, he reflected, after we get Runciter into the cold-pac, we can send out an assist call, back to New York, to everyone at the firm. In fact, to all the prudence organizations. If we can't take off they can come to get us.

But in reality it wouldn't work that way. Because by the time someone from the Society got to Luna, everyone trapped sub-surface, in the elevator shaft and aboard the ship, would be dead. So there really was no chance.

Tito Apostos said, "You could have let more of them into the elevator. We could have squeezed the rest of the women in." He glared at Joe accusingly, his hands shaking with agitation.

"We'll be more exposed to assassination than they will," Joe said. "Hollis will expect any survivors of the blast to make use of the elevator, as we're doing. That's probably why they left the power on. They know we have to get back to our ship."

Wendy Wright said, "You already told us that, Joe."

"I'm trying to rationalize what I'm doing," he said. "Leaving the rest of them down there."

"What about that new girl's talent?" Wendy said. "That sullen, dark girl with the disdainful attitude; Pat something. You could have had her go back into the past, before Runciter's injury; she could have changed all this. Did you forget about her ability?"

"Yes," Joe said tightly. He had, in the aimless, smoky confusion.

"Let's go back down," Tito Apostos said. "Like you say, Hollis' people will be waiting for us at ground level; like you said, we're in more danger by—"

"We're at the surface," Don Denny said. "The elevator's stopped." Wan and stiff, he licked his lips apprehensively as the doors automatically slid aside.

They faced a moving sidewalk that led upward to a concourse, at the end of which, beyond air-membrane doors, the base of their upright ship could be distinguished. Exactly as they had left it. And no one stood between them and it.

Peculiar, Joe Chip thought. Were they sure the exploding humanoid bomb would get us all? Something in the way they planned it must have gone wrong, first in the blast itself, then in their leaving the power on—and now this empty corridor.

"I think," Don Denny said, as Al Hammond and Joe carried Runciter from the elevator and onto the moving sidewalk, "the fact that the bomb floated to the ceiling fouled them up. It seemed to be a fragmentation type, and most of the flak hit the walls above our heads. I think it never occurred to them that any of us might survive; that would be why they left the power on."

"Well, thank god it floated up then," Wendy Wright said. "Good lord, it's chilly. The bomb must have put this place's heating system out of action." She trembled visibly.

The moving sidewalk carried them forward with shattering slowness; it seemed to Joe that five or more minutes passed before the sidewalk evicted them at the two-stage air-membrane doors. The crawl forward, in some ways, seemed to him the worst part of everything which had happened, as if Hollis had arranged this purposely.

"Wait!" a voice called from behind them; footsteps sounded, and Tito Apostos turned, his gun raised, then lowered.

"The rest of them," Don Denny said to Joe, who could not turn around; he and Al Hammond had begun maneuvering Runciter's body through the intricate system of the air-membrane doors. "They're all there; it's okay." With his gun he waved them toward him. "Come on!"

The connecting plastic tunnel still linked their ship with the concourse; Joe heard the characteristic dull clunk under his feet and wondered, *Are they letting us go?* Or, he thought, Are they waiting for us in the ship? It's as if, he thought, some malicious force is playing with us, letting us scamper and twitter like debrained mice. We amuse it. Our efforts entertain it. And when we get just so far its fist will close around us and drop our squeezed remains, like Runciter's, onto the slow-moving floor.

"Denny," he said. "You go into the ship first. See if they're waiting for us."

"And if they are?" Denny said.

"Then you come back," Joe said bitingly, "and tell us and we give up. And then they kill the rest of us."

Wendy Wright said, "Ask Pat whatever her name is to use her ability." Her voice was low but insistent. "Please, Joe."

"Let's try to get into the ship," Tito Apostos said. "I don't like that girl; I don't trust her talent."

"You don't understand her or it," Joe said. He watched skinny, small Don Denny scamper up the tunnel, fiddle with the switching arrangement which controlled the entrance port of the ship, then disappear inside. "He'll never come back," he said, panting; the weight of Glen Runciter seemed to have grown; he could hardly hold onto him. "Let's set Runciter down here," he said to Al Hammond. Together, the two of them lowered Runciter to the floor of the tunnel. "For an old man he's heavy," Joe said, standing erect again. To Wendy he said, "I'll talk to Pat." The others had caught up now; all of them crowded agitatedly into the connecting tunnel. "What a fiasco," he gasped. "Instead of what we hoped to be our big enterprise. You never know. Hollis really got us this time." He motioned Pat up beside him. Her face was smudged and her synthetic sleeveless blouse had been ripped; the elastic band which—fashionably—compressed her breasts could be seen: It had elegant embossed pale-pink fleurs-de-lis imprinted on it, and for no logical reason the perception of this unrelated, meaningless sense-datum registered in his mind. "Listen," he said to her, putting his hand on her shoulder and looking into her eyes; she calmly returned his gaze. "Can you go back? To a time before the bomb was detonated? And restore Glen Runciter?"

"It's too late now," Pat said.

"Why?"

"That's it. Too much time has passed. I would have had to do it right away."

"Why didn't you?" Wendy Wright asked her, with hostility.

Swinging her gaze, Pat eyed her. "Did *you* think of it? If you did, you didn't say. Nobody said."

"You don't feel any responsibility, then," Wendy said. "For Runciter's death. When your talent could have obviated it."

Pat laughed.

Returning from the ship, Don Denny said, "It's empty."

"Okay," Joe said, motioning to Al Hammond. "Let's get him into the ship and into cold-pac." He and Al once more picked up the dense, hard-to-manage body; they continued on into the ship; the inertials scrambled and shoved around him, eager for sanctuary—he experienced the pure physical emanation of their fear, the field surrounding them—and himself too. The possibility that they might actually leave Luna alive made them more rather than less desperate; their stunned resignation had now completely gone.

"Where's the key?" Jon Ild shrilled in Joe's ear as he and Al Hammond stumbled groggily toward the cold-pac chamber. He plucked at Joe's arm. "The key, Mr. Chip."

Al Hammond explained, "The ignition key. For the ship. Runciter must have it on him; get it before we drop him into the cold-pac, because after that we won't be able to touch him."

Digging in Runciter's various pockets, Joe found a leather key case; he passed it to Jon Ild. "Now we can put him into cold-pac?" he said with savage anger. "Come on, Hammond; for chrissakes, help me get him into the 'pac." But we didn't move swiftly enough, he said to himself. It's all over. We failed. Well, he thought wearily, so it goes.

The initial rockets came on with a roar; the ship shuddered as, at the control console, four of the inertials haltingly collaborated in the task of programing the computerized command-receptors.

Why did they let us go? Joe asked himself as he and Al

Hammond stood Runciter's lifeless—or apparently lifeless—body upright in the floor-to-ceiling cold-pac chamber; automatic clamps closed about Runciter's thighs and shoulders, supporting him, while the cold, glistening with its own simulated life, sparkled and shone, dazzling Joe Chip and Al Hammond. "I don't understand it," he said.

"They fouled up," Hammond said. "They didn't have any back-up planned behind the bomb. Like the bomb plotters who tried to kill Hitler; when they saw the explosion go off in the bunker all of them assumed—"

"Before the cold kills us," Joe said, "let's get out of this chamber." He prodded Hammond ahead of him; once outside, the two of them together twisted the locking wheel into place. "God, what a feeling," he said. "To think that a force like that preserves life. Of a sort."

Francy Spanish, her long braids scorched, halted him as he started toward the fore section of the ship. "Is there a communication circuit in the cold-pac?" she asked. "Can we consult with Mr. Runciter now?"

"No consultation," Joe said, shaking his head. "No earphone, no microphone. No protophasons. No half-life. Not until we get back to Earth and transfer him to a moratorium."

"Then, how can we tell if we froze him soon enough?" Don Denny asked.

"We can't," Joe said.

"His brain may have deteriorated," Sammy Mundo said, grinning. He giggled.

"That's right," Joe said. "We may never hear the voice or the thoughts of Glen Runciter again. We may have to run Runciter Associates without him. We may have to depend on what's left of Ella; we may have to move our offices to the Beloved Brethren Moratorium at Zürich and operate out of there." He seated himself in an aisle seat where he could watch the four inertials haggling over the correct way to direct the ship. Somnambulantly, engulfed by the dull, dreary ache of shock, he got out a bent cigarette and lit it.

The cigarette, dry and stale, broke apart as he tried to hold it between his fingers. Strange, he thought.

"The bomb blast," Al Hammond said, noticing. "The heat."

"Did it age us?" Wendy asked, from behind Hammond; she stepped past him and seated herself beside Joe. "I feel old. I *am* old; your package of cigarettes is old; we're all old, as of today, because of what has happened. This was a day for us like no other."

With dramatic energy the ship rose from the surface of Luna, carrying with it, absurdly, the plastic connective tunnel.

7

*Perk up pouting household sur-
faces with new miracle Ubik, the
easy-to-apply, extra-shiny, non-
stick plastic coating. Entirely
harmless if used as directed. Saves
endless scrubbing, glides you right
out of the kitchen!*

"Our best move," Joe Chip said, "seems to be this. We'll land at Zürich." He picked up the microwave audiophone provided by Runciter's expensive, well-appointed ship and dialed the regional code for Switzerland. "By putting him in the same moratorium as Ella we can consult both of them simultaneously; they can be linked up electronically to function in unison."

"Protophasonically," Don Denny corrected.

Joe said, "Do any of you know the name of the manager of the Beloved Brethren Moratorium?"

"Herbert something," Tippy Jackson said. "A German name."

Wendy Wright, pondering, said, "Herbert Schoenheit von Vogelsang. I remember it because Mr. Runciter once told me it means 'Herbert, the beauty of the song of birds.' I wish I had been named that. I remember thinking that at the time."

"You could marry him," Tito Apostos said.

"I'm going to marry Joe Chip," Wendy said in a somber, introspective voice, with childlike gravity.

"Oh?" Pat Conley said. Her light-saturated black eyes ignited. "Are you really?"

"Can you change that too?" Wendy said. "With your talent?"

Pat said, "I'm living with Joe. I'm his mistress. Under our arrangement I pay his bills. I paid his front door, this morning, to let him out. Without me he'd still be in his conapt."

"And our trip to Luna," Al Hammond said, "would not have taken place." He eyed Pat, a complex expression on his face.

"Perhaps not today," Tippy Jackson pointed out, "but eventually. What difference does it make? Anyhow, I think that's fine for Joe to have a mistress who pays his front door." She nudged Joe on the shoulder, her face beaming with what struck Joe as salacious approval. A sort of vicarious enjoying of his private, personal activities; in Mrs. Jackson a voyeur dwelt beneath her extroverted surface.

"Give me the ship's over-all phone book," he said. "I'll notify the moratorium to expect us." He studied his wrist watch. Ten more minutes of flight.

"Here's the phone book, Mr. Chip," Jon Ild said, after a search; he handed him the heavy square box with its keyboard and microscanner.

Joe typed out SWITZ, then ZUR, then BLVD BRETH MORA. "Like Hebrew," Pat said from behind him. "Semantic condensations." The microscanner whisked back and forth, selecting and discarding; at last its mechanism popped up a punch card, which Joe fed into the phone's receptor slot.

The phone said tinnily, "This is a recording." It expelled the punch card vigorously. "The number which you have given me is obsolete. If you need assistance, place a red card in—"

"What's the date on that phone book?" Joe asked Ild, who was returning it to its handy storage shelf.

Ild examined the information stamped on the rear of the box. "1990. Two years old."

"That can't be," Edie Dorn said. "This ship didn't exist two years ago. Everything on it and in it is new."

Tito Apostos said, "Maybe Runciter cut a few corners."

"Not at all," Edie said. "He lavished care, money and engineering skill on *Pratfall II*. Everybody who ever worked for him knows that; this ship is his pride and joy."

"*Was* his pride and joy," Francy Spanish corrected.

"I'm not ready to admit that," Joe said. He fed a red card into the phone's receptor slot. "Give me the current number of the Beloved Brethren Moratorium in Zürich, Switzerland," he said. To Francy Spanish he said, "This ship is still his pride and joy because he still exists."

A card, punched into significance by the phone, leaped out; he transferred it to its receptor slot. This time the phone's computerized workings responded without irritation; on the screen a sallow, conniving face formed, that of the unctuous busybody who ran the Beloved Brethren Moratorium. Joe remembered him with dislike.

"I am Herr Herbert Schoenheit von Vogelsang. Have you come to me in your grief, sir? May I take your name and address, were it to happen that we got cut off?" The moratorium owner poised himself.

Joe said, "There's been an accident."

"What we deem an 'accident,' " von Vogelsang said, "is ever yet a display of god's handiwork. In a sense, all life could be called an 'accident.' And yet in fact—"

"I don't want to engage in a theological discussion," Joe said. "Not at this time."

"This is the time, out of all times, when the consolations of theology are most soothing. Is the deceased a relative?"

"Our employer," Joe said. "Glen Runciter of Runciter Associates, New York. You have his wife Ella there. We'll be landing in eight or nine minutes; can you have one of your transport cold-pac vans waiting?"

"He is in cold-pac now?"

"No," Joe said. "He's warming himself on the beach at Tampa, Florida."

"I assume your amusing response indicates yes."

"Have a van at the Zürich spaceport," Joe said, and rang

off. Look who we've got to deal through, he reflected, from now on. "We'll get Ray Hollis," he said to the inertials grouped around him.

"Get him instead of Mr. Vogelsang?" Sammy Mundo asked.

"Get him in the manner of getting him dead," Joe said. "For bringing this about." Glen Runciter, he thought, frozen upright in a transparent plastic casket ornamented with plastic rosebuds. Wakened into half-life activity one hour a month. Deteriorating, weakening, growing dim . . . Christ, he thought savagely. Of all the people in the world. A man that vital. And vitalic.

"Anyhow," Wendy said, "he'll be closer to Ella."

"In a way," Joe said, "I hope we got him into the cold-pac too —" He broke off, not wanting to say it. "I don't like moratoriums," he said. "Or moratorium owners. I don't like Herbert Schoenheit von Vogelsang. Why does Runciter prefer Swiss moratoriums? What's the matter with a moratorium in New York?"

"It is a Swiss invention," Edie Dorn said. "And according to impartial surveys, the average length of half-life of a given individual in a Swiss moratorium is two full hours greater than an individual in one of ours. The Swiss seem to have a special knack."

"The U.N. ought to abolish half-life," Joe said. "As interfering with the natural process of the cycle of birth and death."

Mockingly, Al Hammond said, "If god approved of half-life, each of us would be born in a casket filled with dry ice."

At the control console, Don Denny said, "We're now under the jurisdiction of the Zürich microwave transmitter. It'll do the rest." He walked away from the console, looking glum.

"Cheer up," Edie Dorn said to him. "To be brutally harsh about it, consider how lucky all of us are; we might be dead now. Either by the bomb or by being lasered down after the blast. It'll make you feel better, once we land; we'll be so much safer on Earth."

Joe said, "The fact that we had to go to Luna should have tipped us off." Should have tipped Runciter off, he realized. "Because of that loophole in the law dealing with civil authority on Luna. Runciter always said, 'Be suspicious of any job order requiring us to leave Earth.' If he were alive he'd be saying it now. 'Especially don't bite if it's Luna where they want us. Too many prudence organizations have bitten on that.' " If he does revive at the moratorium, he thought, that'll be the first thing he says. "I always was suspicious of Luna," he'll say. But not quite suspicious enough. The job was too much of a plum; he couldn't resist it. And so, with that bait, they got him. As he always knew they would.

The ship's retrojets, triggered off by the Zürich microwave transmitter, rumbled on; the ship shuddered.

"Joe," Tito Apostos said, "you're going to have to tell Ella about Runciter. You realize that?"

"I've been thinking about it," Joe said, "since we took off and started back."

The ship, slowing radically, prepared by means of its various homeostatic servo-assist systems to land.

"And in addition," Joe said, "I have to notify the Society as to what's happened. They'll rake us over the coals; they'll point out right away that we walked into it like sheep."

Sammy Mundo said, "But the Society is our friend."

"Nobody," Al Hammond said, "after a fiasco like this, is our friend."

A solar-battery-powered chopper marked BELOVED BRETHREN MORATORIUM waited at the edge of the Zürich field. Beside it stood a beetle-like individual wearing a Continental outfit: tweed toga, loafers, crimson sash and a purple airplane-propeller beanie. The proprietor of the moratorium minced toward Joe Chip, his gloved hand extended, as Joe stepped from the ship's ramp onto the flat ground of Earth.

"Not exactly a trip replete with joy, I would judge by your

appearance," von Vogelsang said as they briefly shook hands. "May my workmen go aboard your attractive ship and begin—"

"Yes," Joe said. "Go aboard and get him." Hands in his pockets, he meandered toward the field's coffee shop, feeling bleakly glum. All standard operating procedure from now on, he realized. We got back to Earth; Hollis didn't get us— we're lucky. The Lunar operation, the whole awful, ugly, rat-trap experience, is over. And a new phase begins. One which we have no direct power over.

"Five cents, please," the door of the coffee shop said, remaining shut before him.

He waited until a couple passed by him on their way out; neatly he squeezed by the door, made it to a vacant stool and seated himself. Hunched over, his hands locked together before him on the counter, he read the menu. "Coffee," he said.

"Cream or sugar?" the speaker of the shop's ruling monad turret asked.

"Both."

The little window opened; a cup of coffee, two tiny paper-wrapped sacks of sugar and a test-tube-like container of cream slid forward and came to rest before him on the counter.

"One international poscred, please," the speaker said.

Joe said, "Charge this to the account of Glen Runciter of Runciter Associates, New York."

"Insert the proper credit card," the speaker said.

"They haven't let me carry around a credit card in five years," Joe said. "I'm still paying off what I charged back in—"

"One poscred, please," the speaker said. It began to tick ominously. "Or in ten seconds I will notify the police."

He passed the poscred over. The ticking stopped.

"We can do without your kind," the speaker said.

"One of these days," Joe said wrathfully, "people like me will rise up and overthrow you, and the end of tyranny by the homeostatic machine will have arrived. The day of human values and compassion and simple warmth will return, and when that happens someone like myself who has gone through an ordeal and who genuinely needs hot coffee to pick him up and keep him functioning when he has to function will get the hot coffee whether he happens to have a poscred readily available or not." He lifted the miniature pitcher of cream, then set it down. "And furthermore, your cream or milk or whatever it is, is sour."

The speaker remained silent.

"Aren't you going to do anything?" Joe said. "You had plenty to say when you wanted a poscred."

The pay door of the coffee shop opened and Al Hammond came in; he walked over to Joe and seated himself beside him. "The moratorium has Runciter in their chopper. They're ready to take off and they want to know if you intend to ride with them."

Joe said, "Look at this cream." He held up the pitcher; in it the fluid plastered the sides in dense clots. "This is what you get for a poscred in one of the most modern, technologically advanced cities on Earth. I'm not leaving here until this place makes an adjustment, either returning my poscred or giving me a replacement pitcher of fresh cream so I can drink my coffee."

Putting his hand on Joe's shoulder, Al Hammond studied him. "What's the matter, Joe?"

"First my cigarette," Joe said. "Then the two-year-old obsolete phone book in the ship. And now they're serving me week-old sour cream. I don't get it, Al."

"Drink the coffee black," Al said. "And get over to the chopper so they can take Runciter to the moratorium. The rest of us will wait in the ship until you come back. And then we'll head for the nearest Society office and make a full report to them."

Joe picked up the coffee cup, and found the coffee cold, inert and ancient; a scummy mold covered the surface. He set the cup back down in revulsion. What's going on? he thought. What's happening to me? His revulsion became, all at once, a weird, nebulous panic.

"Come on, Joe," Al said, his hand closing firmly around Joe's shoulder. "Forget the coffee; it isn't important. What matters is getting Runciter to—"

"You know who gave me that poscred?" Joe said. "Pat Conley. And right away I did what I always do with money; I frittered it away on nothing. On last year's cup of coffee." He got down from the stool, urged off it by Al Hammond's hand. "How about coming with me to the moratorium? I need back-up help, especially when I go to confer with Ella. What should we do, blame it on Runciter? Say it was his decision for us all to go to Luna? That's the truth. Or maybe we should tell her something else, tell her his ship crashed or he died of natural causes."

"But Runciter will eventually be linked up to her," Al said. "And he'll tell her the truth. So you have to tell her the truth."

They left the coffee shop and made their way to the chopper belonging to the Beloved Brethren Moratorium. "Maybe I'll let Runciter tell her," Joe said as they boarded. "Why not? It was his decision for us to go to Luna; let him tell her himself. And he's used to talking to her."

"Ready, gentlemen?" von Vogelsang inquired, seated at the controls of the chopper. "Shall we wind our doleful steps in the direction of Mr. Runciter's final home?"

Joe groaned and stared out through the window of the chopper, fixing his attention on the buildings that made up the installations of Zürich Field.

"Yeah, take off," Al said.

As the chopper left the ground the moratorium owner pressed a button on his control panel. Throughout the cabin of the chopper, from a dozen sources, the sound of Beethoven's *Missa Solemnis* rolled forth sonorously, the many voices saying, *"Agnus dei, qui tollis peccata mundi,"* over and over again, accompanied by an electronically augmented symphony orchestra.

"Did you know that Toscanini used to sing along with the singers when be conducted an opera?" Joe said. "That in his recording of *Traviata* you can hear him during the aria 'Sempre Libera'?"

"I didn't know that," Al said. He watched the sleek, sturdy conapts of Zürich move by below, a dignified and stately procession which Joe also found himself watching.

"Libera me, Domine," Joe said.

"What's that mean?"

Joe said, "It means, 'God have mercy on me.' Don't you know that? Doesn't everybody know that?"

"What made you think of it?" Al said.

"The music, the goddam music." To von Vogelsang he said, "Turn the music off. Runciter can't hear it. I'm the only one who can hear it, and I don't feel like hearing it." To Al he said, "You don't want to hear it, do you?"

Al said, "Calm down, Joe."

"We're carrying our dead employer to a place called the Beloved Brethren Moratorium," Joe said, "and he says, 'Calm down.' You know, Runciter didn't have to go with us to Luna; he could have dispatched us and stayed in New York. So now the most life-loving, full-living man I ever met has been—"

"Your dark-skinned companion's advice is good," the moratorium owner chimed in.

"What advice?" Joe said.

"To calm yourself." Von Vogelsang opened the glove compartment of the chopper's control panel; he handed Joe a merry multicolored box. "Chew one of these, Mr. Chip."

"Tranquilizing gum," Joe said, accepting the box; reflexively he opened it. "Peach-flavored tranquilizing gum." To Al he said, "Do I have to take this?"

"You should," Al said.

Joe said, "Runciter would never have taken a tranquilizer under circumstances of this sort. Glen Runciter never took a tranquilizer in his life. You know what I realize now, Al? He gave his life to save ours. In an indirect way."

"Very indirect," Al said. "Here we are," he said; the chopper had begun to descend toward a target painted on a flat roof field below. "You think you can compose yourself?" he asked Joe.

"I can compose myself," Joe said, "when I hear Runciter's voice again. When I know some form of life, half-life, is still there."

The moratorium owner said cheerily, "I wouldn't worry on that score, Mr. Chip. We generally obtain an adequate protophasonic flow. At first. It is later, when the half-life period has expended itself, that the heartache arises. But, with sensible planning, that can be forestalled for many years." He shut off the motor of the chopper, touched a stud which caused the cabin door to slide back. "Welcome to the Beloved Brethren Moratorium," he said; he ushered the two of them out onto the roof field. "My personal secretary, Miss Beason, will escort you to a consultation lounge; if you will wait there, being subliminally influenced into peace of soul by the colors and textures surrounding you, I will have Mr. Runciter brought in as soon as my technicians establish contact with him."

"I want to be present at the whole process," Joe said. "I want to see your technicians bring him back."

To Al, the moratorium owner said, "Maybe, as his friend, you can make him understand."

"We have to wait in the lounge, Joe," Al said.

Joe looked at him fiercely. "Uncle Tom," he said.

"All the moratoriums work this way," Al said. "Come on with me to the lounge."

"How long will it take?" Joe asked the moratorium owner.

"We'll know one way or another within the first fifteen minutes. If we haven't gotten a measurable signal by then—"

"You're only going to try for fifteen minutes?" Joe said. To Al he said, "They're only going to try for fifteen minutes to bring back a man greater than all of us put together." He felt like crying. Aloud. "Come on," he said to Al. "Let's—"

"You come on," Al repeated. "To the lounge."

Joe followed him into the lounge.

"Cigarette?" Al said, seating himself on a synthetic buffalo-hide couch; he held his pack up to Joe.

"They're stale," Joe said. He didn't need to take one, to touch one, to know that.

"Yeah, so they are." Al put the pack away. "How did you know?" He waited. "You get discouraged easier than anyone I ever ran into. We're lucky to be alive; it could be us, all of us, in that cold-pac there. And Runciter sitting out here in this lounge with these nutty colors." He looked at his watch.

Joe said, "All the cigarettes in the world are stale." He examined his own watch. "Ten after." He pondered, having many disjointed and unconnected brooding thoughts; they swam through him like silvery fish. Fears, and mild dislikes, and apprehensions. And all the silvery fish recirculating to begin once more as fear. "If Runciter were alive," he said, "sitting out here in this lounge, everything would be okay. I know it but I don't know why." He wondered what was, at this moment, going on between the moratorium's technicians and the remains of Glen Runciter. "Do you remember dentists?" he asked Al.

"I don't remember, but I know what they were."

"People's teeth used to decay."

"I realize that," Al said.

"My father told me what it used to feel like, waiting in a dentist's office. Every time the nurse opened the door you thought, It's happening. The thing I've been afraid of all my life."

"And that's what you feel now?" Al asked.

"I feel, Christ, why doesn't that halfwit sap who runs this place come in here and say he's alive, Runciter's alive. Or else he's not. One way or another. Yes or no."

"It's almost always yes. Statistically, as Vogelsang said—"

"In this case it'll be no."

"You have no way of knowing that."

Joe said, "I wonder if Ray Hollis has an outlet here in Zürich."

"Of course he has. But by the time you get a precog in here we'll already know anyhow."

"I'll phone up a precog," Joe said. "I'll get one on the line right now." He started to his feet, wondering where he could find a vidphone. "Give me a quarter."

Al shook his head.

"In a manner of speaking," Joe said, "you're my employee; you have to do what I say or I'll fire you. As soon as Runciter died I took over management of the firm. I've been in charge since the bomb went off; it was my decision to bring him here, and it's my decision to rent the use of a precog for a couple of minutes. Let's have the quarter." He held out his hand.

"Runciter Associates," Al said, "being run by a man who can't keep fifty cents on him. Here's a quarter." He got it from his pocket, tossed it to Joe. "When you make out my paycheck add it on."

Joe left the lounge and wandered down a corridor, rubbing his forehead blearily. This is an unnatural place, he thought. Halfway between the world and death. I *am* head of Runciter Associates now, he realized, except for Ella, who isn't alive and can only speak if I visit this place and have her revived. I know the specifications in Glen Runciter's will, which now have automatically gone into effect; I'm supposed to take over until Ella, or Ella and he if he can be revived, decide on someone to replace him. They have to agree; both wills make that mandatory. Maybe, he thought, they'll decide I can do it on a permanent basis.

That'll never come about, he realized. Not for someone who can't manage his own personal fiscal responsibilities. That's something else Hollis' precog would know, he realized. I can find out from them whether or not I'll be upgraded to director of the firm. That would be worth knowing, along with everything else. And I have to hire the precog anyhow.

"Which way to a public vidphone?" he asked a uniformed employee of the moratorium. The employee pointed. "Thanks," he said, and wandered on, coming at last to the pay vidphone. He lifted the receiver, listened for the dial tone, and then dropped in the quarter which Al had given him.

The phone said, "I am sorry, sir, but I can't accept obsolete money." The quarter clattered out of the bottom of the phone and landed at his feet. Expelled in disgust.

"What do you mean?" he said, stooping awkwardly to retrieve the coin. "Since when is a North American Confederation quarter obsolete?"

"I am sorry, sir," the phone said, "the coin which you put into me was not a North American Confederation quarter but a recalled issue of the United States of America's Philadelphia mint. It is of merely numismatical interest now."

Joe examined the quarter and saw, on its tarnished surface, the bas-relief profile of George Washington. And the date. The coin was forty years old. And, as the phone had said, long ago recalled.

"Having difficulties, sir?" a moratorium employee asked, walking over pleasantly. "I saw the phone expel your coin. May I examine it?" He held out his hand and Joe gave him the U.S. quarter. "I will trade you a current Swiss ten-franc token for this. Which the phone will accept."

"Fine," Joe said. He made the trade, dropped the ten-franc piece into the phone and dialed Hollis' international toll-free number.

"Hollis Talents," a polished female voice said in his ear and, on the screen, a girl's face, modified by artificial beauty aids of an advanced nature, manifested itself. "Oh, Mr. Chip," the girl said, recognizing him. "Mr. Hollis left word with us that you'd call. We've been expecting you all afternoon."

Precogs, Joe thought.

"Mr. Hollis," the girl said, "instructed us to put your call through to him; he wants to handle your needs personally.

Would you hold on a moment while I put you through? So just a moment, Mr. Chip; the next voice that you hear will be Mr. Hollis', God willing." Her face vanished; he confronted a blank gray screen.

A grim blue face with recessive eyes swam into focus, a mysterious countenance floating without neck or body. The eyes reminded him of flawed jewels; they shone but the faceting had gone wrong; the eyes scattered light in irregular directions. "Hello, Mr. Chip."

So this is what he looks like, Joe thought. Photographs haven't caught this, the imperfect planes and surfaces, as if the whole brittle edifice had once been dropped, had broken, had then been reglued—but not quite as before. "The Society," Joe said, "will receive a full report on your murder of Glen Runciter. They own a lot of legal talent; you'll be in court the rest of your life." He waited for the face to react, but it did not. "We know you did it," he said, and felt the futility of it, the pointlessness of what he was doing.

"As to the purpose of your call," Hollis said in a slithering voice which reminded Joe of snakes crawling over one another, "Mr. Runciter will not—"

Shaking, Joe hung up the receiver.

He walked back up the corridor along which he had come; he reached the lounge once more where Al Hammond sat morosely picking apart a dry-as-dust former cigarette. There was a moment of silence and then Al raised his head.

"It's no," Joe said.

"Vogelsang came around looking for you," Al said. "He acted very strange, and it was obvious what's been going on back there. Six will get you eight he's afraid to tell you outright; he'll probably go through a long routine but it'll boil down like you say, it'll boil down to no. So what now?" He waited.

"Now we get Hollis," Joe said.

"We won't get Hollis."

"The Society—" He broke off. The owner of the moratorium had sidled into the lounge, looking nervous and haggard but attempting at the same time to emit an aura of detached, austere prowess.

"We did what we could. At such low temperatures the flow of current is virtually unimpeded; there's no perceptible resistance at minus 150g. The signal should have bounced out clear and strong, but all we got from the amplifier was a sixty-cycle hum. Remember, however, that we did not supervise the original cold-pac installation. Bear that in mind."

Al said, "We have it in mind." He rose stiffly to his feet and stood facing Joe. "I guess that's it."

"I'll talk to Ella," Joe said.

"Now?" Al said. "You better wait until you know what you're going to say. Tell her tomorrow. Go home and get some sleep."

"To go home," Joe said, "is to go home to Pat Conley. I'm in no shape to cope with her either."

"Take a hotel room here in Zürich," Al said. "Disappear. I'll go back to the ship, tell the others, and report to the Society. You can delegate it to me in writing." To von Vogelsang he said, "Bring us a pen and a sheet of paper."

"You know who I feel like talking to?" Joe said, as the moratorium owner scuttled off in search of pen and paper. "Wendy Wright. She'll know what to do. I value her opinion. Why is that? I wonder. I barely know her." He noticed then that subtle background music hung over the lounge. It had been there all this time. The same as on the chopper. *"Dies irae, dies illa,"* the voices sang darkly. *"Solvet saeclum in favilla, teste David cum Sybilla."* The Verdi *Requiem,* he realized. Von Vogelsang, probably personally with his own two hands, switched it on at nine A.M. every morning when he arrived for work.

"Once you get your hotel room," Al said, "I could probably talk Wendy Wright into showing up there."

"That would be immoral," Joe said.

"What?" Al stared at him. "At a time like this? When the

whole organization is about to sink into oblivion unless you can pull yourself together? Anything that'll make you function is desirable, in fact necessary. Go back to the phone, call a hotel, come back here and tell me the name of the hotel and the—"

"All our money is worthless," Joe said. "I can't operate the phone, not unless I can find a coin collector who'll trade me another Swiss ten-franc piece of current issue."

"Jeez," Al said; he let out his breath in a groaning sigh and shook his head.

"Is it *my* fault?" Joe said. "Did I make that quarter you gave me obsolete?" He felt anger.

"In some weird way," Al said, "yes, it is your fault. But I don't know how. Maybe one day I'll figure it out. Okay, we'll both go back to *Pratfall II*. You can pick Wendy Wright up there and take her to the hotel with you."

"*Quantus tremor est futurus*," the voices sang. "*Quando judex est venturus, cuncta stricte discussurus.*"

"What'll I pay the hotel with? They won't take our money any more than the phone will."

Cursing, Al yanked out his wallet, examined the bills in it. "These are old but still in circulation." He inspected the coins in his pockets. "These aren't in circulation." He tossed the coins to the carpet of the lounge, ridding himself, as the phone had, in disgust. "Take these bills." He handed the paper currency to Joe. "There's enough there for the hotel room for one night, dinner and a couple of drinks for each of you. I'll send a ship from New York tomorrow to pick you and her up."

"I'll pay you back," Joe said. "As pro tem director of Runciter Associates, I'll draw a higher salary; I'll be able to pay all my debts off, including the back taxes, penalties and fines which the income-tax people—"

"Without Pat Conley? Without her help?"

"I can throw her out now," Joe said.

Al said, "I wonder."

"This is a new start for me. A new lease on life." I can run the firm, he said to himself. Certainly I won't make the mistake that Runciter made; Hollis, posing as Stanton Mick, won't lure me and my inertials off Earth where we can be gotten at.

"In my opinion," Al said hollowly, "you have a will to fail. No combination of circumstances—including this—is going to change that."

"What I actually have," Joe said, "is a will to succeed. Glen Runciter saw that, which is why he specified in his will that I take over in the event of his death and the failure of the Beloved Brethren Moratorium to revive him into half-life, or any other reputable moratorium as specified by me." Within him his confidence rose; he saw now the manifold possibilities ahead, as clearly as if he had precog abilities. And then he remembered Pat's talent, what she could do to precogs, to any attempt to foresee the future.

"Tuba mirum spargens sonum," the voices sang. *"Per sepulchra regionum coget omnes ante thronum."*

Reading his expression, Al said, "You're not going to throw her out. Not with what she can do."

"I'll rent a room at the Zürich Rootes Hotel," Joe decided. "As per your outlined proposal." But, he thought, Al's right. It won't work; Pat, or even something worse, will move in and destroy me. I'm doomed, in the classic sense. An image thrust itself into his agitated, fatigued mind: a bird caught in cobwebs. Age hung about the image, and this frightened him; this aspect of it seemed literal and real. And, he thought, prophetic. But he could not make out exactly how. The coins, he thought. Out of circulation, rejected by the phone. Collectors' items. Like ones found in museums. Is that it? Hard to say. He really didn't know.

"Mors stupebit," the voices sang. *"Et natura, cum resurget creatura, judicanti responsura."* They sang on and on.

8

If money worries have you in the cellar, go visit the lady at Ubik Savings & Loan. She'll take the frets out of your debts. Suppose, for example, you borrow fifty-nine poscreds on an interest-only loan. Let's see, that adds up to—

Daylight rattled through the elegant hotel room, uncovering stately shapes which, Joe Chip blinkingly saw, were articles of furnishings: great hand-printed drapes of a neo-silkscreen sort that depicted man's ascent from the unicellular organisms of the Cambrian Period to the first heavier-than-air flight at the beginning of the twentieth century. A magnificent pseudo-mahogany dresser, four variegated crypto-chrome-plated reclining chairs . . . he groggily admired the splendor of the hotel room and then he realized with a tremor of keen disappointment, that Wendy had not come knocking at the door. Or else he had not heard her; he had been sleeping too deeply.

Thus, the new empire of his hegemony had vanished in the moment it had begun.

With numbing gloom—a remnant of yesterday—pervading him, he lurched from the big bed, found his clothes and dressed. It was cold, unusually so; he noticed that and pondered on it. Then he lifted the phone receiver and dialed for room service.

"—pay him back if at all possible," the receiver declared in his ear. "First, of course, it has to be established whether

Stanton Mick actually involved himself, or if a mere hom-
osimulacric substitute was in action against us, and if so why,
and if not then how—" The voice droned on, speaking to
itself and not to Joe. It seemed as unaware of him as if he
did not exist. "From all our previous reports," the voice
declared, "it would appear that Mick acts generally in a
reputable manner and in accord with legal and ethical practices established throughout the System. In view of this—"

Joe hung up the phone and stood dizzily swaying, trying
to clear his head. *Runciter's voice.* Beyond any doubt. He
again picked up the phone, listened once more.

"—lawsuit by Mick, who can afford and is accustomed to
litigation of that nature. Our own legal staff certainly should
be consulted before we make a formal report to the Society.
It would be libel if made public and grounds for a suit claiming false arrest if—"

"Runciter!" Joe said. He said it loudly.

"—unable to verify probably for at least—"

Joe hung up.

I don't understand this, he said to himself.

Going into the bathroom, he splashed icy water on his
face, combed his hair with a sanitary, free hotel comb, then,
after meditating for a time, shaved with the sanitary, free
hotel throwaway razor. He slapped sanitary, free hotel af-
tershave onto his chin, neck and jowls, unwrapped the sanitary, free hotel glass and drank from it. Did the moratorium
finally manage to revive him? he wondered. And wired him
up to my phone? Runciter, as soon as he came around, would
want to talk to me, probably before anyone else. But if so,
why can't he hear me back? Why does it consist of one-way
transmission only? Is it only a technical defect which will
clear up?

Returning to the phone, he picked up the receiver once
more with the idea of calling the Beloved Brethren Moratorium.

"—not the ideal person to manage the firm, in view of his
confused personal difficulties, particularly—"

I can't call, Joe realized. He hung up the receiver. I can't even get room service.

In a corner of the large room a chime sounded and a tinkling mechanical voice called, "I'm your free homeopape machine, a service supplied exclusively by all the fine Rootes hotels throughout Earth and the colonies. Simply dial the classification of news that you wish, and in a matter of seconds I'll speedily provide you with a fresh, up-to-the-minute homeopape tailored to your individual requirements; and, let me repeat, at no cost to you!"

"Okay," Joe said, and crossed the room to the machine. Maybe by now, he reflected, news of Runciter's murder has gotten out. The news media cover all admissions to moratoriums routinely. He pressed the button marked *high-type interplan info*. At once the machine began to clank out a printed sheet, which he gathered up as fast as it emerged.

No mention of Runciter. Too soon? Or had the Society managed to suppress it? Or Al, he thought; maybe Al slipped a few poscreds to the owner of the moratorium. But—he himself had all of Al's money. Al couldn't buy off anybody to do anything.

A knock sounded on the hotel room door.

Putting down the homeopape, Joe made his way cautiously to the door, thinking, It's probably Pat Conley; she's trapped me here. On the other hand, it might be someone from New York, here to pick me up and take me back there. Theoretically, he conjectured, it could even be Wendy. But that did not seem likely. Not now, not this late.

It could also be an assassin dispatched by Hollis. He could be killing us off one by one.

Joe opened the door.

Quivering with unease, wringing his pulpy hands together, Herbert Schoenheit von Vogelsang stood in the doorway mumbling. "I just don't understand it, Mr. Chip. We worked all night in relays. We just are not getting a single spark. And yet we ran an electroencephalograph and the 'gram shows faint but unmistakable cerebral activity. So the afterlife is there, but we still can't seem to tap it. We've got probes at every part of the cortex now. I don't know what else we can do, sir."

"Is there measurable brain metabolism?" Joe asked.

"Yes, sir. We called in an outside expert from another moratorium, and he detected it, using his own equipment. It's a normal amount too. Just what you'd expect immediately after death."

"How did you know where to find me?" Joe asked.

"We called Mr. Hammond in New York. Then I tried to call you, here at your hotel, but your phone has been busy all morning. That's why I found it necessary to come here in person."

"It's broken," Joe said. "The phone. I can't call out either."

The moratorium owner said, "Mr. Hammond tried to contact you too, with no success. He asked me to give you a message from him, something he wants you to do here in Zürich before you start back to New York."

"He wants to remind me," Joe said, "to consult Ella."

"To tell her about her husband's unfortunate, untimely death."

"Can I borrow a couple of poscreds from you?" Joe said. "So I can eat breakfast?"

"Mr. Hammond warned me that you would try to borrow money from me. He informed me that he already provided you with sufficient funds to pay for your hotel room, plus a round of drinks, as well as—"

"Al based his estimate on the assumption that I would rent a more modest room than this. However, nothing smaller than this was available, which Al did not foresee. You can add it onto the statement which you will be presenting to Runciter Associates at the end of the month. I am, as Al probably told you, now acting director of the firm. You're dealing with a positive-thinking, powerful man here, who has worked his way step by step to the top. I could, as you must well realize, reconsider our basic policy decision as to which moratorium we wish to patronize; we might, for example, prefer one nearer New York."

Grumpily, von Vogelsang reached within his tweed toga and brought out an ersatz alligator-skin wallet, which he dug into.

"It's a harsh world we're living in," Joe said, accepting the money. "The rule is 'Dog eat dog.' "

"Mr. Hammond gave me further information to pass on to you. The ship from your New York office will arrive in Zürich two hours from now. Approximately."

"Fine," Joe said.

"In order for you to have ample time to confer with Ella Runciter, Mr. Hammond will have the ship pick you up at the moratorium. In view of this, Mr. Hammond suggests that I take you back to the moratorium with me. My chopper is parked on the hotel roof."

"Al Hammond said that? That I should return to the moratorium with you?"

"That's right." Von Vogelsang nodded.

"A tall, stoop-shouldered Negro, about thirty years old? With gold-capped front teeth, each with an ornamental design, the one on the left a heart, the next a club, the one on the right a diamond?"

"The man who came with us from Zürich Field yesterday. Who waited with you at the moratorium."

Joe said, "Did he have on green felt knickers, gray golf socks, badger-hide open-midriff blouse and imitation patent-leather pumps?"

"I couldn't see what he wore. I just saw his face on the vidscreen."

"Did he convey any specific code words so I could be sure it was him?"

The moratorium owner, peeved, said, "I don't understand the problem, Mr. Chip. The man who talked to me on the vidphone from New York is the same man you had with you yesterday."

"I can't take a chance," Joe said, "on going with you, on

getting into your chopper. Maybe Ray Hollis sent you. It was Ray Hollis who killed Mr. Runciter."

His eyes like glass buttons, von Vogelsang said, "Did you inform the Prudence Society of this?"

"We will. We'll get around to it in due time. Meanwhile we have to watch out that Hollis doesn't get the rest of us. He intended to kill us too, there on Luna."

"You need protection," the moratorium owner said. "I suggest you go immediately to your phone and call the Zürich police; they'll assign a man to cover you until you leave for New York. And, as soon as you arrive in New York—"

"My phone, as I said, is broken. All I get on it is the voice of Glen Runciter. That's why no one could reach me."

"Really? How very unusual." The moratorium owner undulated past him into the hotel room. "May I listen?" He picked up the phone receiver questioningly.

"One poscred," Joe said.

Digging into the pockets of his tweed toga, the moratorium owner fished out a handful of coins; his airplane-propeller beanie whirred irritably as he handed three of the coins to Joe.

"I'm only charging you what they ask around here for a cup of coffee," Joe said. "This ought to be worth at least that much." Thinking that, he realized that he had had no breakfast, and that he would be facing Ella in that condition. Well, he could take an amphetamine instead; the hotel probably provided them free, as a courtesy.

Holding the phone receiver tightly against his ear, von Vogelsang said, "I don't hear anything. Not even a dial tone. Now I hear a little static. As if from a great distance. Very faint." He held the receiver out to Joe, who took it and also listened.

He, too, heard only the far-off static. From thousands of miles away, he thought. Eerie. As perplexing in its own way as the voice of Runciter—if that was what it had been. "I'll return your poscred," he said, hanging up the receiver.

"Never mind," von Vogelsang said.

"But you didn't get to hear his voice."

"Let's return to the moratorium. As your Mr. Hammond requested."

Joe said, "Al Hammond is my employee. I make policy. I think I'll return to New York before I talk to Ella; in my opinion, it's more important to frame our formal notification to the Society. When you talked to Al Hammond did he say whether all the inertials left Zürich with him?"

"All but the girl who spent the night with you, here in the hotel." Puzzled, the moratorium owner looked around the room, obviously wondering where she was. His peculiar face fused over with concern. "Isn't she here?"

"Which girl was it?" Joe asked; his morale, already low, plunged into the blackest depths of his mind.

"Mr. Hammond didn't say. He assumed you'd know. It would have been indiscreet for him to tell me her name, considering the circumstances. Didn't she—"

"Nobody showed up." Which had it been? Pat Conley? Or Wendy? He prowled about the hotel room, reflexively working off his fear. I hope to god, he thought, that it was Pat.

"In the closet," von Vogelsang said.

"What?" He stopped pacing.

"Maybe you ought to look in there. These more expensive suites have extra-large closets."

Joe touched the stud of the closet door; its spring-loaded mechanism sent it flying open.

On the floor of the closet a huddled heap, dehydrated, almost mummified, lay curled up. Decaying shreds of what seemingly had once been cloth covered most of it, as if it had, by degrees, over a long period of time, retracted into what remained of its garments. Bending, he turned it over. It weighed only a few pounds; at the push of his hand its limbs folded out into thin bony extensions that rustled like paper. Its hair seemed enormously long; wiry and tangled, the black cloud of hair obscured its face. He crouched, not moving, not wanting to see who it was.

In a strangled voice von Vogelsang rasped, "That's old. Completely dried-out. Like it's been here for centuries. I'll go downstairs and tell the manager."

"It can't be an adult woman," Joe said. These could only be the remnants of a child; they were just too small. "It can't be either Pat or Wendy," he said, and lifted the cloudy hair away from its face. "It's like it was in a kiln," he said. "At a very high temperature, for a long time." The blast, he thought. The severe heat from the bomb.

He stared silently then at the shriveled, heat-darkened little face. And knew who this was. With difficulty he recognized her.

Wendy Wright.

Sometime during the night, he reasoned, she had come into the room, and then some process had started in her or around her. She had sensed it and had crept off, hiding herself in the closet, so he wouldn't know; in her last few hours of life—or perhaps minutes; he hoped it was only minutes—this had overtaken her, but she had made no sound. She hadn't wakened him. Or, he thought, she tried and she couldn't do it, couldn't attract my attention. Maybe it was after that, after trying and failing to wake me, that she crawled into this closet.

I pray to god, he thought, that it happened fast.

"You can't do anything for her?" he asked von Vogelsang. "At your moratorium?"

"Not this late. There wouldn't be any residual half-life left, not with this complete deterioration. Is—she the girl?"

"Yes," he said, nodding.

"You better leave this hotel. Right now. For your own safety. Hollis—it *is* Hollis, isn't it?—will do this to you too."

"My cigarettes," Joe said. "Dried out. The two-year-old phone book in the ship. The soured cream and coffee with scum on it, mold on it. The antiquated money." A common thread: age. "She said that back on Luna, after we made it up to the ship; she said, 'I feel old.' " He pondered, trying to control his fear; it had begun now to turn into terror. But the voice on the phone, he thought. Runciter's voice. What did that mean?

He saw no underlying pattern, no meaning. Runciter's voice on the vidphone fitted no theory which he could summon up or imagine.

"Radiation," von Vogelsang said. "It would seem to me that she was exposed to extensive radioactivity, probably some time ago. An enormous amount of it, in fact."

Joe said, "I think she died because of the blast. The explosion that killed Runciter." Cobalt particles, he said to himself. Hot dust that settled on her and which she inhaled. But, then, we're all going to die this way; it must have settled on all of us. I have it in my own lungs; so does Al; so do the other inertials. There's nothing that can be done in that case. It's too late. We didn't think of that, he realized. It didn't occur to us that the explosion consisted of a micronic nuclear reaction.

No wonder Hollis allowed us to leave. And yet—

That explained Wendy's death and it explained the dried-out cigarettes. But not the phone book, not the coins, not the corruption of the cream and coffee.

Nor did it explain Runciter's voice, the yammering monologue on the hotel room's vidphone. Which ceased when von Vogelsang lifted the receiver. When someone else tried to hear it, he realized.

I've got to get back to New York, he said to himself. All of us who were there on Luna—all of us who were present when the bomb blast went off. We have to work this out together; in fact, it's probably the only way it can be worked out. Before the rest of us die, one by one, the way Wendy did. Or in a worse way, if that's possible.

"Have the hotel management send a polyethylene bag up here," he said to the moratorium owner. "I'll put her in it and take her with me to New York."

"Isn't this a matter for the police? A horrible murder like this; they should be informed."

Joe said, "Just get me the bag."

"All right. It's your employee." The moratorium owner started off down the hall.

"Was once," Joe said. "Not any more." It would have to be her first, he said to himself. But maybe, in a sense, that's better. Wendy, he thought, I'm taking you with me, taking you home.

But not as he had planned.

To the other inertials seated around the massive genuine oak conference table Al Hammond said, breaking abruptly into the joint silence, "Joe should be back anytime now." He looked at his wrist watch to make certain. It appeared to have stopped.

"Meanwhile," Pat Conley said, "I suggest we watch the late afternoon news on TV to see if Hollis has leaked out the news of Runciter's death."

"It wasn't in the 'pape today," Edie Dorn said.

"The TV news is much more recent," Pat said. She handed Al a fifty-cent piece with which to start up the TV set mounted behind curtains at the far end of the conference room, an impressive 3-D color polyphonic mechanism which had been a source of pride to Runciter.

"Want me to put it in the slot for you, Mr. Hammond?" Sammy Mundo asked eagerly.

"Okay," Al said; broodingly, he tossed the coin to Mundo, who caught it and trotted toward the set.

Restlessly, Walter W. Wayles, Runciter's attorney, shifted about in his chair, fiddled with his fine-veined, aristocratic hands at the clasp lock of his briefcase and said, "You people should not have left Mr. Chip in Zürich. We can do nothing until he arrives here, and it's extremely vital that all matters pertaining to Mr. Runciter's will be expedited."

"You've read the will," Al said. "And so has Joe Chip.

We know who Runciter wanted to take over management of the firm."

"But from a legal standpoint—" Wayles began.

"It won't take much longer," Al said brusquely. With his pen he scratched random lines along the borders of the list he had made; preoccupied, he embroidered the list, then read it once again.

> STALE CIGARETTES
> OUT-OF-DATE PHONE BOOK
> OBSOLETE MONEY
> PUTREFIED FOOD
> AD ON MATCHFOLDER

"I'm going to pass this list around the table once more," he said aloud. "And see if this time anyone can spot a connective link between these five occurrences . . . or whatever you want to call them. These five things that are—" He gestured.

"Are wrong," Jon Ild said.

Pat Conley said, "It's easy to see the connective between the first four. But not the matchfolder. That doesn't fit in."

"Let me see the matchfolder again," Al said, reaching out his hand. Pat gave him the matchfolder and, once again, he read the ad.

> AMAZING OPPORTUNITY FOR ADVANCEMENT
> TO ALL WHO CAN QUALIFY!

> Mr. Glen Runciter of the Beloved Brethren Moratorium of Zürich, Switzerland, doubled his income within a week of receiving our free shoe kit with detailed information as to how you also can sell our authentic simulated-leather loafers to friends, relatives, business associates. Mr. Runciter, although helplessly frozen in cold-pac, earned four hundred

Al stopped reading; he pondered, meanwhile picking at a lower tooth with his thumbnail. Yes, he thought; this is different, this ad. The others consist of obsolescence and decay. But not this.

"I wonder," he said aloud, "what would happen if we answered this matchfolder ad. It gives a box number in Des Moines, Iowa."

"We'd get a free shoe kit," Pat Conley said. "With detailed information as to how we too can—"

"Maybe," Al interrupted, "we'd find ourselves in contact with Glen Runciter." Everyone at the table, including Walter W. Wayles, stared at him. "I mean it," he said. "Here." He handed the matchfolder to Tippy Jackson. "Write them 'stant mail."

"And say what?" Tippy Jackson asked.

"Just fill out the coupon," Al said. To Edie Dorn he said, "Are you absolutely sure you've had that matchfolder in your purse since late last week? Or could you have picked it up somewhere today?"

Edie Dorn said, "I put several matchfolders into my purse on Wednesday. As I told you, this morning on my way here I happened to notice this one as I was lighting a cigarette. It definitely has been in my purse from before we went to Luna. From several days before."

"With that ad on it?" Jon Ild asked her.

"I never noticed what the matchfolders said before; I only noticed this today. I can't say anything about it before. Who can?"

"Nobody can," Don Denny said. "What do you think, Al? A gag by Runciter? Did he have them printed up before his death? Or Hollis, maybe? As a sort of grotesque joke— knowing that he was going to kill Runciter? That by the time we noticed the matchfolder Runciter would be in cold-pac, in Zürich, like the matchfolder says?"

Tito Apostos said, "How would Hollis know we'd take Runciter to Zürich? And not to New York?"

"Because Ella's there," Don Denny answered.

At the TV set Sammy Mundo stood silently inspecting the

fifty-cent piece which Al had given him. His underdeveloped, pale forehead had wrinkled up into a perplexed frown.

"What's the matter, Sam?" Al said. He felt himself tense up inwardly; he foresaw another happening.

"Isn't Walt Disney's head supposed to be on the fifty-cent piece?" Sammy said.

"Either Disney's," Al said, "or if it's an older one, then Fidel Castro's. Let's see it."

"Another obsolete coin," Pat Conley said, as Sammy carried the fifty-cent piece to Al.

"No," Al said, examining the coin. "It's last year's; perfectly good datewise. Perfectly acceptable. Any machine in the world would take it. The TV set would take it."

"Then, what's the matter?" Edie Dorn asked timidly.

"Exactly what Sam said," Al answered. "It has the wrong head on it." He got up, carried the coin over to Edie, deposited it in her moist open hand. "Who does it look like to you?"

After a pause Edie said, "I—don't know."

"Sure, you know," Al said.

"Okay," Edie said sharply, goaded into replying against her will. She pushed the coin back at him, ridding herself of it with a shiver of aversion.

"*It's Runciter,*" Al said to all of them seated around the big table.

After a pause Tippy Jackson said, "Add that to your list." Her voice was barely audible.

"I see two processes at work," Pat said presently, as Al reseated himself and began to make the addendum on his piece of paper. "One, a process of deterioration; that seems obvious. We agree on that."

Raising his head, Al said to her, "What's the other?"

"I'm not quite sure." Pat hesitated. "Something to do with Runciter. I think we should look at all our other coins. And paper money too. Let me think a little longer."

One by one, the people at the table got out their wallets, purses, rummaged in their pockets.

"I have a five-poscred note," Jon Ild said, "with a beautiful steel-engraving portrait of Mr. Runciter. The rest—" He took a long look at what he held. "They're normal; they're okay. Do you want to see the five-poscred note, Mr. Hammond?"

Al said, "I've got two of them. Already. Who else?" He looked around the table. Six hands had gone up. "Eight of us," he said, "have what I guess we should call Runciter money, now, to some extent. Probably by the end of the day all the money will be Runciter money. Or give it two days. Anyhow, Runciter money will work; it'll start machines and appliances and we can pay our debts with it."

"Maybe not," Don Denny said. "Why do you think so? This, what you call Runciter money—" He tapped a bill he held. "Is there any reason why the banks should honor it? It's not legitimate issue; the Government didn't put it out. It's funny money; it's not real."

"Okay," Al said reasonably. "Maybe it's not real; maybe the banks will refuse it. But that's not the real question."

"The real question," Pat Conley said, "is, What does this second process consist of, these manifestations of Runciter?"

"That's what they are." Don Denny nodded. " 'Manifestations of Runciter'—that's the second process, along with the decay. Some coins get obsolete; others show up with Runciter's portrait or bust on them. You know what I think? I think these processes are going in opposite directions. One is a going-away, so to speak. A going-out-of-existence. That's process one. The second process is a coming-into-existence. But of something that's never existed before."

"Wish fulfillment," Edie Dorn said faintly.

"Pardon?" Al said.

"Maybe these are things Runciter wished for," Edie said. "To have his portrait on legal tender, on all our money, including metal coins. It's grandiose."

Tito Apostos said, "But *matchfolders?*"

"I guess not," Edie agreed. "That's not very grandiose."

"The firm already advertises on matchfolders," Don

Denny said. "And on TV, and in the 'papes and mags. And with junk mail. Our PR department handles all that. Generally, Runciter didn't give a damn about that end of the business, and he certainly didn't give a damn about matchfolders. If this were some sort of materialization of his psyche you'd expect his face to appear on TV, not on money or matchfolders."

"Maybe it *is* on TV," Al said.

"That's right," Pat Conley said. "We haven't tried it. None of us have had time to watch TV."

"Sammy," Al said, handing him back the fifty-cent piece, "go turn the TV set on."

"I don't know if I want to look," Edie said, as Sammy Mundo dropped the coin into the slot and stood off to one side, jiggling the tuning knobs.

The door of the room opened. Joe Chip stood there, and Al saw his face.

"Shut the TV set off," Al said and got to his feet. Everyone in the room watched as he walked toward Joe. "What happened, Joe?" he said. He waited. Joe said nothing. "What's the matter?"

"I chartered a ship to bring me back here," Joe said huskily.

"You and Wendy?"

Joe said, "Write out a check for the ship. It's on the roof. I don't have enough money for it."

To Walter W. Wayles, Al said, "Are you able to disburse funds?"

"For something like that I can. I'll go settle with the ship." Taking his briefcase with him, Wayles left the room. Joe remained in the doorway, again silent. He looked a hundred years older than when Al had last seen him.

"In my office." Joe turned away from the table; he blinked, hesitated. "I—don't think you should see. The man from the moratorium was with me when I found her. He said he couldn't do anything; it had been too long. Years."

" 'Years'?" Al said, chilled.

Joe said, "We'll go down to my office." He led Al out of the conference room, into the hall, to the elevator. "On the trip back here the ship fed me tranquilizers. That's part of the bill. Actually, I feel a lot better. In a sense, I don't feel anything. It must be the tranquilizers. I guess when they wear off I'll feel it again."

The elevator came. Together they descended, neither of them saying anything until they reached the third floor, where Joe had his office.

"I don't advise you to look." Joe unlocked his office, led Al inside. "It's up to you. If *I* got over it, *you* probably will." He switched on the overhead lighting.

After a pause Al said, "Lord god."

"Don't open it," Joe said.

"I'm not going to open it. This morning or last night?"

"Evidently, it happened early, before she even reached my room. We—that moratorium owner and I—found bits of cloth in the corridor. Leading to my door. But she must have been all right, or nearly all right, when she crossed the lobby; anyhow, nobody noticed anything. And in a big hotel like that they keep somebody watching. And the fact that she managed to reach my room—"

"Yeah, that indicates she must have been at least able to walk. That seems probable, anyhow."

Joe said, "I'm thinking about the rest of us."

"In what way?"

"The same thing. Happening to us."

"How could it?"

"How could it happen to her? Because of the blast. We're going to die like that one after another. One by one. Until none of us are left. Until each of us is ten pounds of skin and hair in a plastic bag, with a few dried-up bones thrown in."

"All right," Al said. "There's some force at work producing rapid decay. It's been at work since—or started with—the blast there on Luna. We already knew that. We also know, or think we know, that another force, a contra-force, is at work, moving things in an opposite direction. Something connected with Runciter. Our money is beginning to have his picture on it. A matchfolder—"

"He was on my vidphone," Joe said. "At the hotel."

"*On* it? How?"

"I don't know; he just was. Not on the screen, not the video part. Only his voice."

"What'd he say?"

"Nothing in particular."

Al studied him. "Could he hear you?" he asked finally.

"No. I tried to get through. It was one-way entirely; I was listening in, and that was all."

"So that's why I couldn't get through to you."

"That's why." Joe nodded.

"We were trying the TV when you showed up. You realize there's nothing in the 'papes about his death. What a mess." He did not like the way Joe Chip looked. Old, small and tired, he reflected. Is this how it begins? *We've got to establish contact with Runciter,* he said to himself. Being able to hear him isn't enough; evidently, he's trying to reach us, but—

If we're going to live through this we'll have to reach him.

Joe said, "Picking him up on TV isn't going to do us any good. It'll just be like the phone all over again. Unless he can tell us how to communicate back. Maybe he *can* tell us; maybe he knows. Maybe he understands what's happened."

"He would have to understand what's happened to himself. Which is something we don't know." In some sense, Al thought, he must be alive, even though the moratorium failed to rouse him. Obviously, the moratorium owner did his best with a client of this much importance. "Did von Vogelsang hear him on the phone?" he asked Joe.

"He tried to hear him. But all he got was silence and then static, apparently from a long way off. I heard it too. Nothing. The sound of absolute nothing. A very strange sound."

"I don't like that," Al said. He was not sure why. "I'd feel better about it if von Vogelsang had heard it too. At least that way we could be sure it was there, that it wasn't an hallucination on your part." Or, for that matter, he thought, on all our parts. As in the case of the matchfolder.

But some of the happenings had definitely not been hallucinations; machines had rejected antiquated coins—objective machines geared to react only to physical properties. No psychological elements came into play there. Machines could not imagine.

"I'm leaving this building for a while," Al said. "Think of a city or a town at random, one that none of us have anything to do with, one where none of us ever go or have ever gone."

"Baltimore," Joe said.

"Okay, I'm going to Baltimore. I'm going to see if a store picked at random will accept Runciter currency."

"Buy me some new cigarettes," Joe said.

"Okay. I'll do that too; I'll see if cigarettes in a random store in Baltimore have been affected. I'll check other products as well; I'll make random samplings. Do you want to come with me, or do you want to go upstairs and tell them about Wendy?"

Joe said, "I'll go with you."

"Maybe we should never tell them about her."

"I think we should," Joe said. "Since it's going to happen again. It may happen before we get back. It may be happening now."

"Then we better get our trip to Baltimore over as quickly as possible," Al said. He started out of the office. Joe Chip followed.

9

My hair is so dry, so unmanageable. What's a girl to do? Simply rub in creamy Ubik hair conditioner. In just five days you'll discover new body in your hair, new glossiness. And Ubik hairspray, used as directed, is absolutely safe.

They selected the Lucky People Supermarket on the periphery of Baltimore.

At the counter Al said to the autonomic, computerized checker, "Give me a pack of Pall Malls."

"Wings are cheaper," Joe said.

Irritated, Al said, "They don't make Wings any more. They haven't for years."

"They make them," Joe said, "but they don't advertise. It's an honest cigarette that claims nothing." To the checker he said, "Change that from Pall Malls to Wings."

The pack of cigarettes slid from the chute and onto the counter. "Ninety-five cents," the checker said.

"Here's a ten-poscred bill." Al fed the bill to the checker, whose circuits at once whirred as it scrutinized the bill. "Your change, sir," the checker said; it deposited a neat heap of coins and bills before Al. "Please move along now."

So Runciter money is acceptable, Al said to himself as he and Joe got out of the way of the next customer, a heavy-set old lady wearing a blueberry-colored cloth coat and carrying a Mexican rope shopping bag. Cautiously, he opened the pack of cigarettes.

The cigarettes crumbled between his fingers.

"It would have proved something," Al said, "if this had been a pack of Pall Malls. I'm getting back in line." He started to do so—and then discovered that the heavy-set old lady in the dark coat was arguing violently with the autonomic checker.

"It was dead," she asserted shrilly, "by the time I got it home. Here; you can have it back." She set a pot on the counter; it contained, Al saw, a lifeless plant, perhaps an azalea—in its moribund state it showed few features.

"I can't give you a refund," the checker answered. "No warranty goes with the plant life which we sell. 'Buyer beware' is our rule. Please move along now."

"And the *Saturday Evening Post*," the old lady said, "that I picked up from your newsstand, it was over a year old. What's the matter with you? And the Martian grubworm TV dinner—"

"Next customer," the checker said; it ignored her.

Al got out of line. He roamed about the premises until he came to the cartons of cigarettes, every conceivable brand, stacked to heights of eight feet or more. "Pick a carton," he said to Joe.

"Dominoes," Joe said. "They're the same price as Wings."

"Christ, don't pick an offbrand; pick something like Winstons or Kools." He himself yanked out a carton. "It's empty." He shook it. "I can tell by the weight." Something, however, inside the carton bounced about, something weightless and small; he tore the carton open and looked within it.

A scrawled note. In handwriting familiar to him, and to Joe. He lifted it out and together they both read it.

Essential I get in touch with you. Situation serious and certainly will get more so as time goes on. There are several possible explanations, which I'll discuss with you. Anyhow, don't give up. I'm sorry about Wendy Wright; in that connection we did all we could.

Al said, "So he knows about Wendy. Well, maybe that means it won't happen again, to the rest of us."

"A random carton of cigarettes," Joe said, "at a random store in a city picked at random. And we find a note directed at us from Glen Runciter. What do the other cartons have in them? The same note?" He lifted down a carton of L&Ms, shook it, then opened it. Ten packs of cigarettes plus ten more below them; absolutely normal. Or is it? Al asked himself. He lifted out one of the packs. "You can see they're okay," Joe said; he pulled out a carton from the middle of the stacks. "This one is full too." He did not open it; instead, he reached for another. And then another. All had packs of cigarettes in them.

And all crumbled into fragments between Al's fingers.

"I wonder how he knew we'd come here," Al said. "And how he knew we'd try that one particular carton." It made no sense. And yet, here, too, the pair of opposing forces were at work. Decay versus Runciter, Al said to himself. Throughout the world. Perhaps throughout the universe. Maybe the sun will go out, Al conjectured, and Glen Runciter will place a substitute sun in its place. If he can.

Yes, he thought; that's the question. How much can Runciter do?

Put another way—how far can the process of decay go?

"Let's try something else," Al said; he walked along the aisle, past cans, packages and boxes, coming at last to the appliance center of the store. There, on impulse, he picked up an expensive German-made tape recorder. "This looks all right," he said to Joe, who had followed him. He picked up a second one, still in its container. "Let's buy this and take it back to New York with us."

"Don't you want to open it?" Joe said. "And try it out before you buy it?"

"I think I already know what we'll find," Al said. "And it's something we can't test out here." He carried the tape recorder toward the checkstand.

...

Back in New York, at Runciter Associates, they turned the tape recorder over to the firm's shop.

Fifteen minutes later the shop foreman, having taken apart the mechanism, made his report. "All the moving parts in the tape-transport stage are worn. The rubber drive-tire has flat spots on it; pieces of rubber are all over the insides. The brakes for high-speed wind and rewind are virtually gone. It needs cleaning and lubricating throughout; it's seen plenty of use—in fact, I would say it needs a complete overhaul, including new belts."

Al said, "Several years of use?"

"Possibly. How long you had it?"

"I bought it today," Al said.

"That isn't possible," the shop foreman said. "Or if you did they sold you—"

"I know what they sold me," Al said. "I knew when I got it, before I opened the carton." To Joe he said, "A brand-new tape recorder, completely worn out. Bought with funny money that the store is willing to accept. Worthless money, worthless article purchased; it has a sort of logic to it."

"This is not my day," the shop foreman said. "This morning when I got up my parrot was dead."

"Dead of what?" Joe asked.

"I don't know, just dead. Stiff as a board." The shop foreman waggled a bony finger at Al. "I'll tell you something you don't know about your tape recorder. It isn't just worn out; it's forty years obsolete. They don't use rubber drive-tires any more, or belt-run transports. You'll never get parts for it unless somebody handmakes them. And it wouldn't be worth it; the damn thing is antiquated. Junk it. Forget about it."

"You're right," Al said. "I didn't know." He accompanied Joe out of the shop and into the corridor. "Now we're talking about something other than decay; this is a different matter.

And we're going to have trouble finding edible food, anywhere, of any kind. How much of the food sold in super-
markets would be good after that many years?"

"The canned goods," Joe said. "And I saw a lot of canned
goods at that supermarket in Baltimore."

"And now we know why," Al said. "Forty years ago su-
permarkets sold a far greater proportion of their commodities
in cans, rather than frozen. That may turn out to be our sole
source; you're right." He cogitated. "But in one day it's
jumped from two years to forty years; by this time tomorrow
it may be a hundred years. And no food is edible a hundred
years after it's packaged, cans or otherwise."

"Chinese eggs," Joe said. "Thousand-year-old eggs that
they bury in the ground."

"And it's not just us," Al said. "That old woman in Baltimore; it's affecting what she bought too: her azalea." Is
the whole world going to starve because of a bomb blast on
Luna? he asked himself. *Why is everyone involved instead of
just us?*

Joe said, "Here comes—"

"Be quiet a second," Al said. "I have to think something
out. Maybe Baltimore is only there when one of us goes
there. And the Lucky People Supermarket; as soon as we
left, it passed out of existence. It could still be that only we
who were on Luna are really experiencing this."

"A philosophical problem of no importance or meaning,"
Joe said. "And incapable of being proved one way or the
other."

Al said caustically, "It would be important to that old lady
in the blueberry-colored cloth coat. And to all the rest of
them."

"Here's the shop foreman," Joe said.

"I've just been looking at the instruction manual," the
shop foreman said, "that came with your tape recorder." He
held the booklet out to Al, a complicated expression on his
face. "Take a look." All at once he grabbed it back. "I'll

save you the trouble of reading; look here on the last page, where it tells who made the damn thing and where to send it for factory repairs."

" 'Made by Runciter of Zürich,' " Al read aloud. "And a maintenance station in the North American Confederation—in Des Moines. The same as on the matchfolder." He passed the booklet to Joe and said, "We're going to Des Moines. This booklet is the first manifestation that links the two locations." I wonder why Des Moines, he said to himself. "Can you recall," he said to Joe, "any connection that Runciter ever had, during his lifetime, with Des Moines?"

Joe said, "Runciter was born there. He spent his first fifteen years there. Every once in a while he used to mention it."

"So now, after his death, he's gone back there. In some manner or other." Runciter is in Zürich, he thought, and also in Des Moines. In Zürich he has measurable brain metabolism; his physical, half-life body is suspended in coldpac in the Beloved Brethren Moratorium, and yet he can't be reached. In Des Moines he has no physical existence and yet, evidently, there contact can be established—in fact, by such extensions as this instruction booklet, *has* been established, at least in one direction, from him to us. And meanwhile, he thought, our world declines, turns back onto itself, bringing to the surface past phases of reality. By the end of the week we may wake up and find ancient clanging streetcars moving down Fifth Avenue. Trolley Dodgers, he thought, and wondered what that meant. An abandoned verbal term, rising from the past; a hazy, distant emanation, in his mind, canceling out current reality. Even this indistinct perception, still only subjective, made him uneasy; it had already become too real, an entity which he had never known about before this moment. "Trolley Dodgers," he said aloud. A hundred years ago at least. Obsessively, the term remained lodged within awareness; he could not forget it.

"How come you know that?" the shop foreman asked.

"Nobody knows that any more; that's the old name for the Brooklyn Dodgers." He eyed Al suspiciously.

Joe said, "We better go upstairs. And make sure they're all right. Before we take off for Des Moines."

"If we don't get to Des Moines soon," Al said, "it may turn out to be an all-day trip or even a two-day trip." As methods of transportation devolve, he thought. From rocket propulsion to jet, from jet to piston-driven aircraft, then surface travel as the coal-fed steam train, horse-drawn cart— but it couldn't regress that far, he said to himself. And yet we've already got on our hands a forty-year-old tape recorder, run by rubber drive-tire and belts. Maybe it could really be.

He and Joe walked rapidly to the elevator; Joe pressed the button and they waited, both of them on edge, saying nothing; both withdrew into their own thoughts.

The elevator arrived clatteringly; the racket awoke Al from his introspection. Reflexively he pushed aside the iron-grill safety door.

And found himself facing an open cage with polished brass fittings, suspended from a cable. A dull-eyed uniformed operator sat on a stool, working the handle; he gazed at them with indifference. It was not indifference, however, that Al felt. "Don't get in," he said to Joe, holding him back. "Look at it and think; try to remember the elevator we rode in earlier today, the hydraulic-powered, closed, self-operated, absolutely silent—"

He ceased talking. Because the elderly clanking contraption had dimmed, and, in its place, the familiar elevator resumed its existence. And yet he sensed the presence of the other, older elevator; it lurked at the periphery of his vision, as if ready to ebb forward as soon as he and Joe turned their attention away. It wants to come back, he realized. It intends to come back. We can delay it temporarily: a few hours, probably, at the most. The momentum of the retrograde force is increasing; archaic forms are moving toward domination more rapidly than we thought. It's now a question of a hundred years at one swing. The elevator we just now saw must have been a century old.

And yet, he thought, we seem able to exert some control over it. We did force the actual contemporary elevator back into being. If all of us stay together, if we function as an entity of—not two—but twelve minds—

"What did you see?" Joe was saying to him. "That made you tell me not to get in the elevator?"

Al said, "Didn't you see the old elevator? Open cage, brass, from around 1910? With the operator sitting on his stool?"

"No," Joe said.

"Did you see *anything?*"

"This." Joe gestured. "The normal elevator I see every day when I come to work. I saw what I always see, what I see now." He entered the elevator, turned and stood facing Al.

Then our perceptions are beginning to differ, Al realized. He wondered what that meant.

It seemed ominous; he did not like it at all. In its dire, obscure way it seemed to him potentially the most deadly change since Runciter's death. They were no longer regressing at the same rate, and he had an acute, intuitive intimation that Wendy Wright had experienced exactly this before her death.

He wondered how much time he himself had left.

Now he became aware of an insidious, seeping, cooling-off which at some earlier and unremembered time had begun to explore him—investigating him as well as the world around him. It reminded him of their final minutes on Luna. The chill debased the surfaces of objects; it warped, expanded, showed itself as bulblike swellings that sighed audibly and popped. Into the manifold open wounds the cold drifted, all the way down into the heart of things, the core which made them live. What he saw now seemed to be a desert of ice from which stark boulders jutted. A wind spewed across the plain which reality had become; the wind congealed into deeper ice, and the boulders disappeared for the most part. And darkness presented itself off at the edges of his vision; he caught only a meager glimpse of it.

But, he thought, this is projection on my part. It isn't the universe which is being entombed by layers of wind, cold, darkness and ice; all this is going on within me, and yet I seem to see it outside. Strange, he thought. Is the whole world inside me? Engulfed by my body? When did that happen? It must be a manifestation of dying, he said to himself. The uncertainty which I feel, the slowing down into entropy—that's the process, and the ice which I see is the result of the success of the process. When I blink out, he thought, the whole universe will disappear. But what about the various lights which I should see, the entrances to new wombs? Where in particular is the red smoky light of fornicating couples? And the dull dark light signifying animal greed? All I can make out, he thought, is encroaching darkness and utter loss of heat, a plain which is cooling off, abandoned by its sun.

This can't be normal death, he said to himself. This is unnatural; the regular momentum of dissolution has been replaced by another factor imposed upon it, a pressure arbitrary and forced.

Maybe I can understand it, he thought, if I can just lie down and rest, if I can get enough energy to think.

"What's the matter?" Joe asked, as, together, they ascended in the elevator.

"Nothing," Al said curtly. They may make it, he thought, but I'm not going to.

He and Joe continued on up in empty silence.

As he entered the conference room Joe realized that Al was no longer with him. Turning, he looked back down the corridor; he made out Al standing alone, not coming any farther. "What's the matter?" he asked again. Al did not move. "Are you all right?" Joe asked, walking back toward him.

"I feel tired," Al said.

"You don't look good," Joe said, feeling deeply uneasy.

Al said, "I'm going to the men's room. You go ahead and join the others; make sure they're okay. I'll be along pretty soon." He started vaguely away; he seemed, now, confused. "I'll be okay," he said. He moved along the corridor haltingly, as if having difficulty seeing his way.

"I'll go with you," Joe said. "To make sure you get there."

"Maybe if I splash some warm water on my face," Al said; he found the toll-free door to the men's room, and, with Joe's help, opened it and disappeared inside. Joe remained in the corridor. Something's the matter with him, he said to himself. Seeing the old elevator made a change in him. He wondered why.

Al reappeared.

"What is it?" Joe said, seeing the expression on his face.

"Take a look at this," Al said; he led Joe into the men's room and pointed at the far wall. "Graffiti," he said. "You know, words scrawled. Like you find all the time in the men's room. Read it."

In crayon, or purple ballpoint pen ink, the words read:

> JUMP IN THE URINAL AND STAND ON YOUR HEAD.
> I'M THE ONE THAT'S ALIVE. YOU'RE ALL DEAD.

"Is it Runciter's writing?" Al asked. "Do you recognize it?"

"Yes," Joe said, nodding. "It's Runciter's writing."

"So now we know the truth," Al said.

"Is it the truth?"

Al said, "Sure. Obviously."

"What a hell of a way to learn it. From the wall of a men's room." He felt bitter resentment rather than anything else.

"That's how graffiti is; harsh and direct. We might have
watched the TV and listened to the vidphone and read the
'papes for months—forever, maybe—without finding out.
Without being told straight to the point like this."

Joe said, "But we're not dead. Except for Wendy."

"We're in half-life. Probably still on *Pratfall II*; we're probably on our way back to Earth from Luna, after the explosion
that killed us—killed *us*, not Runciter. And he's trying to
pick up the flow of protophasons from us. So far he's failed;
we're not getting across from our world to his. But he's
managed to reach us. We're picking him up everywhere, even
places we choose at random. His presence is invading us on
every side, him and only him because he's the sole person
trying to—"

"He and only he," Joe interrupted. "Instead of 'him'; you
said 'him.' "

"I'm sick," Al said. He started water running in the basin,
began splashing it onto his face. It was not hot water, however, Joe saw; in the water fragments of ice crackled and
splintered. "You go back to the conference room. I'll be
along when I feel better, assuming I ever do feel better."

"I think I ought to stay here with you," Joe said.

"No, goddam it—get out of here!" His face gray and filled
with panic, Al shoved him toward the door of the men's
room; he propelled Joe out into the corridor. "Go on, make
sure they're all right!" Al retreated back into the men's room,
clutching at his own eyes; bent over, he disappeared from
view as the door swung shut.

Joe hesitated. "Okay," he said, "I'll be in the conference
room with them." He waited, listening; heard nothing. "Al?"
he said. Christ, he thought. This is terrible. Something is
really the matter with him. "I want to see with my own eyes,"
he said, pushing against the door, "that you're all right."

In a low, calm voice Al said, "It's too late, Joe. Don't
look." The men's room had become dark; Al evidently had
managed to turn the light off. "You can't do anything to

help me," he said in a weak but steady voice. "We shouldn't have separated from the others; that's why it happened to Wendy. You can stay alive at least for a while if you go find them *and stick with them*. Tell them that; make sure all of them understand. Do you understand?"

Joe reached for the light switch.

A blow, feeble and weightless, cuffed his hand in the darkness; terrified, he withdrew his hand, shocked by the impotence of Al's punch. It told him everything. He no longer needed to see.

"I'll go join the others," he said. "Yes, I understand. Does it feel very bad?"

Silence, and then a listless voice whispered, "No, it doesn't feel very bad. I just—" The voice faded out. Once more only silence.

"Maybe I'll see you again sometime," Joe said. He knew it was the wrong thing to say—it horrified him to hear himself prattle out such an inanity. But it was the best he could do. "Let me put it another way," he said, but he knew Al could no longer hear him. "I hope you feel better," he said. "I'll check back after I tell them about the writing on the wall in there. I'll tell them not to come in here and look at it because it might—" He tried to think it out, to say it right. "They might bother you," he finished.

No response.

"Well, so long," Joe said, and left the darkness of the men's room. He walked unsteadily down the corridor, back to the conference room; halting a moment he took a deep, irregular breath and then pushed open the conference-room door.

The TV set mounted in the far wall blared out a detergent commercial; on the great color 3-D screen a housewife critically examined a synthetic otter-pelt towel and in a penetrating, shrill voice declared it unfit to occupy a place in her bathroom. The screen then displayed her bathroom—and picked up graffiti on her bathroom wall too. The same familiar scrawl, this time reading:

LEAN OVER THE BOWL
AND THEN TAKE A DIVE.
ALL OF YOU ARE DEAD. I AM ALIVE.

Only one person in the big conference room watched, however. Joe stood alone in an otherwise empty room. The others, the entire group of them, had gone.

He wondered where they were. And if he would live long enough to find them. It did not seem likely.

10

Has perspiration odor taken you out of the swim? Ten-day Ubik deodorant spray or Ubik roll-on ends worry of offending, brings you back where the happening is. Safe when used as directed in a conscientious program of body hygiene.

The television announcer said, "And now back to Jim Hunter and the news."

On the screen the sunny, hairless face of the newscaster appeared. "Glen Runciter came back today to the place of his birth, but it was not the kind of return which gladdened anyone's heart. Yesterday tragedy struck at Runciter Associates, probably the best-known of Earth's many prudence organizations. In a terrorist blast at an undisclosed subsurface installation on Luna, Glen Runciter was mortally wounded and died before his remains could be transferred to cold-pac. Brought to the Beloved Brethren Moratorium in Zürich, every effort was made to revive Runciter to half-life, but in vain. In acknowledgment of defeat these efforts have now ceased, and the body of Glen Runciter has been returned here to Des Moines, where it will lie in state at the Simple Shepherd Mortuary."

The screen showed an old-fashioned white wooden building, with various persons roaming about outside.

I wonder who authorized the transfer to Des Moines, Joe Chip said to himself.

"It was the sad but inexorably dictated decision by the wife of Glen Runciter," the newscaster's voice continued, "which brought about this final chapter which we are now viewing. Mrs. Ella Runciter, herself in cold-pac, whom it had been hoped her husband would join—revived to face this calamity. Mrs. Runciter learned this morning of the fate which had overtaken her husband, and gave the decision to abandon efforts to awaken belated half-life in the man whom she had expected to merge with, a hope disappointed by reality." A still photo of Ella, taken during her lifetime, appeared briefly on the TV screen. "In solemn ritual," the newscaster continued, "grieving employees of Runciter Associates assembled in the chapel of the Simple Shepherd Mortuary, preparing themselves as best they could, under the circumstances, to pay last respects."

The screen now showed the roof field of the mortuary; a parked upended ship opened its hatch and men and women emerged. A microphone, extended by newsmen, halted them.

"Tell me, sir," a newsmanish voice said, "in addition to working for Glen Runciter, did you and these other employees also know him personally? Know him not as a boss but as a man?"

Blinking like a light-blinded owl, Don Denny said into the extended microphone, "We all knew Glen Runciter as a man. As a good individual and citizen whom we could trust. I know I speak for the others when I say this."

"Are all of Mr. Runciter's employees, or perhaps I should say former employees, here, Mr. Denny?"

"Many of us are here," Don Denny said. "Mr. Len Niggelman, Prudence Society chairman, approached us in New York and informed us that he had heard of Glen Runciter's death. He informed us that the body of the deceased was being brought here to Des Moines, and he said we ought to come here, and we agreed, so he brought us in his ship. This is his ship." Denny indicated the ship out of which he and the others had stepped. "We appreciated him notifying us of the change of location from the moratorium in Zürich to the mortuary here. Several of us are not here, however, because they weren't at the firm's New York offices; I refer in particular to inertials Al Hammond and Wendy Wright and the firm's field tester, Mr. Chip. The whereabouts of the three of them is unknown to us, but perhaps along with—"

"Yes," the news announcer with the microphone said. "Perhaps they will see this telecast, which is being beamed by satellite over all of Earth, and will come here to Des Moines for this tragic occasion, as I am sure—and as you undoubtedly are sure—Mr. Runciter and also Mrs. Runciter would want them to. And now back to Jim Hunter at newsroom central."

Jim Hunter, reappearing on the screen, said, "Ray Hollis, whose psionically talented personnel are the object of inertial nullification and hence the target of the prudence organizations, said today in a statement released by his office that he regretted the accidental death of Glen Runciter and would if possible attend the funeral services in Des Moines. It may be, however, that Len Niggelman, representing the Prudence Society (as we told you earlier), will ask that he be barred in view of the implication on the part of some prudence-organization spokesmen that Hollis originally reacted to news of Runciter's death with ill-disguised relief." Newscaster Hunter paused, picked up a sheet of paper and said, "Turning now to other news—"

With his foot Joe Chip tripped the pedal which controlled the TV set; the screen faded and the sound ebbed into silence.

This doesn't fit in with the graffiti on the bathroom walls, Joe reflected. Maybe Runciter is dead, after all. The TV people think so. Ray Hollis thinks so. So does Len Niggelman. They all consider him dead, and all we have that says otherwise is the two rhymed couplets, which could have been scrawled by anyone—despite what Al thought.

The TV screen relit. Much to his surprise; he had not repressed the pedal switch. And in addition, it changed channels: Images flitted past, of one thing and then another, until at last the mysterious agency was satisfied. The final image remained.

The face of Glen Runciter.

"Tired of lazy tastebuds?" Runciter said in his familiar gravelly voice. "Has boiled cabbage taken over your world of food? That same old, stale, flat, Monday-morning odor no matter how many dimes you put into your stove? Ubik changes all that; Ubik wakes up food flavor, puts hearty taste back where it belongs, and restores fine food smell." On the screen a brightly colored spray can replaced Glen Runciter. "One invisible puff-puff whisk of economically priced Ubik banishes compulsive obsessive fears that the entire world is turning into clotted milk, worn-out tape recorders and obsolete iron-cage elevators, plus other, further, as-yet-unglimpsed manifestations of decay. You see, world deterioration of this regressive type is a normal experience of many half-lifers, especially in the early stages when ties to the real reality are still very strong. A sort of lingering universe is retained as a residual charge, experienced as a pseudo environment but highly unstable and unsupported by any ergic substructure. This is particularly true when several memory systems are fused, as in the case of you people. But with today's new, more-powerful-than-ever Ubik, all this is changed!"

Dazed, Joe seated himself, his eyes fixed on the screen; a cartoon fairy zipped airily in spirals, squirting Ubik here and there.

A hard-eyed housewife with big teeth and horse's chin replaced the cartoon fairy; in a brassy voice she bellowed, "I came over to Ubik after trying weak, out-of-date reality supports. My pots and pans were turning into heaps of rust. The floors of my conapt were sagging. My husband Charley put his foot right through the bedroom door. But now I use economical new powerful today's Ubik, and with miraculous results. Look at this refrigerator." On the screen appeared an antique turret-top G.E. refrigerator. "Why, it's devolved back eighty years."

"Sixty-two years," Joe corrected reflexively.

"But now look at it," the housewife continued, squirting the old turret top with her spray can of Ubik. Sparkles of magic light lit up in a nimbus surrounding the old turret top and, in a flash, a modern six-door pay refrigerator replaced it in splendid glory.

"Yes," Runciter's dark voice resumed, "by making use of the most advanced techniques of present-day science, the reversion of matter to earlier forms *can* be reversed, and at a price any conapt owner can afford. Ubik is sold by leading home-art stores throughout Earth. Do not take internally. Keep away from open flame. Do not deviate from printed procedural approaches as expressed on label. So look for it, Joe. Don't just sit there; go out and buy a can of Ubik and spray it all around you night and day."

Standing up, Joe said loudly, "You know I'm here. Does that mean you can hear and see me?"

"Of course, I can't hear you and see you. This commercial message is on videotape; I recorded it two weeks ago, specifically, twelve days before my death. I knew the bomb blast was coming; I made use of precog talents."

"Then you are really dead."

"Of course, I'm dead. Didn't you watch the telecast from Des Moines just now? I know you did, because my precog saw that too."

"What about the graffiti on the men's-room wall?"

Runciter, from the audio system of the TV set, boomed, "Another deterioration phenomenon. Go buy a can of Ubik and it'll stop happening to you; all those things will cease."

"Al thinks we're dead," Joe said.

"Al is deteriorating." Runciter laughed, a deep, re-echoing pulsation that made the conference room vibrate. "Look, Joe, I recorded this goddam TV commercial to assist you, to guide you—you in particular because we've always been friends. And I knew you'd be very confused, which is exactly what you are right now, totally confused. Which isn't very surprising, considering your usual condition. Anyhow, try to hang on; maybe once you get to Des Moines and see my body lying in state you'll calm down."

"What's this 'Ubik'?" Joe asked.

"I think, though, it's too late to help Al."

Joe said, "What is Ubik made of? How does it work?"

"As a matter of fact, Al probably induced the writing on the men's-room wall. You wouldn't have seen it except for him."

"You really are on videotape, aren't you?" Joe said. "You can't hear me. It's true."

Runciter said, "And in addition, Al—"

"Rats," Joe said in weary disgust. It was no use. He gave up.

The horse-jawed housewife returned to the TV screen, winding up the commercial; her voice softer now, she trilled, "If the home-art store that you patronize doesn't yet carry Ubik, return to your conapt, Mr. Chip, and you'll find a free sample has arrived by mail, a free introductory sample, Mr. Chip, that will keep you going until you can buy a regular-size can." She then faded out. The TV set became opaque and silent. The process that had turned it on had turned it back off.

So I'm supposed to blame Al, Joe thought. The idea did not appeal to him; he sensed the peculiarity of the logic, its perhaps deliberate misdirectedness. Al the fall-guy; Al made into the patsy, everything explained in terms of Al. Senseless, he said to himself. And—had Runciter been able to hear him? *Had Runciter only pretended to be on videotape?* For a time, during the commercial, Runciter had seemed to respond to his questions; only at the end had Runciter's words become malappropriate. He felt all at once like an ineffectual moth, fluttering at the windowpane of reality, dimly seeing it from outside.

A new thought struck him, an eerie idea. Suppose Runciter had made the videotape recording under the assumption, based on inaccurate precog information, that the bomb blast would kill him and leave the rest of them alive. The tape had been made honestly but mistakenly; Runciter had not died: *They* had died, as the graffiti on the men's-room wall had said, and Runciter still lived. Before the bomb blast he had given instructions for the taped commercial to be played at this time, and the network had so done, Runciter having failed to countermand his original order. That would explain the disparity between what Runciter had said on the tape and what he had written on the bathroom walls; it would in fact explain both. Which, as far as he could make out, no other explanation would.

Unless Runciter was playing a sardonic game with them, trifling with them, first leading them in one direction, then the other. An unnatural and gigantic force, haunting their lives. Emanating either within the living world or the half-life world; or, he thought suddenly, perhaps both. In any case, controlling what they experienced, or at least a major part of it. Perhaps not the decay, he decided. Not that. *But why not?* Maybe, he thought, that, too. But Runciter wouldn't admit it. Runciter and Ubik. *Ubiquity,* he realized all at once; that's the derivation of the made-up word, the name of Runciter's alleged spray-can product. Which probably did not even exist. It was probably a further hoax, to bewilder them that much more.

And, in addition, if Runciter were alive, then not one but *two* Runciters existed: the genuine one in the real world who was striving to reach them, and the phantasmagoric Runciter who had become a corpse in this half-life world, the body lying in state in Des Moines, Iowa. And, to carry the logic of this out to its full extent, other persons here, such as Ray Hollis and Len Niggelman, were also phantasmagoria— while their authentic counterparts remained in the world of the living.

Very confusing, Joe Chip said to himself. He did not like it at all. Granted it had a satisfying symmetrical quality, but on the other hand, it struck him as untidy.

I'll zip over to my conapt, he decided, pick up the free sample of Ubik, then head for Des Moines. After all, that's what the TV commercial urged me to do. I'll be safer carrying a can of Ubik with me, as the ad pointed out in its own jingly, clever way.

One has to pay attention to such admonitions, he realized, if one expects to stay alive—or half-alive.

Whichever it is.

The taxi let him off on the roof field of his conapt building; he descended by moving ramp and arrived at his own door. With a coin that someone had given him—Al or Pat, he could not knowingly remember—he opened the door and entered.

The living room smelled faintly of burned grease, an odor he had not come across since childhood. Going into the kitchen he discovered the reason. His stove had reverted. Back to an ancient Buck natural-gas model with clogged burners and encrusted oven door which did not close entirely. He gazed at the old, much-used stove dully—then discovered that the other kitchen appliances had undergone similar metamorphoses. The homeopape machine had vanished entirely. The toaster had dissolved sometime during the day and reformed itself as a rubbishy, quaint, nonautomatic model. Not even pop-up, he discovered as he poked bleakly at it. The refrigerator that greeted him was an enormous belt-driven model, a relic that had floated into being from god knew what distant past; it was even more obsolete than the turret-top G.E. shown in the TV commercial. The coffeepot had undergone the least change; as a matter of fact, in one respect it had improved—it lacked the coin slot, operating obviously toll-free. This aspect was true of all the appliances, he realized. All that remained, anyhow. Like the homeopape machine, the garbage-disposal unit had entirely vanished. He tried to remember what other appliances he had owned, but already memory had become vague; he gave up and returned to the living room.

The TV set had receded back a long way; he found himself

confronted by a dark, wood-cabinet, Atwater-Kent tuned radio-frequency oldtime AM radio, complete with antenna and ground wires. God in heaven, he said to himself, appalled.

But why hadn't the TV set reverted instead to formless metals and plastics? Those, after all, were its constituents; it had been constructed out of them, not out of an earlier radio. Perhaps this weirdly verified a discarded ancient philosophy, that of Plato's ideal objects, the universals which, in each class, were real. The form *TV set* had been a template imposed as a successor to other templates, like the procession of frames in a movie sequence. Prior forms, he reflected, must carry on an invisible, residual life in every object. The past is latent, is submerged, but still there, capable of rising to the surface once the later imprinting unfortunately—and against ordinary experience—vanished. The man contains— not the boy—but earlier men, he thought. History began a long time ago.

The dehydrated remnants of Wendy. The procession of forms that normally takes place—that procession ceased. And the last form wore off, with nothing subsequent: no newer form, no next stage of what we see as growth, to take its place. This must be what we experience as old age; from this absence comes degeneration and senility. Only in this instance it happened abruptly—in a matter of hours.

But this old theory—didn't Plato think that something survived the decline, something inner not able to decay? The ancient dualism: body separated from soul. The body ending as Wendy did, and the soul—out of its nest the bird, flown elsewhere. Maybe so, he thought. To be reborn again, as the *Tibetan Book of the Dead* says. It really is true. Christ, I hope so. Because in that case we all can meet again. In, as in *Winnie-the-Pooh*, another part of the forest, where a boy and his bear will always be playing . . . a category, he thought, imperishable. Like all of us. We will all wind up with Pooh, in a clearer, more durable new place.

For curiosity's sake he turned on the prehistoric radio set;

the yellow celluloid dial glowed, the set gave off a loud sixty-cycle hum, and then, amid static and squeals, a station came on.

"Time for Pepper Young's Family," the announcer said, and organ music gurgled. "Brought to you by mild Camay, the soap of beautiful women. Yesterday Pepper discovered that the labor of months had come to an unexpected end, due to the—" Joe shut the radio off at that point. A pre-World War Two soap opera, he said to himself, marveling. Well, it followed the logic of the form reversions taking place in this, the dying half-world—or whatever it was.

Looking around the living room he discovered a baroque-legged, glass-topped coffee table on which a copy of *Liberty* magazine rested. Also pre-World War Two; the magazine featured a serial entitled "Lightning in the Night," a futuristic fantasy supposing an atomic war. He turned the pages numbly, then studied the room as a whole, seeking to identify other changes.

The tough, neutral-colored floor had become wide, soft-wood boards; in the center of the room a faded Turkish rug lay, impregnated with years of dust.

One single picture remained on the wall, a glass-covered framed print in monochrome showing a dying Indian on horseback. He had never seen it before. It stirred no memories. And he did not care for it one bit.

The vidphone had been replaced by a black, hook-style, upright telephone. Pre-dial. He lifted the receiver from the hook and heard a female voice saying, "Number, please." At that he hung up.

The thermostatically controlled heating system had evidently departed. At one end of the living room he perceived a gas heater, complete with large tin flue running up the wall almost to the ceiling.

Going into the bedroom, he looked in the closet, rummaged, then assembled an outfit: black Oxfords, wool socks, knickers, blue cotton shirt, camel's-hair sports coat and golf cap. For more formal wear he laid out on the bed a pinstriped, blue-black, double-breasted suit, suspenders, wide floral necktie and white shirt with celluloid collar. Jeez, he said to himself in dismay as, in the closet, he came across a golf bag with assorted clubs. What a relic.

Once more he returned to the living room. This time he noticed the spot where his polyphonic audio components had formerly been assembled. The multiplex FM tuner, the high-hysteresis turntable and weightless tracking arm—speakers, horns, multitrack amplifier, all had vanished. In their place a tall, tan wooden structure greeted him; he made out the crank handle and did not need to lift the lid to know what his sound system now consisted of. Bamboo needles, a pack of them on the bookcase beside the Victrola. And a ten-inch 78-speed black-label Victor record of Ray Noble's orchestra playing "Turkish Delight." So much for his tape and LP collection.

And by tomorrow he would probably find himself equipped with a cylinder phonograph, screw-driven. And, to play on it, a shouted recitation of the Lord's Prayer.

A fresh-looking newspaper lying at the far end of the overstuffed sofa attracted his attention. He picked it up and read the date: Tuesday, September 12, 1939. He scanned the headlines.

FRENCH CLAIM SIEGFRIED LINE DENTED
REPORT GAINS IN AREA NEAR SAARBRUCKEN
Major battle said to be shaping up
along Western Front

Interesting, he said to himself. World War Two had just begun. And the French thought they were winning it. He read another headline.

POLISH REPORT CLAIMS GERMAN FORCES HALTED
SAY INVADERS THROW NEW FORCES INTO
BATTLE WITHOUT NEW GAINS

The newspaper had cost three cents. That interested him
too. What could you get now for three cents? he asked himself. He tossed the newspaper back down, and marveled once
again at its freshness. A day or so old, he guessed. No more
than that. So I now have a time fix; I know precisely how
far back the regression has carried.

Wandering about the conapt, searching out the various
changes, he found himself facing a chest of dresser drawers
in the bedroom. On the top rested several framed, glass-
covered photographs.

All were of Runciter. *But not the Runciter he knew.* These
were of a baby, a small boy, then a young man. Runciter as
he once had been, but still recognizable.

Getting out his wallet, he found only snapshots of Runciter, none of his family, none of friends. Runciter everywhere! He returned the wallet to his pocket, then realized
with a jolt that it had been made of natural cowhide, not
plastic. Well, that fitted. In the old days there had been
organic leather available. So what? he said to himself. Bringing the wallet out once more, he somberly scrutinized it; he
rubbed the cowhide and experienced a new tactile sensation,
a pleasant one. Infinitely superior to plastic, he decided.

Back in the living room again, he poked about, searching
for the familiar mail slot, the recessed wall cavity which
should have contained today's mail. It had vanished; it no
longer existed. He pondered, trying to envision oldtime mail
practices. On the floor outside the conapt door? No. In a
box of some kind; he recalled the term *mailbox*. Okay, it
would be in the mailbox, but where had mailboxes been
located? At the main entrance of the building? That—
dimly—seemed right. He would have to leave his conapt.
The mail would be found on the ground floor, twenty stories
below.

"Five cents, please," his front door said when he tried to
open it. One thing, anyhow, hadn't changed. The toll door
had an innate stubbornness to it; probably it would hold out
after everything else. After everything except it had long

since reverted, perhaps in the whole city . . . if not the whole world.

He paid the door a nickel, hurried down the hall to the moving ramp which he had used only minutes ago. The ramp, however, had now reverted to a flight of inert concrete stairs. Twenty flights down, he reflected. Step by step. Impossible; no one could walk down that many stairs. The elevator. He started toward it, then remembered what had happened to Al. *Suppose this time I see what he saw*, he said to himself. An old iron cage hanging from a wire cable, operated by a senile borderline moron wearing an official elevator-operator's cap. Not a vision of 1939 but a vision of 1909, a regression much greater than anything I've run into so far.

Better not to risk it. Better to take the stairs.

Resigned, he began to descend.

He had gotten almost halfway down when something ominous flicked alive in his brain. There was no way by which he could get back up—either to his conapt or to the roof field where the taxi waited. Once on the ground floor he would be confined there, maybe forever. Unless the spray can of Ubik was potent enough to restore the elevator or the moving ramp. Surface travel, he said to himself. What the hell will that consist of by the time I get down there? Train? Covered wagon?

Clattering down two steps at a time, he morosely continued his descent. Too late now to change his mind.

When he reached ground level he found himself confronted by a large lobby, including a marble-topped table, very long, on which two ceramic vases of flowers—evidently iris—rested. Four wide steps led down to the curtained front door; he grasped the faceted glass knob of the door and swung it open.

More steps. And, on the right, a row of locked brass mailboxes, each with a name, each requiring a key. He had been right; this was as far as the mail was brought. He located his own box, finding a strip of paper at the bottom of it reading

JOSEPH CHIP 2075, plus a button which, when pressed, evidently rang upstairs in his conapt.

The key. He had no key. Or did he? Fishing in his pockets, he discovered a ring on which several diversely shaped metal keys dangled; perplexed, he studied them, wondering what they were for. The lock on the mailbox seemed unusually small; obviously, it took a similar-size key. Selecting the most meager key on the ring, he inserted it in the lock of the mailbox, turned it. The brass door of the box fell open. He peered inside.

Within the box lay two letters and a square package wrapped in brown paper, sealed with brown tape. Purple three-cent stamps with a portrait of George Washington; he paused to admire these unusual memorabilia from the past and then, ignoring the letters, tore open the square package, finding it rewardingly heavy. But, he realized suddenly, It's the wrong shape for a spray can; it's not tall enough. Fear touched him. What if it was not a free sample of Ubik? It had to be; it just had to be. Otherwise—Al all over again. *Mors certa et hora certa*, he said to himself as he dropped the brown-paper wrappings and examined the pasteboard container within.

UBIK LIVER AND KIDNEY BALM

Inside the container he found a blue glass jar with a large lid. The label read: DIRECTIONS FOR USE. This unique analgesic formula, developed over a period of forty years by Dr. Edward Sonderbar, is guaranteed to end forever annoying getting up at night. You will sleep peacefully for the first time, and with superlative comfort. Merely dissolve a teaspoonful of UBIK LIVER AND KIDNEY BALM in a glass of warm water and drink immediately one-half hour before retiring. If pain or irritation persists, increase dosage to one tablespoonful. Do not give to children. Contains processed oleander leaves, saltpeter, oil of peppermint, N-Acetyl-p-aminophenol, zinc oxide, charcoal, cobalt chloride, caffeine, extract of digitalis, steroids in trace amounts, sodium citrate, ascorbic acid, artificial coloring and flavoring. UBIK LIVER AND KIDNEY BALM is potent and effective if handled as per instructions. Inflammable. Use rubber gloves. Do not allow to get in eyes. Do not splash on skin. Do not inhale over long periods of time. Warning: prolonged or excessive use may result in habituation.

This is insane, Joe said to himself. He read the list of ingredients once more, feeling growing, baffled anger. And a mounting helpless sensation that took root and spread through every part of him. I'm finished, he said to himself. This stuff isn't what Runciter advertised on TV; this is some arcane mixture of old-time patent medicines, skin salves, pain killers, poisons, inert nothings—plus, of all things, cortisone. Which didn't exist before World War Two. Obviously, the Ubik which he described to me in the taped TV commercial, this sample of it anyhow, has reverted. An irony that is just plain too much: The substance created to reverse the regressive change process has itself regressed. I should have known as soon as I saw the old purple three-cent stamps.

He looked up and down the street. And saw, parked at the curb, a classic, museum-piece surface car. A LaSalle.

Can I get to Des Moines in a 1939 LaSalle automobile? he asked himself. Eventually, if it remains stable, perhaps a week from now. But by then it won't matter. And, anyhow, the car won't remain stable. Nothing—except maybe my front door—will.

However, he walked over to the LaSalle to examine it at close range. Maybe it's mine, he said to himself; maybe one of my keys fits its ignition. Isn't that how surface cars operated? On the other hand, how am I going to drive it? I don't know how to pilot an oldtime automobile, especially one with—what did they call it?—manual transmission. He opened the door and slid onto the seat behind the driver's steering wheel; there he sat, plucking aimlessly at his lower lip and trying to think the situation through.

Maybe I ought to drink down a tablespoon of Ubik liver and kidney balm, he said to himself grimly. With those ingredients it ought to kill me fairly thoroughly. But it did not strike him as the kind of death he could welcome. The cobalt chloride would do it, very slowly and agonizingly, unless the digitalis managed it first. And there were, of course, the oleander leaves. They could hardly be overlooked. The whole combination would melt his bones into jelly. Inch by inch.

Wait a minute, he thought. Air transportation existed in 1939. If I could get to the New York Airport—possibly in this car—I could charter a flight. Rent a Ford trimotor plane complete with pilot. That would get me to Des Moines.

He tried his various keys and at last found one which switched on the car's ignition. The starter motor cranked away, and then the engine caught; with a healthy rumble the engine continued to turn over, and the sound of it pleased him. Like the genuine cowhide wallet, this particular regression struck him as an improvement; being completely silent, the transportation of his own time lacked this palpable touch of sturdy realism.

Now the clutch, he said to himself. Over on the left. With his foot he located it. Clutch down to the floor, then shift the lever into gear. He tried it—and obtained a horrid clashing noise, metal whirring against metal. Evidently, he had managed to let up on the clutch. He tried it again. This time he successfully got it into gear.

Lurching, the car moved forward; it bucked and shuddered but it moved. It limped erratically up the street, and he felt within him a certain measured renewal of optimism. And now let's see if we can find the goddam airfield, he said to himself. Before it's too late, before we're back to the days of the Gnome rotary engine with its revolving outside cylinders and its castor-oil lubricant. Good for fifty miles of hedge-hopping flight at seventy-five miles per hour.

. . .

An hour later he arrived at the airfield, parked and surveyed the hangars, the windsock, the old biplanes with their huge wooden props. What a sight, he reflected. An indistinct page out of history. Re-created remnants of another millennium, lacking any connection with the familiar, real world. A phantasm that had drifted into sight only momentarily; this, too, would be gone soon: it would no more survive than had contemporary artifacts. The process of devolution would sweep this away like it had everything else.

He got shakily from the LaSalle—feeling acutely carsick—and trudged toward the main buildings of the airfield.

"What can I charter with this?" he asked, laying all his money out on the counter before the first official-looking person he caught sight of. "I want to get to Des Moines as quickly as possible. I want to take off right away."

The field official, bald-headed, with a waxed mustache and small, round, gold-rimmed eyeglasses, inspected the bills silently. "Hey, Sam," he called with a turn of his apple-like round head. "Come here and look at this money."

A second individual, wearing a striped shirt with billowing sleeves, shiny seersucker trousers and canvas shoes, stumped over. "Fake money," he said after he had taken his look. "Play money. Not George Washington and not Alexander Hamilton." Both officials scrutinized Joe.

Joe said, "I have a '39 LaSalle parked in the parking lot. I'll trade it for a one-way flight to Des Moines on any plane that'll get me there. Does that interest you?"

Presently the official with the little gold-rimmed glasses said meditatively, "Maybe Oggie Brent would be interested."

"Brent?" the official in the seersucker pants said, raising his eyebrows. "You mean that Jenny of his? That plane's over twenty years old. It wouldn't get to Philadelphia."

"How about McGee?"

"Sure, but he's in Newark."

"Then, maybe Sandy Jespersen. That Curtiss-Wright of his would make it to Iowa. Sooner or later." To Joe the official said, "Go out by hangar three and look for a red and white Curtiss biplane. You'll see a little short guy, sort of fat, fiddling around with it. If he don't take you up on it nobody here will, unless you want to wait till tomorrow for Ike McGee to come back here in his Fokker trimotor."

"Thanks," Joe said, and left the building; he strode rapidly toward hangar three, already seeing what looked like a red and white Curtiss-Wright biplane. At least I won't be making the trip in a World War JN training plane, he said to himself. And then he thought, *How did I know that "Jenny" is a nickname for a JN trainer?* Good god, he thought. Elements of this period appear to be developing corresponding coordinates in my mind. No wonder I was able to drive the LaSalle; I'm beginning to phase mentally with this time-continuum in earnest!

A short fat man with red hair puttered with an oily rag at the wheels of his biplane; he glanced up as Joe approached.

"Are you Mr. Jespersen?" Joe asked.

"That's right." The man surveyed him, obviously mystified by Joe's clothes, which had not reverted. "What can I do for you?" Joe told him.

"You want to trade a LaSalle, a new LaSalle, for a one-way trip to Des Moines?" Jespersen cogitated, his brows knitting. "Might as well be both ways; I got to fly back here anyway. Okay, I'll take a look at it. But I'm not promising anything; I haven't made up my mind."

Together they made their way to the parking lot.

"I don't see any '39 LaSalle," Jespersen said suspiciously.

The man was right. The LaSalle had disappeared. In its place Joe saw a fabric-top Ford coupé, a tinny and small car, very old, 1929, he guessed. A black 1929 Model-A Ford. Nearly worthless; he could tell that from Jespersen's expression.

Obviously, it was now hopeless. He would never get to Des Moines. And, as Runciter had pointed out in his TV commercial, this meant death—the same death that had overtaken Wendy and Al.

It would be only a matter of time.

Better, he thought, to die another way. Ubik, he thought. He opened the door of his Ford and got in.

There, on the seat beside him, rested the bottle which he had received in the mail. He picked it up—

And discovered something which did not really surprise him. The bottle, like the car, had again regressed. Seamless and flat, with scratch marks on it, the kind of bottle made in a wooden mold. Very old indeed; the cap appeared to be handmade, a soft tin screw-type dating from the late nineteenth century. The label, too, had changed; holding the bottle up, he read the words printed on it.

> ELIXIR OF UBIQUE. GUARANTEED TO RESTORE LOST MAN-
> LINESS AND TO BANISH VAPORS OF ALL KNOWN KINDS
> AS WELL AS TO RELIEVE REPRODUCTIVE COMPLAINTS IN
> BOTH MEN AND WOMEN. A BENEFICENT AID TO MANKIND
> WHEN SEDULOUSLY EMPLOYED AS INDICATED.

And, in smaller type, a further inscription; he had to squint in order to read the smudged, minute script.

> *Don't do it, Joe. There's another way.*
> *Keep trying. You'll find it. Lots of luck.*

Runciter, he realized. Still playing his sadistic cat-and-mouse games with us. Goading us into keeping going a little longer. Delaying the end as long as possible. God knows why. Maybe, he thought, Runciter enjoys our torment. But that isn't like him; that's not the Glen Runciter I knew.

However, Joe put the Elixir of Ubique bottle down, abandoning the idea of making use of it.

And wondered what Runciter's elusive, hinted at other way might be.

11

Taken as directed, Ubik provides uninterrupted sleep without morning-after grogginess. You awaken fresh, ready to tackle all those little annoying problems facing you. Do not exceed recommended dosage.

"Hey, that bottle you have," Jespersen said; he peered into the car, an unusual note in his voice. "Can I look at it?"

Joe Chip wordlessly passed the aviator the flat bottle of Elixir of Ubique.

"My grandmother used to talk about this," Jespersen said, holding the bottle up to the light. "Where'd you get it? They haven't made this since around the time of the Civil War."

"I inherited it," Joe said.

"You must have. Yeah, you don't see these handmade flasks any more. The company never put out very many of these in the first place. This medicine was invented in San Francisco around 1850. Never sold in stores; the customers had to order it made up. It came in three strengths. This what you have here, this is the strongest of the three." He eyed Joe. "Do you know what's in this?"

"Sure," Joe said. "Oil of peppermint, zinc oxide, sodium citrate, charcoal—"

"Let it go," Jespersen interrupted. Frowning, he appeared to be busily turning something over in his mind. Then, at last, his expression changed. He had come to a decision. "I'll fly you to Des Moines in exchange for this flask of Elixir of

Ubique. Let's get started; I want to do as much of the flying as possible in daylight." He strode away from the '29 Ford, taking the bottle with him.

Ten minutes later the Curtiss-Wright biplane had been gassed, the prop manually spun, and, with Joe Chip and Jespersen aboard, it began weaving an erratic, sloppy path down the runway, bouncing into the air and then collapsing back again. Joe gritted his teeth and hung on.

"We're carrying so much weight," Jespersen said without emotion; he did not seem alarmed. The plane at last wobbled up into the air, leaving the runway permanently behind; noisily it droned over the rooftops of buildings, on its way west.

Joe yelled, "How long will it take to get there?"

"Depends on how much tailwind we get. Hard to say. Probably around noon tomorrow if our luck holds out."

"Will you tell me now," Joe yelled, "what's in the bottle?"

"Gold flakes suspended in a base composed mostly of mineral oil," the pilot yelled back.

"How much gold? Very much?"

Jespersen turned his head and grinned without answering. He did not have to say; it was obvious.

The old Curtiss-Wright biplane blurpled on, in the general direction of Iowa.

At three in the afternoon the following day they reached the airfield at Des Moines. Having landed the plane, the pilot sauntered off for parts unknown, carrying his flask of gold flakes with him. With aching, cramped stiffness, Joe climbed from the plane, stood for a time rubbing his numb legs, and then unsteadily headed toward the airport office, as little of it as there was.

"Can I use your phone?" he asked an elderly rustic official who sat hunched over a weather map, absorbed in what he was doing.

"If you got a nickel." The official, with a jerk of his cowlick head, indicated the public phone.

Joe sorted through his money, casting out all the coins which had Runciter's profile on them; at last he found an authentic buffalo nickel of the period and laid it before the elderly official.

"Ump," the official grunted without looking up.

Locating the local phone book, Joe extracted from it the number of the Simple Shepherd Mortuary. He gave the number to the operator, and presently his party responded.

"Simple Shepherd Mortuary. Mr. Bliss speaking."

"I'm here to attend the services for Glen Runciter," Joe said. "Am I too late?" He prayed silently that he was not.

"Services for Mr. Runciter are in progress right now," Mr. Bliss said. "Where are you, sir? Would you like us to send a vehicle to fetch you?" He seemed fussily disapproving.

"I'm at the airport," Joe said.

"You should have arrived earlier," Mr. Bliss chided. "I doubt very much if you'll be able to attend any of the service. However, Mr. Runciter will be lying in state for the balance of today and tomorrow morning. Watch for our car, Mr.—"

"Chip," Joe said.

"Yes, you have been expected. Several of the bereaved have asked that we maintain a vigil for you as well as for Mr. Hammond and a"—he paused—"a Miss Wright. Are they with you?"

"No," Joe said. He hung up, then seated himself on a curved, polished wooden bench where he could watch cars approaching the airport. Anyhow, he said to himself, I'm here in time to join the rest of the group. They haven't left town yet, and that's what matters.

The elderly official called, "Mister, come over here a sec."

Getting up, Joe crossed the waiting room. "What's wrong?"

"This nickel you gave me." The official had been scrutinizing it all this time.

"It's a buffalo nickel," Joe said. "Isn't that the right coin for this period?"

"This nickel is dated 1940." The elderly official eyed him unblinkingly.

With a groan Joe got out his remaining coins, again sorted among them; at last he found a 1938 nickel and tossed it down before the official. "Keep them both," he said, and once more seated himself on the polished, curved bench.

"We get counterfeit money every now and then," the official said.

Joe said nothing; he turned his attention to the semi-highboy Audiola radio playing by itself off in a corner of the waiting room. The announcer was plugging a toothpaste called Ipana. I wonder how long I'm going to have to wait here, Joe asked himself. It made him nervous, now that he had come so close physically to the inertials. I'd hate to make it this far, he thought, within a few miles, and then— He stopped his thoughts at that point and simply sat.

Half an hour later a 1930 Willys-Knight 87 put-putted onto the airfield's parking lot; a hempen home-spun individual wearing a conspicuously black suit emerged and shaded his eyes with the flat of his hand in order to see into the waiting room.

Joe approached him. "Are you Mr. Bliss?" he asked.

"Certainly, I am." Bliss briefly shook hands with him, meanwhile emitting a strong smell of Sen-sen, then got back at once into the Willys-Knight and restarted the motor. "Come along, Mr. Chip. Please hurry. We may still be able to attend a part of the service. Father Abernathy generally speaks quite a while on such important occasions as this."

Joe got into the front seat beside Mr. Bliss. A moment later they clanked onto the road leading to downtown Des Moines, rushing along at speeds sometimes reaching forty miles an hour.

"You're an employee of Mr. Runciter?" Bliss asked.

"Right," Joe said.

"Unusual line of business that Mr. Runciter was in. I'm not quite sure I understand it." Bliss honked at a red setter which had ventured onto the asphalt pavement; the dog retreated, giving the Willys-Knight its pompous right of way. "What does 'psionic' mean? Several of Mr. Runciter's employees have used the term."

"Parapsychological powers," Joe said. "Mental force operating directly, without any intervening physical agency."

"Mystical powers, you mean? Like knowing the future? The reason I ask that is that several of you people have talked about the future as if it already exists. Not to me; they didn't say anything about it except to each other, but I overheard— you know how it is. Are you people mediums, is that it?"

"In a manner of speaking."

"What do you foresee about the war in Europe?"

Joe said, "Germany and Japan will lose. The United States will get into it on December 7th, 1941." He lapsed into silence then, not feeling inclined to discuss it; he had his own problems to occupy his attention.

"I'm a Shriner, myself," Bliss said.

What is the rest of the group experiencing? Joe wondered. This reality? The United States of 1939? Or, when I rejoin them, will my regression be reversed, placing me at a later period? A good question. Because, collectively, they would have to find their way back fifty-three years, to the reasonable and proper form-constituents of contemporary, unregressed time. If the group as a whole had experienced the same amount of regression as he had, then his joining them would not help him or them—except in one regard: He might be spared the ordeal of undergoing further world decay. On the other hand, this reality of 1939 seemed fairly stable; in the last twenty-four hours it had managed to remain virtually constant. But, he reflected, that might be due to my drawing nearer to the group.

On the other hand, the 1939 jar of Ubik liver and kidney balm had reverted back an additional eighty-odd years: from spray can to jar to wooden-mold bottle within a few hours. Like the 1908 cage elevator which Al alone had seen—

But that wasn't so. The short, fat pilot, Sandy Jespersen, had also seen the wooden-mold bottle, the Elixir of Ubique, as it had become finally. *This was not a private vision; it had, in fact, gotten him here to Des Moines.* And the pilot had seen the reversion of the LaSalle as well. Something entirely different had overtaken Al, it would seem. At least, he hoped so. Prayed so.

Suppose, he reflected, we can't reverse our regression; suppose we remain here the balance of our lives. *Is that so bad?* We can get used to nine-tube screen-grid highboy Philco radios, although they won't really be necessary, inasmuch as the superheterodyne circuit has already been invented—although I haven't as yet run across one. We can learn to drive American Austin motorcars selling for $445—a sum that had popped into his mind seemingly at random but which, he intuited, was correct. Once we get jobs and earn money of this period, he said to himself, we won't be traveling aboard antique Curtiss-Wright biplanes; after all, four years ago, in 1935, transpacific service by four-engine China clippers was inaugurated. The Ford trimotor is an eleven-year-old plane by now; to these people it's a relic, and the biplane I came here on is—even to them—a museum piece. That LaSalle I had, before it reverted, was a considerable piece of machinery; I felt real satisfaction driving it.

"What about Russia?" Mr. Bliss was asking. "In the war, I mean. Do we wipe out those Reds? Can you see that far ahead?"

Joe said, "Russia will fight on the same side as the U.S.A." And all the other objects and entities and artifacts of this world, he mulled. Medicine will be a major drawback; let's see—just about now they should be using the sulfa drugs. It's going to be serious for us when we become ill. And— dental work isn't going to be much fun either; they're still working with hot drills and novocaine. Fluoride toothpastes haven't even come into being; that's another twenty years in the future.

"On our side?" Bliss sputtered. "The Communists? That's impossible; they've got that pact with the Nazis."

"Germany will violate that pact," Joe said. "Hitler will attack the Soviet Union in June 1941."

"And wipe it out, I hope."

Startled out of his preoccupations, Joe turned to look closely at Mr. Bliss driving his nine-year-old Willys-Knight.

Bliss said, "Those Communists are the real menace, not the Germans. Take the treatment of the Jews. You know who makes a lot out of that? Jews in this country, a lot of them not citizens but refugees living on public welfare. I think the Nazis certainly have been a little extreme in some of the things they've done to the Jews, but basically there's been the Jewish question for a long time, and something, although maybe not so vile as those concentration camps, had to be done about it. We have a similar problem here in the United States, both with Jews and with the niggers. Eventually we're going to have to do something about both."

"I never actually heard the term 'nigger' used," Joe said, and found himself appraising this era a little differently, all at once. I forgot about this, he realized.

"Lindbergh is the one who's right about Germany," Bliss said. "Have you ever listened to him speak? I don't mean what the newspapers write it up like, but actually—" He slowed the car to a stop for a semaphore-style stop signal. "Take Senator Borah and Senator Nye. If it wasn't for them, Roosevelt would be selling munitions to England and getting us into a war that's not our war. Roosevelt is so darn interested in repealing the arms embargo clause of the neutrality bill; he wants us to get into the war. The American people aren't going to support him. The American people aren't interested in fighting England's war or anybody else's war." The signal clanged and a green semaphore swung out. Bliss shifted into low gear and the Willys-Knight bumbled forward, melding with downtown Des Moines' midday traffic.

"You're not going to enjoy the next five years," Joe said.

"Why not? The whole state of Iowa is behind me in what I believe. You know what I think about you employees of

Mr. Runciter? From what you've said and from what those others said, what I overheard, I think you're professional agitators." Bliss glanced at Joe with uncowed bravado.

Joe said nothing; he watched the oldtime brick and wood and concrete buildings go by, the quaint cars—most of which appeared to be black—and wondered if he was the only one of the group who had been confronted by this particular aspect of the world of 1939. In New York, he told himself, it'll be different; this is the Bible Belt, the isolationist Middle West. We won't be living here; we'll be on either the East Coast or the West.

But instinctively he sensed that a major problem for all of them had exposed itself just now. We know too much, he realized, to live comfortably in this time segment. If we had regressed twenty years, or thirty years, we could probably make the psychological transition; it might not be interesting to once more live through the Gemini spacewalks and the creaking first Apollo flights, but at least it would be possible. But at this point in time—

They're still listening to ten-inch 78 records of "Two Black Crows." And Joe Penner. And "Mert and Marge." The Depression is still going on. In our time we maintain colonies on Mars, on Luna; we're perfecting workable interstellar flight—these people have not been able to cope with the Dust Bowl of Oklahoma.

This is a world that lives in terms of William Jennings Bryan's oratory; the Scopes "Monkey Trial" is a vivid reality here. He thought, There is no way we can adapt to their viewpoint, their moral, political, sociological environment. To them we're professional agitators, more alien than the Nazis, probably even more of a menace than the Communist Party. We're the most dangerous agitators that this time segment has yet had to deal with. Bliss is absolutely right.

"Where are you people from?" Bliss was asking. "Not from any part of the United States; am I correct?"

Joe said, "You're correct. We're from the North American Confederation." From his pocket he brought forth a Runciter quarter, which he handed to Bliss. "Be my guest," he said.

Glancing at the coin, Bliss gulped and quavered, "the profile on this coin—this is the deceased! This is Mr. Runciter!" He took another look and blanched. "And the date. 1990."

"Don't spend it all in one place," Joe said.

When the Willys-Knight reached the Simple Shepherd Mortuary the service had already ended. On the wide, white, wooden steps of the two-story frame building a group of people stood, and Joe recognized all of them. There at last they were: Edie Dorn, Tippy Jackson, Jon Ild, Francy Spanish, Tito Apostos, Don Denny, Sammy Mundo, Fred Zafsky and—Pat. My wife, he said to himself, impressed once again by the sight of her, the dramatic dark hair, the intense coloring of her eyes and skin, all the powerful contrasts radiating from her.

"No," he said aloud as he stepped from the parked car. "She's not my wife; she wiped that out." But, he remembered, she kept the ring. The unique wrought-silver and jade wedding ring which she and I picked out . . . that's all that remains. But what a shock to see her again. To regain, for an instant, the ghostly shroud of a marriage that has been abolished. That had in fact never existed—except for this ring. And, whenever she felt like it, she could obliterate the ring too.

"Hi, Joe Chip," she said in her cool, almost mocking voice; her intense eyes fixed on him, appraising him.

"Hello," he said awkwardly. The others greeted him too, but that did not seem so important; Pat had snared his attention.

"No Al Hammond?" Don Denny asked.

Joe said, "Al's dead. Wendy Wright is dead."

"We know about Wendy," Pat said. Calmly.

"No, we didn't know," Don Denny said. "We assumed but we weren't sure. *I* wasn't sure." To Joe he said, "What happened to them? What killed them?"

"They wore out," Joe said.

"Why?" Tito Apostos said hoarsely, crowding into the circle of people surrounding Joe.

Pat Conley said, "The last thing you said to us, Joe Chip, back in New York, before you went off with Hammond—"

"I know what I said," Joe said.

Pat continued, "You said something about years. 'It had been too long,' you said. What does that mean? Something about time."

"Mr. Chip," Edie Dorn said agitatedly, "since we came here to this place, this town has radically changed. None of us understand it. Do you see what we see?" With her hand she indicated the mortuary building, then the street and the other buildings.

"I'm not sure," Joe said, "what it is you see."

"Come on, Chip," Tito Apostos said with anger. "Don't mess around; simply tell us, for chrissakes, what this place looks like to you. That vehicle." He gestured toward the Willys-Knight. "You arrived in that. Tell us what it is; tell us what you arrived in." They all waited, all of them intently watching Joe.

"Mr. Chip," Sammy Mundo stammered, "that's a real old automobile, that's what it is; right?" He giggled. "How old is it exactly?"

After a pause Joe said, "Sixty-two years old."

"That would make it 1930," Tippy Jackson said to Don Denny. "Which is pretty close to what we figured."

"We figured 1939," Don Denny said to Joe in a level voice. A moderate, detached, mature, baritone voice. Without undue emotionality. Even under these circumstances.

Joe said, "It's fairly easy to establish that. I took a look at a newspaper at my conapt back in New York. September 12th. So today is September 13th, 1939. The French think they've breached the Siegfried Line."

"Which, in itself," Jon Ild said, "is a million laughs."

"I hoped," Joe said, "that you as a group were experiencing a later reality. Well, so it goes."

"If it's 1939 it's 1939," Fred Zafsky said in a squeaky, highpitched voice. "Naturally, we all experience it; what else can we do?" He flapped his long arms energetically, appealing to the others for their agreement.

"Flurk off, Zafsky," Tito Apostos said with annoyance.

To Pat, Joe Chip said, "What do you say about this?"

She shrugged.

"Don't shrug," he said. "Answer."

"We've gone back in time," Pat said.

"Not really," Joe said.

"Then what have we done?" Pat said. "Gone forward in time, is that it?"

Joe said, "We haven't gone anywhere. We're where we've always been. But for some reason—for one of several possible reasons—reality has receded; it's lost its underlying support and it's ebbed back to previous forms. Forms it took fifty-three years ago. It may regress further. I'm more interested, at this point, in knowing if Runciter has manifested himself to you."

"Runciter," Don Denny said, this time with undue emotionality, "is lying inside this building in his casket, dead as a herring. That's the only manifestation we've had of him, and that's the only one we're going to get."

"Does the word 'Ubik' mean anything to you, Mr. Chip?" Francesca Spanish said.

It took him a moment to absorb what she had said. "Jesus Christ," he said then. "Can't you distinguish manifestations of—"

"Francy has dreams," Tippy Jackson said. "She's always had them. Tell him your Ubik dream, Francy." To Joe she said, "Francy will now tell you her Ubik dream, as she calls it. She had it last night."

"I call it that because that's what it is," Francesca Spanish said fiercely; she clasped her hands together in a spasm of excited agitation. "Listen, Mr. Chip, it wasn't like any dream I've ever had before. A great hand came down from the sky, like the arm and hand of God. Enormous, the size of a mountain. And I knew at the time how important it was; the hand was closed, made into a rocklike fist, and I knew it contained something of value so great that my life and the lives of everyone else on Earth depended on it. And I waited for the fist to open, and it did open. And I saw what it contained."

"An aerosol spray can," Don Denny said dryly.

"On the spray can," Francesca Spanish continued, "there was one word, great golden letters, glittering; golden fire spelling out UBIK. Nothing else. Just that strange word. And then the hand closed up again around the spray can and the hand and arm disappeared, drawn back up into a sort of gray overcast. Today before the funeral services I looked in a dictionary and I called the public library, but no one knew that word or even what language it is and it isn't in the dictionary. It isn't English, the librarian told me. There's a Latin word very close to it: *ubique*. It means—"

"Everywhere," Joe said.

Francesca Spanish nodded. "That's what it means. But no Ubik, and that's how it was spelled in the dream."

"They're the same word," Joe said. "Just different spellings."

"How do you know that?" Pat Conley said archly.

"Runciter appeared to me yesterday," Joe said. "In a taped TV commercial that he made before his death." He did not elaborate; it seemed too complex to explain, at least at this particular time.

"You miserable fool," Pat Conley said to him.

"Why?" he asked.

"Is that your idea of a manifestation of a dead man? You might as well consider letters he wrote before his death 'manifestations.' Or interoffice memos that he transcribed over the years. Or even—"

Joe said, "I'm going inside and take a last look at Runciter." He departed from the group, leaving them standing there, and made his way up the wide board steps and into the dark, cool interior of the mortuary.

Emptiness. He saw no one, only a large chamber with pewlike rows of seats and, at the far end, a casket surrounded by flowers. Off in a small sideroom an old-fashioned reed pump organ and a few wooden folding chairs. The mortuary smelled of dust and flowers, a sweet, stale mixture that repelled him. Think of all the Iowans, he thought, who've embraced eternity in this listless room. Varnished floors, handkerchiefs, heavy dark wool suits . . . everything but pennies placed over the dead eyes. And the organ playing symmetric little hymns.

He reached the casket, hesitated, then looked down.

A singed, dehydrated heap of bones lay at one end of the casket, culminating in a paper-like skull that leered up at him, the eyes recessed like dried grapes. Tatters of cloth with bristle-like woven spines had collected near the tiny body, as if blown there by wind. As if the body, breathing, had cluttered itself with them by its wheezing, meager processes—inhalation and exhalation which had now ceased. Nothing stirred. The mysterious change, which had also degraded Wendy Wright and Al, had reached its end, evidently a long time ago. Years ago, he thought, remembering Wendy.

Had the others in the group seen this? Or had it happened since the services? Joe reached out, took hold of the oak lid of the casket and shut it; the thump of wood against wood echoed throughout the empty mortuary, but no one heard it. No one appeared.

Blinded by tears of fright, he made his way back out of the dust-stricken, silent room. Back into the weak sunlight of late afternoon.

"What's the matter?" Don Denny asked him as he rejoined the group.

Joe said, "Nothing."

"You look scared out of your goony wits," Pat Conley said acutely.

"Nothing!" He stared at her with deep, infuriated hostility.

Tippy Jackson said to him, "While you were in there did you by any chance happen to see Edie Dorn?"

"She's missing," Jon Ild said by way of explanation.

"But she was just out here," Joe protested.

"All day she's been saying she felt terribly cold and tired," Don Denny said. "It may be that she went back to the hotel; she said something about it earlier, that she wanted to lie down and take a nap right after the services. She's probably all right."

Joe said, "She's probably dead." To all of them he said, "I thought you understood. If any one of us gets separated from the group he won't survive; what happened to Wendy and Al and Runciter—" He broke off.

"Runciter was killed in the blast," Don Denny said.

"We were all killed in the blast," Joe said. "I know that because Runciter told me; he wrote it on the wall of the men's room back at our New York offices. And I saw it again on—"

"What you're saying is insane," Pat Conley said sharply, interrupting him. "Is Runciter dead or isn't he? Are we dead or aren't we? First you say one thing, then you say another. Can't you be consistent?"

"Try to be consistent," Jon Ild put in. The others, their faces pinched and creased with worry, nodded in mute agreement.

Joe said, "I can tell you what the graffiti said. I can tell you about the worn-out tape recorder, the instructions that came with it; I can tell you about Runciter's TV commercial, the note in the carton of cigarettes in Baltimore—I can tell you about the label on the flask of Elixir of Ubique. But I can't make it all add up. In any case, we have to get to your hotel to try to reach Edie Dorn before she withers away and irreversibly expires. Where can we get a taxi?"

"The mortuary has provided us with a car to use while we're here," Don Denny said. "That Pierce-Arrow sitting over there." He pointed.

They hurried toward it.

"We're not all of us going to be able to fit in," Tippy Jackson said as Don Denny tugged the solid iron door open and got inside.

"Ask Bliss if we can take the Willys-Knight," Joe said; he started up the engine of the Pierce-Arrow and, as soon as everyone possible had gotten into the car, drove out onto the busy main street of Des Moines. The Willys-Knight followed close behind, its horn honking dolefully to tell Joe it was there.

12

*Pop tasty Ubik into your toaster,
made only from fresh fruit and
healthful all-vegetable shortening.
Ubik makes breakfast a feast, puts
zing into your thing! Safe when
handled as directed.*

One by one, Joe Chip said to himself as he piloted the big
car through traffic, we're succumbing. *Something is wrong
with my theory.* Edie, by being with the group, should have
been immune. And I—

It should have been me, he thought. Sometime during my
slow flight from New York.

"What we'll have to do," he said to Don Denny, "is make
sure that anyone who feels tired—that seems to be the first
warning—tells the rest of us. And isn't allowed to wander
away."

Twisting around to face those in the back seat, Don
said, "Do you all hear that? As soon as any of you feels
tired, even a little bit, report it to either Mr. Chip or myself." He turned back toward Joe. "And then what?" he
asked.

"And then what, Joe?" Pat Conley echoed. "What do we
do then? Tell us how we do it, Joe. We're listening."

Joe said to her, "It seems strange to me that your talent
isn't coming into play. This situation appears to me to be
made for it. Why can't you go back fifteen minutes and

compel Edie Dorn not to wander off? Do what you did when
I first introduced you to Runciter."

"G. G. Ashwood introduced me to Mr. Runciter," Pat
said.

"So you're not going to do anything," Joe said.

Sammy Mundo giggled and said, "They had a fight last
night while we were eating dinner, Miss Conley and Miss
Dorn. Miss Conley doesn't like her; that's why she won't
help."

"I liked Edie," Pat said.

"Do you have any reason for not making use of your
talent?" Don Denny asked her. "Joe's right; it's very strange
and difficult to understand—at least for me—why exactly
you don't try to help."

After a pause Pat said, "My talent doesn't work any more.
It hasn't since the bomb blast on Luna."

"Why didn't you say so?" Joe said.

Pat said, "I didn't feel like saying so, goddam it. Why
should I volunteer information like that, that I can't do anything? I keep trying and it keeps not working; nothing happens. And it's never been that way before. I've had the talent
virtually my entire life."

"When did—" Joe began.

"With Runciter," Pat said. "On Luna, right away. Before
you asked me."

"So you knew that long ago," Joe said.

"I tried again in New York, after you showed up from
Zürich and it was obvious that something awful had happened to Wendy. And I've been trying now; I started as soon
as you said Edie was probably dead. Maybe it's because we're
back in this archaic time period; maybe psionic talents don't
work in 1939. But that wouldn't explain Luna. Unless we
had already traveled back here and we didn't realize it." She
lapsed into brooding, introverted silence; dully, she gazed
out at the streets of Des Moines, a bitter expression on her
potent, wild face.

It fits in, Joe said to himself. Of course, her time-traveling talent no longer functions. This is not really 1939, and we are outside of time entirely; this proves that Al was right. The graffiti was right. This is half-life, as the couplets told us.

He did not, however, say this to the others with him in the car. Why tell them it's hopeless? he said to himself. They're going to find it out soon enough. The smarter ones, such as Denny, probably understand it already. Based on what I've said and what they themselves have gone through.

"This really bothers you," Don Denny said to him, "that her talent no longer works."

"Sure." He nodded. "I hoped it might change the situation."

"There's more," Denny said with acute intuition. "I can tell by your"—he gestured—"tone of voice, maybe. Anyhow, I know. This means something. It's important. It tells you something."

"Do I keep going straight here?" Joe said, slowing the Pierce-Arrow at an intersection.

"Turn right," Tippy Jackson said.

Pat said, "You'll see a brick building with a neon sign going up and down. The Meremont Hotel, it's called. A terrible place. One bathroom for every two rooms, and a tub instead of a shower. And the food. Incredible. And the only drink they sell is something called Nehi."

"I liked the food," Don Denny said. "Genuine cowmeat, rather than protein synthetics. Authentic salmon—"

"Is your money good?" Joe asked. And then he heard a high-pitched whine, echoing up and down the street behind him. "What's that mean?" he asked Denny.

"I don't know," Denny said nervously.

Sammy Mundo said, "It's a police siren. You didn't give a signal before you turned."

"How could I?" Joe said. "There's no lever on the steering column."

"You should have made a hand signal," Sammy said. The

siren had become very close now; Joe, turning his head, saw a motorcycle pulling up abreast with him. He slowed the car, uncertain as to what he should do. "Stop at the curb," Sammy advised him.

Joe stopped the car at the curb.

Stepping from his motorcycle, the cop strolled up to Joe, a young, rat-faced man with hard, large eyes; he studied Joe and then said, "Let me see your license, mister."

"I don't have one," Joe said. "Make out the ticket and let us go." He could see the hotel now. To Don Denny he said, "You better get over there, you and everyone else." The Willys-Knight continued on toward it. Don Denny, Pat, Sammy Mundo and Tippy Jackson abandoned the car; they trotted after the Willys-Knight, which had begun to slow to a stop across from the hotel, leaving Joe to face the cop alone.

The cop said to Joe, "Do you have any identification?"

Joe handed him his wallet. With a purple indelible pencil the cop wrote out a ticket, tore it from his pad and passed it to Joe. "Failure to signal. No operator's license. The citation tells where and when to appear." The cop slapped his ticket book shut, handed Joe his wallet, then sauntered back to his motorcycle. He revved up his motor and then zoomed out into traffic without looking back.

For some obscure reason Joe glanced over the citation before putting it away in his pocket. And read it once again—slowly. In purple indelible pencil the familiar scrawled handwriting said:

> *You are in much greater danger than*
> *I thought. What Pat Conley said is*

There the message ceased. In the middle of a sentence. He wondered how it would have continued. Was there anything more on the citation? He turned it over, found nothing, returned again to the front side. No further handwriting, but,

in squirrel agate type at the bottom of the slip of paper, the
following inscription:

> Try Archer's Drugstore for reliable
> household remedies and medicinal
> preparations of tried and tested
> value. Economically priced.

Not much to go on, Joe reflected. But still—not what
should have appeared at the bottom of a Des Moines traffic
citation; it was, clearly, another manifestation, as was the
purple handwriting above it.

Getting out of the Pierce-Arrow, he entered the nearest
store, a magazine, candy and tobacco-supply shop. "May I
use your phone book?" he asked the broad-beamed, middle-
aged proprietor.

"In the rear," the proprietor said amiably, with a jerk of
his heavy thumb.

Joe found the phone book and, in the dim recesses of the
dark little store, looked up Archer's Drugstore. He could
not find it listed.

Closing the phone book, he approached the proprietor,
who at the moment was engaged in selling a roll of Necco
wafers to a boy. "Do you know where I can find Archer's
Drugstore?" Joe asked him.

"Nowhere," the proprietor said. "At least, not any more."

"Why not?"

"It's been closed for years."

Joe said, "Tell me where it was. Anyhow. Draw me a
map."

"You don't need a map; I can tell you where it was." The
big man leaned forward, pointing out the door of his shop.
"You see that barber pole there? Go over there and then
look north. That's north." He indicated the direction.
"You'll see an old building with gables. Yellow in color.
There's a couple of apartments over it still being used, but
the store premises downstairs, they're abandoned. You'll be

able to make out the sign, though: Archer's Drugs. So you'll know when you've found it. What happened is that Ed Archer came down with throat cancer and—"

"Thanks," Joe said, and started out of the store, back into the pale midafternoon sunlight; he walked rapidly across the street to the barber pole, and, from that position, looked due north.

He could see the tall, peeling yellow building at the periphery of his range of vision. But something about it struck him as strange. A shimmer, an unsteadiness, as if the building faded forward into stability and then retreated into insubstantial uncertainty. An oscillation, each phase lasting a few seconds and then blurring off into its opposite, a fairly regular variability as if an organic pulsation underlay the structure. As if, he thought, it's alive.

Maybe, he thought, I've come to the end. He began to walk toward the abandoned drugstore, not taking his eyes from it; he watched it pulse, he watched it change between its two states, and then, as he got closer and closer to it, he discerned the nature of its alternate conditions. At the amplitude of greater stability it became a retail home-art outlet of his own time period, homeostatic in operation, a self-service enterprise selling ten-thousand commodities for the modern conapt; he had patronized such highly functional computer-controlled pseudo merchants throughout his adult life.

And, at the amplitude of insubstantiality, it resolved itself into a tiny, anachronistic drugstore with rococo ornamentation. In its meager window displays he saw hernia belts, rows of corrective eyeglasses, a mortar and pestle, jars of assorted tablets, a hand-printed sign reading LEECHES, huge glass-stoppered bottles that contained a Pandora's heritage of patent medicines and placebos . . . and, painted on a flat wood board running across the top of the windows, the words ARCHER'S DRUGSTORE. No sign whatever of an empty, abandoned, closed-up store; its 1939 stage had somehow been excluded. He thought, So in entering it I either revert further or I find myself back roughly in my own time. And—it's the further reversion, the pre-1939 phase, that I evidently need.

Presently he stood before it, experiencing physically the tidal tug of the amplitudes; he felt himself drawn back, then ahead, then back again. Pedestrians clumped by, taking no notice; obviously, none of them saw what he saw: They perceived neither Archer's Drugstore nor the 1992 home-art outlet. That mystified him most of all.

As the structure swung directly into its ancient phase he stepped forward, crossed the threshold. And entered Archer's Drugstore.

To the right a long marble-topped counter. Boxes on the shelves, dingy in color; the whole store had a black quality to it, not merely in regard to the absence of light but rather a protective coloration, as if it had been constructed to blend, to merge with shadows, to be at all times opaque. It had a heavy, dense quality; it pulled him down, weighing on him like something installed permanently on his back. And it had ceased to oscillate. At least for him, now that he had entered it. He wondered if he had made the right choice; now, too late, he considered the alternative, what it might have meant. A return—possibly—to his own time. Out of this devolved world of constantly declining time-binding capacity—out, perhaps, forever. Well, he thought, so it goes. He wandered about the drugstore, observing the brass and the wood, evidently walnut . . . he came at last to the prescription window at the rear.

A wispy young man, wearing a gray, many-buttoned suit with vest, appeared and silently confronted him. For a long time Joe and the man looked at each other, neither speaking. The only sound came from a wall clock with Latin numerals on its round face; its pendulum ticked back and forth inexorably. After the fashion of clocks. Everywhere.

Joe said, "I'd like a jar of Ubik."

"The salve?" the druggist said. His lips did not seem properly synchronized with his words; first Joe saw the man's mouth open, the lips move, and then, after a measurable interval, he heard the words.

"Is it a salve?" Joe said. "I thought it was for internal use."

The druggist did not respond for an interval. As if a gulf separated the two of them, an epoch of time. Then at last his mouth again opened, his lips again moved. And, presently, Joe heard words. "Ubik has undergone many alterations as the manufacturer has improved it. You may be familiar with the old Ubik, rather than the new." The druggist turned to one side, and his movement had a stop-action quality; he flowed in a slow, measured, dancelike step, an esthetically pleasing rhythm but emotionally jolting. "We have had a great deal of difficulty obtaining Ubik of late," he said as he flowed back; in his right hand he held a flat leaded tin which he placed before Joe on the prescription counter. "This comes in the form of a powder to which you add coal tar. The coal tar comes separate; I can supply that to you at very little cost. The Ubik powder, however, is dear. Forty dollars."

"What's in it?" Joe asked. The price chilled him.

"That is the manufacturer's secret."

Joe picked up the sealed tin and held it to the light. "Is it all right if I read the label?"

"Of course."

In the dim light entering from the street he at last managed to make out the printing on the label of the tin. It continued the handwritten message on the traffic citation, picking up at the exact point at which Runciter's writing had abruptly stopped.

> *absolutely untrue. She did not—repeat,*
> *not—try to use her talent following the*
> *bomb blast. She did not try to restore*
> *Wendy Wright or Al Hammond or Edie Dorn.*
> *She's lying to you, Joe, and that makes*
> *me rethink the whole situation. I'll*
> *let you know as soon as I come to a*

> *conclusion. Meanwhile be very careful.*
> *By the way: Ubik powder is of universal*
> *healing value if directions for use are*
> *rigorously and conscientiously followed.*

"Can I make you out a check?" Joe asked the druggist. "I don't have forty dollars with me and I need the Ubik badly. It's literally a matter hanging between life and death." He reached into his jacket pocket for his checkbook.

"You're not from Des Moines, are you?" the druggist said. "I can tell by your accent. No, I'd have to know you to take a check that large. We've had a whole rash of bad checks the last few weeks, all by people from out of town."

"Credit card, then?"

The druggist said, "What is a 'credit card'?"

Laying down the tin of Ubik, Joe turned and walked wordlessly out of the drugstore onto the sidewalk. He crossed the street, starting in the direction of the hotel, then paused to look back at the drugstore.

He saw only a dilapidated yellow building, curtains in its upstairs windows, the ground floor boarded up and deserted; through the spaces between the boards he saw gaping darkness, the cavity of a broken window. Without life.

And that is that, he realized. The opportunity to buy a tin of Ubik powder is gone. Even if I were to find forty dollars lying on the pavement. But, he thought, I did get the rest of Runciter's warning. For what it's worth. It may not even be true. It may be only a deformed and misguided opinion by a dying brain. Or by a totally dead brain—as in the case of the TV commercial. Christ, he said to himself dismally. Suppose it *is* true?

Persons here and there on the sidewalk stared up absorbedly at the sky. Noticing them, Joe looked up too. Shielding his eyes against the slanting shafts of sun, he distinguished a dot exuding white trails of smoke: a high-flying monoplane industriously skywriting. As he and the other pedestrians watched, the already dissipating streamers spelled out a message.

KEEP THE OLD SWIZER UP, JOE!

Easy to say, Joe said to himself. Easy enough to write out in the form of words.

Hunched over with uneasy gloom—and the first faint intimations of returning terror—he shuffled off in the direction of the Meremont Hotel.

Don Denny met him in the high-ceilinged, provincial, crimson-carpeted lobby. "We found her," he said. "It's all over—for her, anyhow. And it wasn't pretty, not pretty at all. Now Fred Zafsky is gone. I thought he was in the other car, and they thought he went along with us. Apparently, he didn't get into either car; he must be back at the mortuary."

"It's happening faster now," Joe said. He wondered how much difference Ubik—dangled toward them again and again in countless different ways but always out of reach—would have made. I guess we'll never know, he decided. "Can we get a drink here?" he asked Don Denny. "What about money? Mine's worthless."

"The mortuary is paying for everything. Runciter's instructions to them."

"The hotel tab too?" It struck him as odd. How had that been managed? "I want you to look at this citation," he said to Don Denny. "While no one else is with us." He passed the slip of paper over to him. "I have the rest of the message; that's where I've been: getting it."

Denny read the citation, then reread it. Then, slowly, handed it back to Joe. "Runciter thinks Pat Conley is lying," he said.

"Yes," Joe said.

"You realize what that would mean?" His voice rose

sharply. "It means she could have nullified all this. Everything that's happened to us, starting with Runciter's death."

Joe said, "It could mean more than that."

Eying him, Denny said, "You're right. Yes, you're absolutely right." He looked startled and, then, acutely responsive. Awareness glittered in his face. Of an unhappy, stricken kind.

"I don't particularly feel like thinking about it," Joe said. "I don't like anything about it. It's worse. A lot worse than what I thought before, what Al Hammond believed, for example. Which was bad enough."

"But this could be it," Denny said.

"Throughout all that's been happening," Joe said, "I've kept trying to understand why. I was sure if I knew why—" But Al never thought of this, he said to himself. Both of us let it drop out of our minds. For a good reason.

Denny said, "Don't say anything to the rest of them. This may not be true; and even if it is, knowing it isn't going to help them."

"Knowing what?" Pat Conley said from behind them. "What isn't going to help them?" She came around in front of them now, her black, color-saturated eyes wise and calm. Serenely calm. "It's a shame about Edie Dorn," she said. "And Fred Zafsky; I guess he's gone too. That doesn't really leave very many of us, does it? I wonder who'll be next." She seemed undisturbed, totally in control of herself. "Tippy is lying down in her room. She didn't say she felt tired, but I think we must assume she is. Don't you agree?"

After a pause Don Denny said, "Yes, I agree."

"How did you make out with your citation, Joe?" Pat said. She held out her hand. "Can I take a look at it?"

Joe passed it to her. The moment, he thought, has come; everything is now; rolled up into the present. Into one instant.

"How did the policeman know my name?" Pat asked, after she had glanced over it; she raised her eyes, looked intently at Joe and then at Don Denny. "Why is there something here about me?"

She doesn't recognize the writing, Joe said to himself. Because she's not familiar with it. As the rest of us are. "Runciter," he said. "You're doing it, aren't you, Pat?" he said. "It's you, your talent. We're here because of you."

"And you're killing us off," Don Denny said to her. "One by one. But why?" To Joe he said, "What reason could she have? She doesn't even know us, not really."

"Is this why you came to Runciter Associates?" Joe asked her. He tried—but failed—to keep his voice steady; in his ears it wavered and he felt abrupt contempt for himself. "G. G. Ashwood scouted you and brought you in. Was he working for Hollis, is that it? Is that what really happened to us—*not the bomb blast but you?*"

Pat smiled.

And the lobby of the hotel blew up in Joe Chip's face.

13

*Lift your arms and be all at once
curvier! New extra-gentle Ubik bra
and longline Ubik special bra
mean, Lift your arms and be all at
once curvier! Supplies firm, relax-
ing support to bosom all day long
when fitted as directed.*

Darkness hummed about him, clinging to him like coagu-
lated, damp, warm wool. The terror he had felt as intimation
fused with the darkness became whole and real. I wasn't
careful, he realized. I didn't do what Runciter told me to do;
I let her see the citation.

"What's the matter, Joe?" Don Denny's voice, edged with
great worry. "What's wrong?"

"I'm okay." He could see a little now; the darkness had
grown horizontal lines of gray, as if it had begun to decom-
pose. "I just feel tired," he said, and realized how really
tired his body had become. He could not remember such
fatigue. Never before in his life.

Don Denny said, "Let me help you to a chair." Joe felt
his hand clamped over his shoulder; he felt Denny guiding
him, and this made him afraid, this need to be led. He pulled
away.

"I'm okay," he repeated. The shape of Denny had started
to form near him; he concentrated on it, then once again
distinguished the turn-of-the-century lobby with its ornate
crystal chandelier and its complicated yellow light. "Let me

sit down," he said and, groping, found a cane-bottomed chair.

To Pat, Don Denny said harshly, "What did you do to him?"

"She didn't do anything to me," Joe said, trying to make his voice firm. But it dipped shrilly, with unnatural overtones. As if it's speeded up, he thought. High-pitched. Not my own.

"That's right," Pat said. "I didn't do anything to him or to anybody else."

Joe said, "I want to go upstairs and lie down."

"I'll get you a room," Don Denny said nervously; he hovered near Joe, appearing and then disappearing as the lights of the lobby ebbed. The light waned into dull red, then grew stronger, then waned once more. "You stay there in that chair, Joe; I'll be right back." Denny hurried off in the direction of the desk. Pat remained.

"Anything I can do for you?" Pat asked pleasantly.

"No," he said. It took vast effort, saying the word aloud; it clung to the internal cavern lodged in his heart, a hollowness which grew with each second. "A cigarette, maybe," he said, and saying the full sentence exhausted him; he felt his heart labor. The difficult beating increased his burden; it was a further weight pressing down on him, a huge hand squeezing. "Do you have one?" he said, and managed to look up at her through the smoky red light. The fitful, flickering glow of an unrobust reality.

"Sorry," Pat said. "No got."

Joe said, "What's—the matter with me?"

"Cardiac arrest, maybe," Pat said.

"Do you think there's a hotel doctor?" he managed to say.

"I doubt it."

"You won't see? You won't look?"

Pat said, "I think it's merely psychosomatic. You're not really sick. You'll recover."

Returning, Don Denny said, "I've got a room for you, Joe. On the second floor, Room 203." He paused, and Joe felt his scrutiny, the concern of his gaze. "Joe, you look awful. Frail. Like you're about to blow away. My god, Joe, do you know what you look like? You look like Edie Dorn looked when we found her."

"Oh, nothing like that," Pat said. "Edie Dorn is dead. Joe isn't dead. Are you, Joe?"

Joe said, "I want to go upstairs. I want to lie down." Somehow he got to his feet; his heart thudded, seemed to hesitate, to not beat for a moment, and then it resumed, slamming like an upright iron ingot crashing against cement; each pulse of it made his whole body shudder. "Where's the elevator?" he said.

"I'll lead you over to it," Denny said; again his hand clamped over Joe's shoulder. "You're like a feather," Denny said. "What's happening to you, Joe? Can you say? Do you know? Try to tell me."

"He doesn't know," Pat said.

"I think he should have a doctor," Denny said. "Right away."

"No," Joe said. Lying down will help me, he said to himself; he felt an oceanic pull, an enormous tide tugging at him: It urged him to lie down. It compelled him toward one thing alone, to stretch out, on his back, alone, upstairs in his hotel room. Where no one could see him. I have to get away, he said to himself. I've got to be by myself. Why? he wondered. He did not know; it had invaded him as an instinct, non-rational, impossible to understand or explain.

"I'll go get a doctor," Denny said. "Pat, you stay here with him. Don't let him out of your sight. I'll be back as soon as I can." He started off; Joe dimly saw his retreating form. Denny appeared to shrink, to dwindle. And then he was entirely gone. Patricia Conley remained, but that did not make him feel less alone. His isolation, in spite of her physical presence, had become absolute.

"Well, Joe," she said. "What do you want? What can I do for you? Just name it."

"The elevator," he said.

"You want me to lead you over to the elevator? I'll be glad to." She started off, and, as best he could, he followed. It seemed to him that she walked unusually fast; she did not wait and she did not look back—he found it almost impossible to keep her in sight. Is it my imagination, he asked himself, that she's moving so rapidly? It must be me; I'm slowed down, compressed by gravity. His world had assumed the attribute of pure mass. He perceived himself in one mode only: that of an object subjected to the pressure of weight. One quality, one attribute. And one experience. Inertia.

"Not so fast," he said. He could not see her now; she had lithely trotted beyond his range of vision. Standing there, not able to move any farther, he panted; he felt his face drip and his eyes sting from the salty moisture. "Wait," he said.

Pat reappeared. He distinguished her face as she bent to peer at him. Her perfect and tranquil expression. The disinterestedness of her attention, its scientific detachment. "Want me to wipe your face?" she asked; she brought out a handkerchief, small and dainty and lace-edged. She smiled, the same smile as before.

"Just get me into the elevator." He compelled his body to move forward. One step. Two. Now he could make out the elevator, with several persons waiting for it. The old-fashioned dial above the sliding doors with its clock hand. The hand, the baroque needle, wavered between three and four; it retired to the left, reaching the three, then wavered between three and two.

"It'll be here in a sec," Pat said. She got her cigarettes and lighter from her purse, lit up, exhaled trails of gray smoke from her nostrils. "It's a very ancient kind of elevator," she said to him, her arms folded sedately. "You know what I think? I think it's one of those old open iron cages. Do they scare you?"

The needle had passed two now; it hovered above one, then plunged down firmly. The doors slid aside.

Joe saw the grill of the cage, the latticework. He saw the uniformed attendant, seated on a stool, his hand on the rotating control. "Going up," the attendant said. "Move to the back, please."

"I'm not going to get into it," Joe said.

"Why not?" Pat said. "Do you think the cable will break? Is that what frightens you? I can see you're frightened."

"This is what Al saw," he said.

"Well, Joe," Pat said, "the only other way up to your room is the stairs. And you aren't going to be able to climb stairs, not in your condition."

"I'll go up by the stairs." He started away, seeking to locate the stairs. I can't see! he said to himself. I can't find them! The weight on him crushed his lungs, making it difficult and painful to breathe; he had to halt, concentrating on getting air into him—that alone. Maybe it is a heart attack, he thought. I can't go up the stairs if it is. But the longing within him had grown even greater, the overpowering need to be alone. Locked in an empty room, entirely unwitnessed, silent and supine. Stretched out, not needing to speak, not needing to move. Not required to cope with anyone or any problem. And no one will even know where I am, he told himself. That seemed, unaccountably, very important; he wanted to be unknown and invisible, to live unseen. Pat especially, he thought; not her; she can't be near me.

"There we are," Pat said. She guided him, turning him slightly to the left. "Right in front of you. Just take hold of the railing and go bump-de-bump upstairs to bed. See?" She ascended skillfully, dancing and twinkling, poising herself, then scrambling weightlessly to the next step. "Can you make it?"

Joe said, "I—don't want you. To come with me."

"Oh, dear." She clucked-clucked with mock dolefulness; her black eyes shone. "Are you afraid I'll take advantage of your condition? Do something to you, something harmful?"

"No." He shook his head. "I—just want. To be. Alone." Gripping the rail, he managed to pull himself up onto the first step. Halting there, he gazed up, trying to make out the top of the flight. Trying to determine how far away it was, how many steps he had left.

"Mr. Denny asked me to stay with you. I can read to you or get you things. I can wait on you."

He climbed another step. "Alone," he gasped.

Pat said, "May I watch you climb? I'd like to see how long it takes you. Assuming you make it at all."

"I'll make it." He placed his foot on the next step, gripped the railing and hoisted himself up. His swollen heart choked off his throat; he shut his eyes and wheezed in strangled air.

"I wonder," Pat said, "if this is what Wendy did. She was the first; right?"

Joe gasped, "I was. In love with. Her."

"Oh, I know. G. G. Ashwood told me. He read your mind. G.G. and I got to be very good friends; we spent a lot of time together. You might say we had an affair. Yes, you could say that."

"Our theory," Joe said, "was right." He took a deeper breath. "One," he succeeded in saying; he ascended another step and then, with tremendous effort, another. "That you and G.G. Worked it out with Ray Hollis. To infiltrate."

"Quite right," Pat agreed.

"Our best inertials. And Runciter. Wipe us all out." He made his way up one more step. "We're not in half-life. We're not—"

"Oh, you can *die*," Pat said. "You're not dead; not you, in particular, I mean. But you are dying off one by one. But why talk about it? Why bring it up again? You said it all a little while ago, and frankly, you bore me, going over it again and again. You're really a very dull, pedantic person, Joe. Almost as dull as Wendy Wright. You two would have made a good pair."

"That's why Wendy died first," he said. "Not because she had separated. From the group. But because—" He cringed as the pain in his heart throbbed up violently; he had tried for another step, but this time he had missed. He stumbled, then found himself seated, huddled like—yes, he thought. Wendy in the closet: huddled like this. Reaching out his hand, he took hold of the sleeve of his coat. He tugged.

The fabric tore. Dried and starved, the material parted like cheap gray paper; it had no strength . . . like something fashioned by wasps. So there was no doubt about it. He would soon be leaving a trail behind him, bits of crumbled cloth. A trail of debris leading to a hotel room and yearned-for isolation. His last labored actions governed by a tropism. An orientation urging him toward death, decay and non-being. A dismal alchemy controlled him: culminating in the grave.

He ascended another step.

I'm going to make it, he realized. The force goading me on is feasting on my body; that's why Wendy and Al and Edie—and undoubtedly Zafsky by now—deteriorated physically as they died, leaving only a discarded husklike weightless shell, containing nothing, no essence, no juices, no substantial density. The force thrust itself against the weight of many gravities, and this is the cost, this using up of the waning body. But the body, as a source supply, will be enough to get me up there; a biological necessity is at work, and probably at this point not even Pat, who set it into motion, can abort it. He wondered how she felt now as she watched him climb. Did she admire him? Did she feel contempt? He raised his head, searched for her; he made her out, her vital face with its several hues. Only interest there. No malevolence. A neutral expression. He did not feel surprise. Pat had made no move to hinder him and no move to help him. It seemed right, even to him.

"Feel any better?" Pat asked.

"No," he said. And, getting halfway up, lunged onto the next step.

"You look different. Not so upset."

Joe said, "Because I can make it. I know that."

"It's not much further," Pat agreed.

"Farther," he corrected.

"You're incredible. So trivial, so small. Even in your own death spasms you—" She corrected herself, catlike and clever. "Or what probably seem subjectively to you as death spasms. I shouldn't have used that term, 'death spasms.' It might depress you. Try to be optimistic. Okay?"

"Just tell me," he said. "How many steps. Left."

"Six." She slid away from him, gliding upward noiselessly, effortlessly. "No; sorry. Ten. Or is it nine? I think it's nine."

Again he climbed a step. Then the next. And the next. He did not talk; he did not even try to see. Going by the hardness of the surface against which he rested, he crept snail-like from step to step, feeling a kind of skill develop in him, an ability to tell exactly how to exert himself, how to use his nearly bankrupt power.

"Almost there," Pat said cheerily from above him. "What do you have to say, Joe? Any comments on your great climb? The greatest climb in the history of man. No, that's not true. Wendy and Al and Edie and Fred Zafsky did it before you. But this is the only one I've actually watched."

Joe said, "Why me?"

"I want to watch you, Joe, because of your low-class little scheme back in Zürich. Of having Wendy Wright spend the night with you in your hotel room. Now, tonight, this will be different. You'll be alone."

"That night, too," Joe said. "I was. Alone." Another step. He coughed convulsively, and out of him, in drops hurled from his streaked face, his remaining capacity expelled itself uselessly.

"She was there; not in your bed but in the room somewhere. You slept through it, though." Pat laughed.

"I'm trying," Joe said. "Not to cough." He made it up two more steps and knew that he had almost reached the top. How long had he been on the stairs? he wondered. No way for him to tell.

He discovered then, with a shock, that he had become cold as well as exhausted. When had this happened? he asked himself. Sometime in the past; it had infiltrated so gradually that before now he had not noticed it. Oh, god, he said to himself and shivered frantically. His bones seemed almost to quake. Worse than on Luna, far worse. Worse, too, than the chill which had hung over his hotel room in Zürich. Those had been harbingers.

Metabolism, he reflected, is a burning process, an active furnace. When it ceases to function, life is over. They must be wrong about hell, he said to himself. Hell is cold; everything there is cold. The body means weight and heat; now weight is a force which I am succumbing to, and heat, my heat, is slipping away. And, unless I become reborn, it will never return. This is the destiny of the universe. So at least I won't be alone.

But he felt alone. It's overtaking me too soon, he realized. The proper time hasn't come; something has hurried this up—some conniving thing has accelerated it, out of malice and curiosity: a polymorphic, perverse agency which likes to watch. An infantile, retarded entity which enjoys what's happening. It has crushed me like a bent-legged insect, he said to himself. A simple bug which does nothing but hug the earth. Which can never fly or escape. Can only descend step by step into what is deranged and foul. Into the world of the tomb which a perverse entity surrounded by its own filth inhabits. The thing we call Pat.

"Do you have your key?" Pat asked. "To your room? Think how awful you'd feel to get up to the second floor and find you had lost your key and couldn't get into your room."

"I have it." He groped in his pockets.

His coat ripped away, tattered and in shreds; it fell from him and, from its top pocket, the key slid. It fell two steps down, below him. Beyond reach.

Pat said briskly, "I'll get it for you." Darting by him she scooped up the key, held it to the light to examine it, then laid it at the top of the flight of stairs, on the railing. "Right up here," she said, "where you can reach it when you're through climbing. Your reward. The room, I think, is to the left, about four doors down the hall. You'll have to move slowly, but it'll be a lot easier once you're off the stairs. Once you don't have to climb."

"I can see," he said. "The key. And the top. I can see the top of the stairs." With both arms grasping the bannister he dragged himself upward, ascended three steps in one agonizing expenditure of himself. He felt it deplete him; the weight on him grew, the cold grew, and the substantiality of himself waned. But—

He had reached the top.

"Goodby, Joe," Pat said. She hovered over him, kneeling slightly so that he could see her face. "You don't want Don Denny bursting in, do you? A doctor won't be able to help you. So I'll tell him that I got the hotel people to call a cab and that you're on your way across town to a hospital. That way you won't be bothered. You can be entirely by yourself. Do you agree?"

"Yes," he said.

"Here's the key." She pushed the cold metal thing into his hand, closed his fingers about it. "Keep your chin up, as they say here in '39. Don't take any wooden nickels. They say that too." She slipped away then, onto her feet; for an instant she stood there, scrutinizing him, and then she darted off down the hall to the elevator. He saw her press the button, wait; he saw the doors slide open, and then Pat disappeared.

Gripping the key he rose lurchingly to a crouched position; he balanced himself against the far wall of the corridor, then turned to the left and began to walk step by step, still supporting himself by means of the wall. Darkness, he thought. It isn't lit. He squeezed his eyes shut, opened them, blinked. Sweat from his face still blinded him, still stung; he could not tell if the corridor were genuinely dark or whether his power of sight was fading out.

By the time he reached the first door he had been reduced to crawling; he tilted his head up, sought for the number on the door. No, not this one. He crept on.

When he found the proper door he had to stand erect, propped up, to insert the key in the lock. The effort finished him. The key still in his hand, he fell; his head struck the door and he flopped back onto the dust-choked carpet, smelling the odor of age and wear and frigid death. I can't get in the room, he realized. I can't stand up any more.

But he had to. Out here he could be seen.

Gripping the knob with both hands he tugged himself onto his feet one more time. He rested his weight entirely against the door as he tremblingly poked the key in the direction of the knob and the lock; this way, once he had turned the key, the door would fall open and he would be inside. And then, he thought, if I can close the door after me and if I can get to the bed, it'll be over.

The lock grated. The metal unit hauled itself back. The door opened and he pitched forward, arms extended. The floor rose toward him and he made out shapes in the carpet, swirls and designs and floral entities in red and gold, but worn into roughness and lusterlessness; the colors had dimmed, and as he struck the floor, feeling little if any pain, he thought, This is very old, this room. When this place was first built they probably did use an open iron cage for an elevator. So I saw the actual elevator, he said to himself, the authentic, original one.

He lay for a time, and then, as if called, summoned into motion, stirred. He lifted himself up onto his knees, placed his hands flat before him . . . my hands, he thought; good god. Parchment hands, yellow and knobby, like the ass of a cooked, dry turkey. Bristly skin, not like human skin; pin-feathers, as if I've devolved back millions of years to something that flies and coasts, using its skin as a sail.

Opening his eyes, he searched for the bed; he strove to identify it. The fat far window, admitting gray light through its web of curtains. A vanity table, ugly, with lank legs. Then the bed, with brass knobs capping its railed sides, bent and irregular, as if years of use had twisted the railings, warped the varnished wooden headboards. I want to get on it even so, he said to himself; he reached toward it, slid and dragged himself farther into the room.

And saw then a figure seated in an overstuffed chair, facing
him. A spectator who had made no sound but who now stood
up and came rapidly toward him.

Glen Runciter.

"I couldn't help you climb the stairs," Runciter said, his
heavy face stern. "She would have seen me. Matter of fact,
I was afraid she'd come all the way into the room with you,
and then we'd be in trouble because she—" He broke off,
bent and hoisted Joe up to his feet as if Joe had no weight
left in him, no remaining material constituents. "We'll talk
about that later. Here." He carried Joe under his arm, across
the room—not to the bed but to the overstuffed chair in
which he himself had been sitting. "Can you hold on a few
seconds longer?" Runciter asked. "I want to shut and lock
the door. In case she changes her mind."

"Yes," Joe said.

Runciter strode in three big steps to the door, slammed it
and bolted it, came at once back to Joe. Opening a drawer
of the vanity table, he hastily brought out a spray can with
bright stripes, balloons and lettering glorifying its shiny surfaces. "Ubik," Runciter said, he shook the can mightily, then
stood before Joe, aiming it at him. "Don't thank me for
this," he said, and sprayed prolongedly left and right; the
air flickered and shimmered, as if bright particles of light had
been released, as if the sun's energy sparkled here in this
worn-out elderly hotel room. "Feel better? It should work
on you right away; you should already be getting a reaction."
He eyed Joe with anxiety.

14

*It takes more than a bag to seal in
food flavor; it takes Ubik plastic
wrap—actually four layers in one.
Keeps freshness in, air and moisture out. Watch this simulated test.*

"Do you have a cigarette?" Joe said. His voice shook, but
not from weariness. Nor from cold. Both had gone. I'm tense,
he said to himself. But I'm not dying. That process has been
stopped by the Ubik spray.

As Runciter said it would, he remembered, in his taped
TV commercial. If I could find it I would be all right; Runciter
promised that. But, he thought somberly, it took a long time.
And I almost didn't get to it.

"No filter tips," Runciter said. "They don't have filtration
devices on their cigarettes in this backward, no-good time
period." He held a pack of Camels toward Joe. "I'll light it
for you." He struck a match and extended it.

"It's fresh," Joe said.

"Oh hell, yes. Christ, I just now bought it downstairs at
the tobacco counter. We're a long way into this. Well past
the stage of clotted milk and stale cigarettes." He grinned
starkly, his eyes determined and bleak, reflecting no light.
"*In* it," he said, "not *out* of it. There's a difference." He lit
a cigarette for himself too; leaning back, he smoked in silence, his expression still grim. And, Joe decided, tired. But
not the kind of tiredness that he himself had undergone.

Joe said, "Can you help the rest of the group?"

"I have exactly one can of this Ubik. Most of it I had to use on you." He gestured with resentment; his fingers convulsed in a tremor of unresigned anger. "My ability to alter things here is limited. I've done what I could." His head jerked as he raised his eyes to glare at Joe. "I got through to you—all of you—every chance I could, every way I could. I did everything that I had the capacity to bring about. Damn little. Almost nothing." He lapsed then into smoldering, brooding silence.

"The graffiti on the bathroom walls," Joe said. "You wrote that we were dead and you were alive."

"I *am* alive," Runciter rasped.

"Are we dead, the rest of us?"

After a long pause, Runciter said, "Yes."

"But in the taped TV commercial—"

"That was for the purpose of getting you to fight. To find Ubik. It made you look and you kept on looking too. I kept trying to get it to you, but you know what went wrong; she kept drawing everyone into the past—she worked on us all with that talent of hers. Over and over again she regressed it and made it worthless." Runciter added, "Except for the fragmentary notes I managed to slip to you in conjunction with the stuff." Urgently, he pointed his heavy, determined finger at Joe, gesturing with vigor. "Look what I've been up against. The same thing that got all of you, that's killed you off one by one. Frankly, it's amazing to me that I was able to do as much as I could."

Joe said, "When did you figure out what was taking place? Did you always know? From the start?"

" 'The start,' " Runciter echoed bitingly. "What's that mean? It started months or maybe even years ago; god knows how long Hollis and Mick and Pat Conley and S. Dole Melipone and G. G. Ashwood have been hatching it up, working it over and reworking it like dough. Here's what happened. We got lured to Luna. We let Pat Conley come with us, a woman we didn't know, a talent we didn't understand—

which possibly even Hollis doesn't understand. An ability anyhow connected with time reversion; not, strictly speaking, the ability to travel through time . . . for instance, she can't go into the future. In a certain sense, she can't go into the past either; what she does, as near as I can comprehend it, is start a counter-process that uncovers the prior stages inherent in configurations of matter. But you know that; you and Al figured it out." He ground his teeth with wrath. "Al Hammond—what a loss. But I couldn't do anything; I couldn't break through then as I've done now."

"Why were you able to now?" Joe asked.

Runciter said, *"Because this is as far back as she is able to carry us.* Normal forward flow has already resumed; we're again flowing from past into present into future. She evidently stretched her ability to its limit. 1939; that's the limit. What she's done now is shut off her talent. Why not? She's accomplished what Ray Hollis sent her to us to do."

"How many people have been affected?"

"Just the group of us who were on Luna there in that subsurface room. Not even Zoe Wirt. Pat can circumscribe the range of the field she creates. As far as the rest of the world is concerned, the bunch of us took off for Luna and got blown up in an accidental explosion; we were put into cold-pac by solicitous Stanton Mick, but no contact could be established—they didn't get us soon enough."

Joe said, "Why wouldn't the bomb blast be enough?"

Lifting an eyebrow, Runciter regarded him.

"Why use Pat Conley at all?" Joe said. He sensed, even in his weary, shaken state, something wrong. "There's no reason for all this reversion machinery, this sinking us into a retrograde time momentum back here to 1939. It serves no purpose."

"That's an interesting point," Runciter said; he nodded slowly, a frown on his rugged, stony face. "I'll have to think about it. Give me a little while." He walked to the window, stood gazing out at the stores across the street.

"It strikes me," Joe said, "that what we appear to be faced with is a malignant rather than a purposeful force. Not so much someone trying to kill us or nullify us, someone trying to eliminate us from functioning as a prudence organization, but—" He pondered; he almost had it. "An irresponsible entity that's enjoying what it's doing to us. The way it's killing us off one by one. It doesn't have to prolong all this. That doesn't sound to me like Ray Hollis; he deals in cold, practical murder. And from what I know about Stanton Mick—"

"Pat herself," Runciter interrupted brusquely; he turned away from the window. "She's psychologically a sadistic person. Like tearing wings off flies. Playing with us." He watched for Joe's reaction.

Joe said, "It sounds to me more like a child."

"But look at Pat Conley; she's spiteful and jealous. She got Wendy first because of emotional animosity. She followed you all the way up the stairs just now, enjoying it; gloating over it, in fact."

"How do you know that?" Joe said. *You were waiting here in this room*, he said to himself; *you couldn't have seen it. And—how had Runciter known he would come to this particular room?*

Letting out his breath in a ragged, noisy rush, Runciter said, "I haven't told you all of it. As a matter of fact . . ." He ceased speaking, chewed his lower lip savagely, then abruptly resumed. "What I've said hasn't been strictly true. I don't hold the same relationship to this regressed world that the rest of you do; you're absolutely right: I know too much. It's because I enter it from outside, Joe."

"Manifestations," Joe said.

"Yes. Thrust down into this world, here and there. At strategic points and times. Like the traffic citation. Like Archer's—"

"You didn't tape that TV commercial," Joe said. "That was live."

Runciter, with reluctance, nodded.

"Why the difference," Joe said, "between your situation and ours?"

"You want me to say?"

"Yes." He prepared himself, already knowing what he would hear.

"I'm not dead, Joe. The graffiti told the truth. You're all in cold-pac and I'm—" Runciter spoke with difficulty, not looking directly at Joe. "I'm sitting in a consultation lounge at the Beloved Brethren Moratorium. All of you are inter-wired, on my instructions; kept together as a group. I'm out here trying to reach you. That's where I am when I say I'm outside; that's why the manifestations, as you call them. For one week now I've been trying to get you all functioning in half-life, but—it isn't working. You're fading out one by one."

After a pause Joe said, "What about Pat Conley?"

"Yeah, she's with you; in half-life, interwired to the rest of the group."

"Are the regressions due to her talent? Or to the normal decay of half-life?" Tensely, he waited for Runciter's answer; everything, as he saw it, hung on this one question.

Runciter snorted, grimaced, then said hoarsely, "The normal decay. Ella experienced it. Everyone who enters half-life experiences it."

"You're lying to me," Joe said. And felt a knife shear through him.

Staring at him, Runciter said, "Joe, my god, I saved your life; I broke through to you enough just now to bring you back into full half-life functioning—you'll probably go on indefinitely now. If I hadn't been waiting here in this hotel room when you came crawling through that door, why, hell— hey, look, goddam it; you'd be lying on that rundown bed dead as a doornail by now if it wasn't for me. I'm Glen Runciter; I'm your boss and I'm the one fighting to save all your lives—I'm the *only* one out here in the real world plug-ging for you." He continued to stare at Joe with heated indignation and surprise. A bewildered, injured surprise, as if he could not fathom what was happening. "That girl," Runciter said, "that Pat Conley, she would have killed you like she killed—" He broke off.

Joe said, "Like she killed Wendy and Al, Edie Dorn, Fred Zafsky, and maybe by now Tito Apostos."

In a low but controlled voice Runciter said, "This situation is very complex, Joe. It doesn't admit to simple answers."

"You don't know the answers," Joe said. "That's the problem. You made up answers; you had to invent them to explain your presence here. All your presences here, your so-called manifestations."

"I don't call them that; you and Al worked out that name. Don't blame me for what you two—"

"You don't know any more than I do," Joe said, "about what's happening to us and who's attacking us. Glen, you can't say who we're up against *because you don't know.*"

Runciter said, "I know I'm alive; I know I'm sitting out here in this consultation lounge at the moratorium."

"Your body in the coffin," Joe said. "Here at the Simple Shepherd Mortuary. Did you look at it?"

"No," Runciter said, "but that isn't really—"

"It had withered," Joe said. "Lost bulk like Wendy's and Al's and Edie's—and, in a little while, mine. Exactly the same for you; no better, no worse."

"In your case I got Ubik—" Again Runciter broke off; a difficult-to-decipher expression appeared on his face: a combination perhaps of insight, fear and—but Joe couldn't tell. "I got you the Ubik," he finished.

"What is Ubik?" Joe said.

There was no answer from Runciter.

"You don't know that either," Joe said. "You don't know what it is or why it works. You don't even know where it comes from."

After a long, agonized pause, Runciter said, "You're right, Joe. Absolutely right." Tremulously, he lit another cigarette. "But I wanted to save your life; that part's true. Hell, I'd like to save all your lives." The cigarette slipped from his fingers; it dropped to the floor, rolled away. With labored effort, Runciter bent over to grope for it. On his face showed extreme and clear-cut unhappiness. Almost a despair.

"We're in this," Joe said, "and you're sitting out there, out in the lounge, and you can't do it; you can't put a stop to the thing we're involved in."

"That's right." Runciter nodded.

"This is cold-pac," Joe said, "but there's something more. Something not natural to people in half-life. There are two forces at work, as Al figured out; one helping us and one destroying us. You're working with the force or entity or person that's trying to help us. You got the Ubik from them."

"Yes."

Joe said, "So none of us know even yet who it is that's destroying us—and who it is that's protecting us; you outside don't know, and we in here don't know. Maybe it's Pat."

"I think it is," Runciter said. "I think there's your enemy."

Joe said, "Almost. But I don't think so." I don't think, he said to himself, that we've met our enemy face to face, or our friend either.

He thought, But I think we will. Before long we will know who they both are.

"Are you sure," he asked Runciter, "absolutely sure, that you're beyond doubt the only one who survived the blast? Think before you answer."

"Like I said, Zoe Wirt—"

"Of *us*," Joe said. "She's not here in this time segment with us. Pat Conley, for example."

"Pat Conley's chest was crushed. She died of shock and a collapsed lung, with multiple internal injuries, including a damaged liver and a leg broken in three places. Physically speaking, she's about four feet away from you; her body, I mean."

"And it's the same for all the rest? They're all here in cold-pac at the Beloved Brethren Moratorium?"

Runciter said, "With one exception. Sammy Mundo. He

suffered massive brain damage and lapsed into a coma out of which they say he'll never emerge. The cortical—"

"Then he's alive. He's not in cold-pac. He's not here."

"I wouldn't call it 'alive.' They've run encephalograms on him; no cortical activity at all. A vegetable, nothing more. No personality, no motion, no consciousness—there's nothing happening in Mundo's brain, nothing in the slightest."

Joe said, "So, therefore, you naturally didn't think to mention it."

"I mentioned it now."

"When I asked you." He reflected. "How far is he from us? In Zürich?"

"We set down here in Zürich, yes. He's at the Carl Jung Hospital. About a quarter mile from this moratorium."

"Rent a telepath," Joe said. "Or use G. G. Ashwood. Have him scanned." A boy, he said to himself. Disorganized and immature. A cruel, unformed, peculiar personality. This may be it, he said to himself. It would fit in with what we're experiencing, the capricious contradictory happenings. The pulling off of our wings and then the putting back. The temporary restorations, as in just now with me here in this hotel room, after my climb up the stairs.

Runciter sighed. "We did that. In brain-injury cases like this it's a regular practice to try to reach the person telepathically. No results; nothing. No frontal-lobe cerebration of any sort. Sorry, Joe." He wagged his massive head in a sympathetic, tic-like motion; obviously, he shared Joe's disappointment.

Removing the plastic disk from its place, its firm adhesion to his ear, Glen Runciter said into the microphone, "I'll talk to you again later." He now set down all the communications apparatus, rose stiffly from the chair and momentarily stood facing the misty, immobile, icebound shape of Joe Chip resting within its transparent plastic casket. Upright and silent, as it would be for the rest of eternity.

"Did you ring for me, sir?" Herbert Schoenheit von Vogelsang scuttled into the consultation lounge, cringing like a medieval toady. "Shall I put Mr. Chip back with the others? You're done, sir?"

Runciter said, "I'm done."

"Did your—"

"Yes, I got through all right. We could hear each other fine this time." He lit a cigarette; it had been hours since he had had one, had found a free moment. By now the arduous, prolonged task of reaching Joe Chip had depleted him. "Do you have an amphetamine dispenser nearby?" he asked the moratorium owner.

"In the hall outside the consultation lounge." The eager-to-please creature pointed.

Leaving the lounge, Runciter made his way to the amphetamine dispenser; he inserted a coin, pushed the choice lever, and, into the drop slot, a small familiar object slid with a tinkling sound.

The pill made him feel better. But then he thought about his appointment with Len Niggelman two hours from now and wondered if he could really make it. There's been too much going on, he decided. I'm not ready to make my formal report to the Society; I'll have to vid Niggelman and ask for a postponement.

Using a pay phone, he called Niggelman back in the North American Confederation. "Len," he said, "I can't do any more today. I've spent the last twelve hours trying to get through to my people in cold-pac, and I'm exhausted. Would tomorrow be okay?"

Niggelman said, "The sooner you file your official, formal statement with us, the sooner we can begin action against Hollis. My legal department says it's open and shut; they're champing at the bit."

"They think they can make a civil charge stick?"

"Civil and criminal. They've been talking to the New York district attorney. But until you make a formal, notarized report to us—"

"Tomorrow," Runciter promised. "After I get some sleep. This has damn near finished me off." This loss of all my best people, he said to himself. Especially Joe Chip. My organization is depleted and we won't be able to resume commercial operations for months, maybe years. God, he thought, where am I going to get inertials to replace those I've lost? And where am I going to find a tester like Joe?

Niggelman said, "Sure, Glen. Get a good night's sleep and then meet me in my office tomorrow, say at ten o'clock our time."

"Thanks," Runciter said. He rang off, then threw himself heavily down on a pink-plastic couch across the corridor from the phone. I can't find a tester like Joe, he said to himself. The fact of the matter is that Runciter Associates is finished.

The moratorium owner came in, then, putting in another of his untimely appearances. "Can I get you anything, Mr. Runciter? A cup of coffee? Another amphetamine, perhaps a twelve-hour spansule? In my office I have some twenty-four-hour spansules; one of those would get you back up into action for hours, if not all night."

"All night," Runciter said, "I intend to sleep."

"Then how about a—"

"Flap away," Runciter grated. The moratorium owner scuttled off, leaving him alone. Why did I have to pick this place? Runciter asked himself. I guess because Ella's here. It is, after all, the best; that's why she's here, and, hence, why they're all here. Think of them, he reflected, so many who were so recently on this side of the casket. What a catastrophe.

Ella, he said to himself, remembering. I'd better talk to her again for a moment, to let her know how things are going. That's, after all, what I told her I'd do.

Getting to his feet, he started off in search of the moratorium owner.

Am I going to get that damn Jory this time? he asked himself. Or will I be able to keep Ella in focus long enough to tell her what Joe said? It's become so hard to hang onto her now, with Jory growing and expanding and feeding on her and maybe on others over there in half-life. The moratorium should do something about him; Jory's a hazard to everyone here. Why do they let him go on? he asked himself.

He thought, Maybe because they can't stop him.

Maybe there's never been anyone in half-life like Jory before.

15

*Could it be that I have bad breath,
Tom? Well, Ed, if you're worried
about that, try today's new Ubik,
with powerful germicidal foaming
action, guaranteed safe when
taken as directed.*

The door of the ancient hotel room swung open. Don Denny, accompanied by a middle-aged, responsible-looking man with neatly trimmed gray hair, entered. Denny, his face strained with apprehension, said, "How are you, Joe? Why aren't you lying down? For chrissake, get onto the bed."

"Please lie down, Mr. Chip," the doctor said as he set his medical bag on the vanity table and opened it up. "Is there pain along with the enervation and the difficult respiration?" He approached the bed with an old-fashioned stethoscope and cumbersome blood-pressure-reading equipment. "Do you have any history of cardiac involvement, Mr. Chip? Or your mother or father? Unbutton your shirt, please." He drew up a wooden chair beside the bed, seated himself expectantly on it.

Joe said, "I'm okay now."

"Let him listen to your heart," Denny said tersely.

"Okay." Joe stretched out on the bed and unbuttoned his shirt. "Runciter managed to get through to me," he said to Denny. "We're in cold-pac; he's on the other side trying to reach us. Someone else is trying to injure us. Pat didn't do it, or, anyhow, she didn't do it alone. Neither she nor Runciter knows what's going on. When you opened the door did you see Runciter?"

"No," Denny said.

"He was sitting across the room from me," Joe said. "Two, three minutes ago. 'Sorry, Joe,' he said; that was the last thing he said to me and then he cut contact, stopped communicating, just canceled himself out. Look on the vanity table and see if he left the spray can of Ubik."

Denny searched, then held up the brightly illuminated can. "Here it is. But it seems empty." Denny shook it.

"Almost empty," Joe said. "Spray what's left on yourself. Go ahead." He gestured emphatically.

"Don't talk, Mr. Chip," the doctor said, listening to his stethoscope. He then rolled up Joe's sleeve and began winding inflatable rubber fabric around his arm in preparation for the blood-pressure test.

"How's my heart?" Joe asked.

"Appears normal," the doctor said. "Although slightly fast."

"See?" Joe said to Don Denny. "I've recovered."

Denny said, "The others are dying, Joe."

Half sitting up, Joe said, "All of them?"

"Everyone that's left." He held the can but did not use it.

"Pat, too?" Joe asked.

"When I got out of the elevator on the second floor here I found her. It had just begun to hit her. She seemed terribly surprised; apparently, she couldn't believe it." He set the can down again. "I guess she thought she was doing it. With her talent."

Joe said, "That's right; that's what she thought. Why won't you use the Ubik?"

"Hell, Joe, we're going to die. You know it, and I know it." He removed his horn-rimmed glasses and rubbed his eyes. "After I saw Pat's condition I went into the other rooms, and that's when I saw the rest of them. Of *us*. That's why we took so long getting here; I had Dr. Taylor examine them. I couldn't believe they'd dwindle away so fast. The acceleration has been so goddam great. In just the last hour—"

"Use the Ubik," Joe said. "Or I'll use it on you."

Don Denny again picked up the can, again shook it, pointed the nozzle toward himself. "All right," he said. "If that's what you want. There really isn't any reason not to. This is the end, isn't it? I mean, they're all dead; only you and I are left, and the Ubik is going to wear off you in a few hours. And you won't be able to get any more. Which will leave me." His decision made, Denny depressed the button of the spray can; the shimmering, palpitating vapor, filled with particles of metallic light that danced nimbly, formed at once around him. Don Denny disappeared, concealed by the nimbus of radiant, ergic excitement.

Pausing in his task of reading Joe's blood pressure, Dr. Taylor twisted his head to see. Both he and Joe watched as the vapor now condensed; puddles of it glistened on the carpet, and down the wall behind Denny it drizzled in bright streaks.

The cloud concealing Denny evaporated.

The person standing there, in the center of the vaporizing stain of Ubik that had saturated the worn and dingy carpet, was not Don Denny.

An adolescent boy, mawkishly slender, with irregular black-button eyes beneath tangled brows. He wore an anachronistic costume: white drip-dry shirt, jeans and laceless leather slippers. Clothes from the middle of the century. On his elongated face Joe saw a smile, but it was a misshapen smile, a thwarted crease that became now almost a jeering leer. No two features matched: His ears had too many convolutions in them to fit with his chitinous eyes. His straight hair contradicted the interwoven, curly bristles of his brows. And his nose, Joe thought, too thin, too sharp, far too long. Even his chin failed to harmonize with the balance of his face; it had a deep chisel mark in it, a cleft obviously penetrating far up into the bone . . . Joe thought, as if at that point the manufacturer of this creature struck it a blow aimed at obliterating it. But the physical material, the base substance, had been too dense; the boy had not fractured and split apart. He existed in defiance of even the force that had constructed him; he jeered at everything else and it, too.

"Who are you?" Joe said.

The boy's fingers writhed, a twitch protecting him evidently from a stammer. "Sometimes I call myself Matt, and sometimes Bill," he said. "But mostly I'm Jory. That's my real name—Jory." Gray, shabby teeth showed as he spoke. And a grubby tongue.

After an interval Joe said, "Where's Denny? He never came into this room, did he?" Dead, he thought, with the others.

"I ate Denny a long time ago," the boy Jory said. "Right at the beginning, before they came here from New York. First I ate Wendy Wright. Denny came second."

Joe said, "How do you mean 'ate'?" Literally? he wondered, his flesh undulating with aversion; the gross physical motion rolled through him, engulfing him, as if his body wanted to shrink away. However, he managed more or less to conceal it.

"I did what I do," Jory said. "It's hard to explain, but I've been doing it a long time to lots of half-life people. I eat their life, what remains of it. There's very little in each person, so I need a lot of them. I used to wait until they had been in half-life awhile, but now I have to have them immediately. If I'm going to be able to live myself. If you come close to me and listen—I'll hold my mouth open—you can hear their voices. Not all of them, but anyhow the last ones I ate. The ones you know." With his fingernail he picked at an upper incisor, his head tilted on one side as he regarded Joe, evidently waiting to hear his reaction. "Don't you have anything to say?" he said.

"It was you who started me dying, down there in the lobby."

"Me and not Pat. I ate her out in the hall by the elevator,

and then I ate the others. I thought you were dead." He
rotated the can of Ubik, which he still held. "I can't figure
this out. What's in it, and where does Runciter get it?" He
scowled. "But Runciter can't be doing it; you're right. He's
on the outside. This originates from within our environment.
It has to, because nothing can come in from outside except
words."

Joe said, "So there's nothing you can do to me. You can't
eat me because of the Ubik."

"I can't eat you for a while. But the Ubik will wear off."

"You don't know that; you don't even know what it is or
where it comes from." I wonder if I can kill you, he thought.
The boy Jory seemed delicate. This is the thing that got
Wendy, he said to himself. I'm seeing it face to face, as I
knew I eventually would. Wendy, Al, the real Don Denny—
all the rest of them. It even ate Runciter's corpse as it lay
in the casket at the mortuary; there must have been a flicker
of residual protophasic activity in or near it, or something,
anyhow, which attracted him.

The doctor said, "Mr. Chip, I didn't have a chance to
finish taking your blood pressure. Please lie back down."

Joe stared at him, then said, "Didn't he see you change,
Jory? Hasn't he heard what you've been saying?"

"Dr. Taylor is a product of my mind," Jory said. "Like
every other fixture in this pseudo world."

"I don't believe it," Joe said. To the doctor he said, "You
heard what he's been saying, didn't you?"

With a hollow whistling pop the doctor disappeared.

"See?" Jory said, pleased.

"What are you going to do when I'm killed off?" Joe asked
the boy. "Will you keep on maintaining this 1939 world, this
pseudo world, as you call it?"

"Of course not. There'd be no reason to."

"Then it's all for me, just for me. This entire world."

Jory said, "It's not very large. One hotel in Des Moines.
And a street outside the window with a few people and cars.
And maybe a couple of other buildings thrown in: stores

across the street for you to look at when you happen to see out."

"So you're not maintaining any New York or Zürich or—"

"Why should I? No one's there. Wherever you and the others of the group went, I constructed a tangible reality corresponding to their minimal expectations. When you flew here from New York I created hundreds of miles of countryside, town after town—I found that very exhausting. I had to eat a great deal to make up for that. In fact, that's the reason I had to finish off the others so soon after you got here. I needed to replenish myself."

Joe said, "Why 1939? Why not our own contemporary world, 1992?"

"The effort; I can't keep objects from regressing. Doing it all alone, it was too much for me. I created 1992 at first, but then things began to break down. The coins, the cream, the cigarettes—all those phenomena that you noticed. And then Runciter kept breaking through from outside; that made it even harder for me. Actually, it would have been better if he hadn't interfered." Jory grinned slyly. "But I didn't worry about the reversion. I knew you'd figure it was Pat Conley. It would seem like her talent because it's sort of like what her talent does. I thought maybe the rest of you would kill her. I would enjoy that." His grin increased.

"What's the point of keeping this hotel and the street outside going for me now?" Joe said. "Now that I know?"

"But I always do it this way." Jory's eyes widened.

Joe said, "I'm going to kill you." He stepped toward Jory in an uncoordinated half-falling motion. Raising his open hands he plunged against the boy, trying to capture the neck, searching for the bent-pipestem windpipe with all his fingers.

Snarling, Jory bit him. The great shovel teeth fastened deep into Joe's right hand. They hung on as, meanwhile, Jory raised his head, lifting Joe's hand with his jaw; Jory stared at him with unwinking eyes, snoring wetly as he tried to close his jaws. The teeth sank deeper and Joe felt the pain of it throughout him. He's eating me, he realized. "You can't," he said aloud; he hit Jory on the snout, punching again and again. "The Ubik keeps you away," he said as he cuffed Jory's jeering eyes. "You can't do it to me."

"Gahm grau," Jory bubbled, working his jaws sideways like a sheep's. Grinding Joe's hand until the pain became too much for Joe to stand. He kicked Jory. The teeth released his hand; he crept backward, looking at the blood rising from the punctures made by the troll teeth. Jesus, he said to himself, appalled.

"You can't do to me," Joe said, "what you did to them." Locating the spray can of Ubik, he pointed the nozzle toward the bleeding wound which his hand had become. He pressed the red plastic stud and a weak stream of particles emerged and settled in a film over the chewed, torn flesh. The pain immediately departed. Before his eyes the wound healed.

"And you can't kill me," Jory said. He still grinned.

Joe said, "I'm going downstairs." He walked unsteadily to the door of the room and opened it. Outside lay the dingy hall; he started forward, step by step, treading carefully. The floor, however, seemed substantial. Not a quasi- or irreal world at all.

"Don't go too far," Jory said from behind him. "I can't keep too great an area going. Like, if you were to get into one of those cars and drive for miles . . . eventually you'd reach a point where it breaks down. And you wouldn't like that any better than I do."

"I don't see what I have to lose." Joe reached the elevator, pressed the down button.

Jory called after him, "I have trouble with elevators. They're complicated. Maybe you should take the stairs."

After waiting a little longer, Joe gave up; as Jory had advised, he descended by the stairs—the same flight up which he had so recently come, step by step, in an agony of effort.

Well, he thought, that's one of the two agencies who're at work; Jory is the one who's destroying us—has destroyed us, except for me. Behind Jory there is nothing; he is the end. Will I meet the other? Probably not soon enough for it to matter, he decided. He looked once more at his hand. Completely well.

Reaching the lobby, he gazed around him, at the people, the great chandelier overhead. Jory, in many respects, had done a good job, despite the reversion to these older forms. Real, he thought, experiencing the floor beneath his feet. I can't get over it.

He thought, Jory must have had experience. He must have done this many times before.

Going to the hotel desk, he said to the clerk, "You have a restaurant that you'd recommend?"

"Down the street," the clerk said, pausing in his task of sorting mail. "To your right. The Matador. You'll find it excellent, sir."

"I'm lonely," Joe said, on impulse. "Does the hotel have any source of supply? Any girls?"

The clerk said in a clipped, disapproving voice, "Not *this* hotel, sir; this hotel does not pander."

"You keep a good clean family hotel," Joe said.

"We like to think so, sir."

"I was just testing you," Joe said. "I wanted to be sure what kind of hotel I was staying in." He left the counter, recrossed the lobby, made his way down the wide marble stairs, through the revolving door and onto the pavement outside.

16

Wake up to a hearty, lip-smacking bowlful of nutritious, nourishing Ubik toasted flakes, the adult cereal that's more crunchy, more tasty, more ummmish. Ubik breakfast cereal, the whole-bowl taste treat! Do not exceed recommended portion at any one meal.

The diversity of cars impressed him. Many years represented, many makes and many models. The fact that they mostly came in black could not be laid at Jory's door; this detail was authentic.

But how did Jory know it?

That's peculiar, he thought; Jory's knowledge of the minutiae of 1939, a period in which none of us lived—except Glen Runciter.

Then all at once he realized why. Jory had told the truth; he had constructed—not this world—but the world, or rather its phantasmagoric counterpart, of their own time. Decomposition back to these forms was not of his doing; they happened despite his efforts. These are natural atavisms, Joe realized, happening mechanically as Jory's strength wanes. As the boy says, it's an enormous effort. This is perhaps the first time he has created a world this diverse, for so many people at once. It isn't usual for so many half-lifers to be interwired.

We have put an abnormal strain on Jory, he said to himself. And we paid for it.

A square old Dodge taxi sputtered past; Joe waved at it,

and the cab floundered noisily to the curb. Let's test out what Jory said, he said to himself, as to the early boundary of this quasi world now. To the driver he said, "Take me for a ride through town; go anywhere you want. I'd like to see as many streets and buildings and people as possible, and then, when you've driven through all of Des Moines, I want you to drive me to the next town and we'll see that."

"I don't go between towns, mister," the driver said, holding the door open for Joe. "But I'll be glad to drive you around Des Moines. It's a nice city, sir. You're from out of state, aren't you?"

"New York," Joe said, getting inside the cab.

The cab rolled back out into traffic. "How do they feel about the war back in New York?" the driver asked presently. "Do you think we'll be getting into it? Roosevelt wants to get us—"

"I don't care to discuss politics or the war," Joe said harshly.

They drove for a time in silence.

Watching the buildings, people and cars go by, Joe asked himself again how Jory could maintain it all. So many details, he marveled. I should be coming to the edge of it soon; it has to be just about now.

"Driver," he said, "are there any houses of prostitution here in Des Moines?'

"No," the driver said.

Maybe Jory can't manage that, Joe reflected. Because of his youth. Or maybe he disapproves. He felt, all at once, tired. Where am I going? he asked himself. And what for? To prove to myself that what Jory told me is true? *I already know it's true;* I saw the doctor wink out. I saw Jory emerge from inside Don Denny; that should have been enough. All I'm doing this way is putting more of a load on Jory, which will increase his appetite. I'd better give up, he decided. This is pointless.

And, as Jory had said, the Ubik would be wearing off anyhow. This driving around Des Moines is not the way I

want to spend my last minutes or hours of life. There must
be something else.

Along the sidewalk a girl moved in a slow, easy gait; she
seemed to be window-shopping. A pretty girl, with gay,
blond pigtails, wearing an unbuttoned sweater over her
blouse, a bright red skirt and high-heeled little shoes. "Slow
the cab," he instructed the driver. "There, by that girl with
the pigtails."

"She won't talk to you," the driver said. "She'll call a
cop."

Joe said, "I don't care." It hardly mattered at this point.

Slowing, the old Dodge bumbled its way to the curb; its
tires protested as they rubbed against the curb. The girl
glanced up.

"Hi, miss," Joe said.

She regarded him with curiosity; her warm, intelligent,
blue eyes widened a little, but they showed no aversion or
alarm. Rather, she seemed slightly amused at him. But in a
friendly way. "Yes?" she said.

"I'm going to die," Joe said.

"Oh, dear," the girl said, with concern. "Are you—"

"He's not sick," the driver put in. "He's been asking after
girls; he just wants to pick you up."

The girl laughed. Without hostility. And she did not de-
part.

"It's almost dinnertime," Joe said to her. "Let me take
you to a restaurant, the Matador; I understand that's nice."
His tiredness now had increased; he felt the weight of it on
him, and then he realized, with muted, weary horror, that
it consisted of the same fatigue which had attacked him in
the hotel lobby, after he had shown the police citation to
Pat. And the cold. Stealthily, the physical experience of the
cold-pac surrounding him had come back. The Ubik is beginning to wear off, he realized. I don't have much longer.

Something must have showed in his face; the girl walked
toward him, up to the window of the cab. "Are you all right?"
she asked.

Joe said, with effort, "I'm dying, miss." The wound on his hand, the teeth marks, had begun to throb once more. And were again becoming visible. This alone would have been enough to fill him with dread.

"Have the driver take you to the hospital," the girl said.

"Can we have dinner together?" Joe asked her.

"Is that what you want to do?" she said. "When you're— whatever it is. Sick? Are you sick?" She opened the door of the cab then. "Do you want me to go with you to the hospital? Is that it?"

"To the Matador," Joe said. "We'll have braised fillet of Martian mole cricket." He remembered then that that imported delicacy did not exist in this time period. "Market steak," he said. "Beef. Do you like beef?"

Getting into the cab, the girl said to the driver, "He wants to go to the Matador."

"Okay, miss," the driver said. The cab rolled out into traffic once more. At the next intersection the driver made a U-turn; now Joe realized, we are on our way to the restaurant. I wonder if I'll make it there. Fatigue and cold had invaded him completely; he felt his body processes begin to close down, one by one. Organs that had no future; the liver did not need to make red blood cells, the kidneys did not need to excrete wastes, the intestines no longer served any purpose. Only the heart, laboring on, and the increasingly difficult breathing; each time he drew air into his lungs he sensed the concrete block that had situated itself on his chest. My gravestone, he decided. His hand, he saw, was bleeding again; thick, slow blood appeared, drop by drop.

"Care for a Lucky Strike?" the girl asked him, extending her pack toward him. " 'They're toasted,' as the slogan goes. The phrase 'L.S.M.F.T.' won't come into existence until—"

Joe said, "My name is Joe Chip."

"Do you want me to tell you my name?"

"Yes," he grated, and shut his eyes; he couldn't speak any further, for a time anyhow. "Do you like Des Moines?" he asked her presently, concealing his hand from her. "Have you lived here a long time?"

"You sound very tired, Mr. Chip," the girl said.

"Oh, hell," he said, gesturing. "It doesn't matter."

"Yes, it does." The girl opened her purse, rummaged briskly within it. "I'm not a deformation of Jory's; I'm not like him—" She indicated the driver. "Or like these little old stores and houses and this dingy street, all these people and their neolithic cars. Here, Mr. Chip." From her purse she brought an envelope, which she passed to him. "This is for you. Open it right away; I don't think either of us should have delayed so long."

With leaden fingers he tore open the envelope.

In it he found a certificate, stately and ornamented. The printing on it, however, swam; he was too weary now to read. "What's it say?" he asked her, laying it down on his lap.

"From the company that manufactures Ubik," the girl said. "It is a guarantee, Mr. Chip, of a free, lifetime supply, free because I know your problem regarding money, your, shall we say, idiosyncrasy. And a list, on the reverse, of all the drugstores which carry it. Two drugstores—and not abandoned ones—in Des Moines are listed. I suggest we go to one first, before we eat dinner. Here, driver." She leaned forward and handed the driver a slip of paper already written out. "Take us to this address. And hurry; they'll be closing soon."

Joe lay back against the seat, panting for breath.

"We'll make it to the drugstore," the girl said, and patted his arm reassuringly.

"Who are you?" Joe asked her.

"My name is Ella. Ella Hyde Runciter. Your employer's wife."

"You're here with us," Joe said. "On this side; you're in cold-pac."

"As you well know. I have been for some time," Ella Runciter said. "Fairly soon I'll be reborn into another womb,

I think. At least, Glen says so. I keep dreaming about a smoky red light, and that's bad; that's not a morally proper womb to be born into." She laughed a rich, warm laugh.

"You're the other one," Joe said. "Jory destroying us, you trying to help us. Behind you there's no one, just as there's no one behind Jory. I've reached the last entities involved."

Ella said caustically, "I don't think of myself as an 'entity'; I usually think of myself as Ella Runciter."

"But it's true," Joe said.

"Yes." Somberly, she nodded.

"Why are you working against Jory?"

"Because Jory invaded me," Ella said. "He menaced me in the same way he's menaced you. We both know what he does; he told you himself, in your hotel room. Sometimes he becomes very powerful; on occasion, he manages to supplant me when I'm active and trying to talk to Glen. But I seem to be able to cope with him better than most half-lifers, with or without Ubik. Better, for instance, than your group, even acting as a collective."

"Yes," Joe said. It certainly was true. Well proved.

"When I'm reborn," Ella said, "Glen won't be able to consult with me any more. I have a very selfish, practical reason for assisting you, Mr. Chip; *I want you to replace me.* I want to have someone whom Glen can ask for advice and assistance, whom he can lean on. You will be ideal; you'll be doing in half-life what you did in full-life. So, in a sense, I'm not motivated by noble sentiments; I saved you from Jory for a good common-sense reason." She added, "And god knows I detest Jory."

"After you're reborn," Joe said, "I won't succumb?"

"You have your lifetime supply of Ubik. As it says on the certificate I gave you."

Joe said, "Maybe I can defeat Jory."

"Destroy him, you mean?" Ella pondered. "He's not invulnerable. Maybe in time you can learn ways to nullify him. I think that's really the best you can hope to do; I doubt if you can truly destroy him—in other words consume him—

as he does to half-lifers placed near him at the moratorium."

"Hell," Joe said. "I'll tell Glen Runciter the situation and have him move Jory out of the moratorium entirely."

"Glen has no authority to do that."

"Won't Schoenheit von Vogelsang—"

Ella said, "Herbert is paid a great deal of money annually, by Jory's family, to keep him with the others and to think up plausible reasons for doing so. And—there are Jorys in every moratorium. This battle goes on wherever you have half-lifers; it's a verity, a rule, of our kind of existence." She lapsed into silence then; for the first time he saw on her face an expression of anger. A ruffled, taut look that disturbed her tranquility. "It has to be fought on our side of the glass," Ella said. "By those of us in half-life, those that Jory preys on. You'll have to take charge, Mr. Chip, after I'm reborn. Do you think you can do that? It'll be hard. Jory will be sapping your strength always, putting a burden on you that you'll feel as—" She hesitated. "The approach of death. Which it will be. Because in half-life we diminish constantly anyhow. Jory only speeds it up. The weariness and cooling-off come anyhow. But not so soon."

To himself Joe thought, I can remember what he did to Wendy. That'll keep me going. That alone.

"Here's the drugstore, miss," the driver said. The square, upright old Dodge wheezed to the curb and parked.

"I won't go in with you," Ella Runciter said to Joe as he opened the door and crept shakily out. "Goodby. Thanks for your loyalty to Glen. Thanks for what you're going to be doing for him." She leaned toward him, kissed him on the cheek; her lips seemed to him ripe with life. And some of it was conveyed to him; he felt slightly stronger. "Good luck with Jory." She settled back, composed herself sedately, her purse on her lap.

Joe shut the cab door, stood, then made his way haltingly into the drugstore. Behind him the cab thub-thubbed off; he heard but did not see it go.

Within the solemn, lamplit interior of the drugstore a bald

pharmacist wearing a formal dark vest, bow tie and sharply pressed sharkskin trousers, approached him. "Afraid we're closing, sir. I was just coming to lock the door."

"But I'm in," Joe said. "And I want to be waited on." He showed the pharmacist the certificate which Ella had given him; squinting through his round, rimless glasses, the pharmacist labored over the gothic printing. "Are you going to wait on me?" Joe asked.

"Ubik," the pharmacist said. "I believe I'm out of that. Let me check and see." He started off.

"Jory," Joe said.

Turning his head the pharmacist said, "Sir?"

"You're Jory," Joe said. I can tell now, he said to himself. I'm learning to know him when I encounter him. "You invented this drugstore," he said, "and everything in it except for the spray cans of Ubik. You have no authority over Ubik; that comes from Ella." He forced himself into motion; step by step he edged his way behind the counter to the shelves of medical supplies. Peering in the gloom over one shelf after the other, he tried to locate the Ubik. The lighting of the store had dimmed; the antique fixtures were fading.

"I've regressed all the Ubik in this store," the pharmacist said in a youthful, high-pitched Jory voice. "Back to the liver and kidney balm. It's no good now."

"I'll go to the other drugstore that has it," Joe said. He leaned against a counter, painfully drawing in slow, irregular gulps of air.

Jory, from within the balding pharmacist, said, "It'll be closed."

"Tomorrow," Joe said. "I can hold out until tomorrow morning."

"You can't," Jory said. "And, anyhow, the Ubik at that drugstore will be regressed too."

"Another town," Joe said.

"Wherever you go, it'll be regressed. Back to the salve or back to the powder or back to the elixir or back to the balm. You'll never see a spray can of it, Joe Chip." Jory, in the

form of the bald-headed pharmacist, smiled, showing cel-
luloid-like dentures.

"I can—" He broke off, gathering his meager vitality to
him. Trying, by his own strength, to warm his stiffening,
cold-numbed body. "Bring it up to the present," he said.
"To 1992."

"Can you, Mr. Chip?" The pharmacist handed Joe a
square pasteboard container. "Here you are. Open it and
you'll see—"

Joe said, "I know what I'll see." He concentrated on the
blue jar of liver and kidney balm. Evolve forward, he said
to it, flooding it with his need; he poured whatever energy
he had left onto the container. It did not change. This is the
regular world, he said to it. "Spray can," he said aloud. He
shut his eyes, resting.

"It's not a spray can, Mr Chip," the pharmacist said.
Going here and there in the drugstore he shut off lights; at
the cash register he punched a key and the drawer rattled
open. Expertly, the pharmacist transferred the bills and
change from the drawer into a metal box with a lock on it.

"You are a spray can," Joe said to the pasteboard container which he held in his hand. "This is 1992," he said,
and tried to exert everything; he put the entirety of himself
into the effort.

The last light blinked out, turned off by the pseudo pharmacist. A dull gleam shone into the drugstore from the street-
lamp outside; by it, Joe could make out the shape of the
object in his hand, its boxlike lines. Opening the door, the
pharmacist said, "Come on, Mr. Chip. Time to go home.
She was wrong, wasn't she? And you won't see her again,
because she's so far on the road to being reborn; she's not
thinking about you any more, or me or Runciter. What Ella
sees now are various lights: red and dingy, then maybe bright
orange—"

"What I hold here," Joe said, "is a spray can."

"No," the pharmacist said. "I'm sorry, Mr. Chip. I really
am. But it's not."

Joe set the pasteboard container down on a nearby counter. He turned, with dignity, and began the long, slow journey across the drugstore to the front door which the pharmacist held open for him. Neither of them spoke until Joe, at last, passed through the doorway and out onto the nocturnal sidewalk.

Behind him the pharmacist emerged too; he bent and locked the door after the two of them.

"I think I'll complain to the manufacturer," Joe said. "About the—" He ceased talking. Something constricted his throat; he could not breathe and he could not speak. Then, temporarily, the blockage abated. "Your regressed drugstore," he finished.

"Goodnight," the pharmacist said. He remained for a moment, eying Joe in the evening gloom. Then, shrugging, he started off.

To his left, Joe made out the dark shape of a bench where people waited for a streetcar. He managed to reach it, to seat himself. The other persons, two or three, whichever it was, squeezed away from him, either out of aversion or to give him room; he could not tell which, and he didn't care. All he felt was the support of the bench beneath him, the release of some of his vast inertial weight. A few more minutes, he said to himself. If I remember right. Christ, what a thing to have to go through, he said to himself. For the second time.

Anyhow, we tried, he thought as he watched the yellow flickering lights and neon signs, the flow of cars going in both directions directly before his eyes. He thought to himself, Runciter kicked and struggled; Ella has been scratching and biting and gouging for a long time. And, he thought, I damn near evolved the jar of Ubik liver and kidney balm back to the present. I almost succeeded. There was something in knowing that, an awareness of his own great strength. His final transcendental attempt.

The streetcar, a clanging metal enormity, came to a grating

halt before the bench. The several people beside Joe rose and hurried out to board it by its rear platform.

"Hey, mister!" the conductor yelled to Joe. "Are you coming or aren't you?"

Joe said nothing. The conductor waited, then jerked his signal cord. Noisily, the streetcar started up; it continued on, and then at last disappeared beyond his range of vision. Lots of luck, Joe said to himself as he heard the racket of the streetcar's wheels die away. And so long.

He leaned back, closed his eyes.

"Excuse me." Bending over him in the darkness a girl in a synthetic ostrich-leather coat; he looked up at her, jarred into awareness. "Mr. Chip?" she said. Pretty and slender, dressed in hat, gloves, suit and high heels. She held something in her hand; he saw the outline of a package. "Of New York? Of Runciter Associates? I don't want to give this to the wrong person."

"I'm Joe Chip," he said. For a moment he thought the girl might be Ella Runciter. But he had never seen her before. "Who sent you?" he said.

"Dr. Sonderbar," the girl said. "The younger Dr. Sonderbar, son of Dr. Sonderbar the founder."

"Who's that?" The name meant nothing to him, and then he remembered where he had seen it. "The Liver and Kidney man," he said. "Processed oleander leaves, oil of peppermint, charcoal, cobalt chloride, zinc oxide—" Weariness overcame him; he stopped talking.

The girl said, "By making use of the most advanced techniques of modern-day science, the reversion of matter to earlier forms can be reversed, and at a price any conapt owner can afford. Ubik is sold by leading home-art stores throughout Earth. So look for it at the place you shop, Mr. Chip."

Fully conscious now, he said, "Look for it *where*?" He struggled to his feet, stood inexpertly swaying. "You're from 1992; what you said came from Runciter's TV commercial."

An evening wind rustled at him and he felt it tug at him, drawing him away with it; he seemed to be like some ragged bundle of webs and cloth, barely holding together.

"Yes, Mr. Chip." The girl handed him a package. "You brought me from the future, by what you did there inside the drugstore a few moments ago. You summoned me directly from the factory. Mr. Chip, I could spray it on you, if you're too weak to. Shall I? I'm an official factory representative and technical consultant; I know how to apply it." She took the package swiftly back from his trembling hands; tearing it open, she immediately sprayed him with Ubik. In the dusk he saw the spray can glint. He saw the happy, colored lettering.

"Thanks," he said after a time. After he felt better. And warmer.

The girl said, "You didn't need as much this time as you did in the hotel room; you must be stronger than before. Here, take the can of it; you might need it before morning."

"Can I get more?" Joe said. "When this runs out?"

"Evidently so. If you got me here once. I would assume you can get me here again. The same way." She moved away from him, merging with the shadows created by the dense walls of closed-up nearby stores.

"What *is* Ubik?" Joe said, wanting her to stay.

"A spray can of Ubik," the girl answered, "is a portable negative ionizer, with a self-contained, high-voltage, low-amp unit powered by a peak-gain helium battery of 25kv. The negative ions are given a counter-clockwise spin by a radically biased acceleration chamber, which creates a centripetal tendency to them so that they cohere rather than dissipate. A negative ion field diminishes the velocity of anti-protophasons normally present in the atmosphere; as soon as their velocity falls they cease to be anti-protophasons and, under the principle of parity, no longer can unite with protophasons radiated from persons frozen in cold-pac; that is, those in half-life. The end result is that the proportion of protophasons not canceled by anti-protophasons increases,

which means—for a specific time, anyhow—an increment in
the net put-forth field of protophasonic activity . . . which
the affected half-lifer experiences as greater vitality plus a
lowering of the experience of low cold-pac temperatures. So
you can see why regressed forms of Ubik failed to—"

Joe said reflexively, "To say 'negative ions' is redundant.
All ions are negative."

Again the girl moved away. "Maybe I'll see you again,"
she said gently. "It was rewarding to bring you the spray
can; maybe next time—"

"Maybe we can have dinner together," Joe said.

"I'll look forward to it." She ebbed farther and farther
away.

"Who invented Ubik?" Joe asked.

"A number of responsible half-lifers whom Jory threat-
ened. But principally by Ella Runciter. It took her and them
working together a long, long time. And there still isn't very
much of it available, as yet." Ebbing from him in her trim,
covert way, she continued to retreat and then, by degrees,
was gone.

"At the Matador," Joe called after her. "I understand Jory
did a good job materializing it. Or regressing it just right,
whatever it is he does." He listened, but the girl did not
answer.

Carefully carrying the spray can of Ubik, Joe Chip walked
out to greet the evening traffic, searching for a cab.

Under a streetlight he held up the spray can of Ubik, read
the printing on the label.

> I THINK HER NAME IS MYRA LANEY.
> LOOK ON REVERSE SIDE OF CONTAINER
> FOR ADDRESS AND PHONE NUMBER.

"Thanks," Joe said to the spray can. We are served by
organic ghosts, he thought, who, speaking and writing, pass
through this our new environment. Watching, wise, physical
ghosts from the full-life world, elements of which have be-

come for us invading but agreeable splinters of a substance that pulsates like a former heart. And of all of them, he thought, thanks to Glen Runciter. In particular. The writer of instructions, labels and notes. Valuable notes.

He raised his arm to slow to a grumpy halt a passing 1936 Graham cab.

17

*I am Ubik. Before the universe
was, I am. I made the suns. I made
the worlds. I created the lives and
the places they inhabit; I move
them here, I put them there. They
go as I say, they do as I tell them.
I am the word and my name is
never spoken, the name which no
one knows. I am called Ubik, but
that is not my name. I am. I shall
always be.*

Glen Runciter could not find the moratorium owner.

"Are you sure you don't know where he is?" Runciter
asked Miss Beason, the moratorium owner's secretary. "It's
essential that I talk to Ella again."

"I'll have her brought out," Miss Beason said. "You may
use office 4-B; please wait there, Mr. Runciter; I will have
your wife for you in a very short time. Try to make yourself
comfortable."

Locating office 4-B, Runciter paced about restlessly. At
last a moratorium attendant appeared, wheeling in Ella's
casket on a handtruck. "Sorry to keep you waiting," the
attendant said; he began at once to set up the electronic
communing mechanism, humming happily as he worked.

In short order the task was completed. The attendant
checked the circuit one last time, nodded in satisfaction, then
started to leave the office.

"This is for you," Runciter said, and handed him several
fifty-cent pieces which he had scrounged from his various
pockets. "I appreciate the rapidity with which you accomplished the job."

"Thank you, Mr. Runciter," the attendant said. He glanced at the coins, then frowned. "What kind of money is this?" he said.

Runciter took a good long look at the fifty-cent pieces. He saw at once what the attendant meant; very definitely, the coins were not as they should be. Whose profile is this? he asked himself. Who's this on all three coins? Not the right person at all. And yet he's familiar. I know him.

And then he recognized the profile. I wonder what this means, he asked himself. Strangest thing I've ever seen. Most things in life eventually can be explained. But—Joe Chip on a fifty-cent piece?

It was the first Joe Chip money he had ever seen.

He had an intuition, chillingly, that if he searched his pockets, and his billfold, he would find more.

This was just the beginning.

ABOUT THE AUTHOR

PHILIP K. DICK was born in Chicago in 1928 and lived most of his life in California. He briefly attended the University of California, but dropped out before completing any classes. In 1952 he began writing professionally and proceeded to write thirty-six novels and five short story collections. He won the Hugo Award for best novel in 1962 for *The Man in the High Castle* and the John W. Campbell Memorial Award for best novel of the year in 1974 for *Flow My Tears the Policeman Said*. Philip K. Dick died of heart failure following a stroke on March 2, 1982, in Santa Ana, California.